HOW TO ROCK BEST FRIENDS AND FRENEMIES

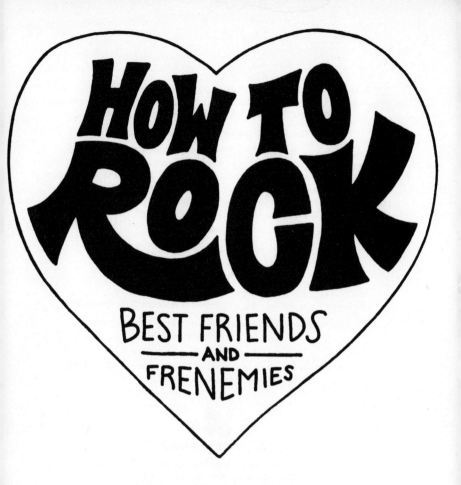

HOW TO ROCK

BEST FRIENDS
— AND —
FRENEMIES

A NOVEL BY MEG HASTON

poppy

LITTLE, BROWN AND COMPANY
New York   Boston

Copyright © 2012 by Alloy Entertainment

Poppy

Hachette Book Group
237 Park Avenue, New York, NY 10017
Visit our website at lb-kids.com

Poppy is an imprint of Little, Brown and Company.
The Poppy name and logo are trademarks of Hachette Book Group, Inc.

The publisher is not responsible for websites (or their content)
that are not owned by the publisher.

First Paperback Edition: December 2013
First published in hardcover in September 2012 as *How to Rock Break-Ups and Make-Ups* by Little, Brown and Company

Produced by Alloy Entertainment
1700 Broadway, New York, NY 10019

"Go Your Own Way" by Lindsey Buckingham (New Sounds Music).
All rights reserved.

Book design by Liz Dresner
Hand-lettering by Carolyn Sewell

ISBN 978-0-316-06827-7

10 9 8 7 6 5 4 3 2 1

RRD-C

Printed in the United States of America

*For Episcopal School of Jacksonville,
where I first learned the power of words
and continue to learn the strength of community.*

CUE THE NEW TRACK
Monday, 6:58 A.M.

I have a unique talent for remembering the soundtrack to every significant life moment in my twelve and a half years, including epiphanies, crises, and unbeatable hair days.

The morning of my very first *Simon Says* television broadcast for Marquette Middle School's Channel M last September, I blasted Beyoncé's "Diva" on my iPod for the entire El ride to school. Four years ago, when my dad told me he was moving from Chicago to Los Angeles and that it was "best for everyone involved," creepy carnival music whistled from the Ferris wheel at Navy Pier.

And as I waited for my best friend, Molly Knight, at Sugar Daddy this morning, the clink of ceramic mugs and the sleepy *chug, chug, ding!* of the old-fashioned cash register blended together in familiar harmony. Outside, my city was starting to rouse, and pinkish light shone on bleary-eyed passersby. For the rest of Chicago, it was just another Monday morning.

The rest of Chicago had no idea how easy they had it.

I sat on one of the cracked turquoise leather couches at the back of the bakery and willed my knees to stop bouncing. But I was too riled up to sit still. Two weeks ago, after a humiliating tumble at Molly's thirteenth birthday party, I'd gone from

KACEY SIMON, SEVENTH-GRADE JOURNALIST,
ADVICE GURU, and MOST POPULAR GIRL
BASICALLY EVER

to

KACEY SIMON, LISPING, BRACES-AND-GLASSES-
WEARING, FRIENDLESS REJECT.

Luckily, my literal fall from grace was yesterday's headline, and now I was back on top, thanks to some major soul-searching and a genius plan I'd executed with my friend Paige Greene. And after I'd saved my best guy friend (and Molly's boyfriend), Zander Jarvis, during the Rock Chicago showcase last Friday night, Zander had even asked me to rejoin Gravity as lead singer.

Friends? Check. Popularity? Check. Band? Check.

Unquenchable crush on my best friend's boyfriend? *Cough*CHECK*cough*.

The scratchy clang of the bell over the door startled me, sending a wave of scalding liquid over the edge of my cup.

"Oww." I licked my thumb and pressed it into the widening heart-shaped stain on the knee of my new bottle-green jeggings.

"Watch it. I'm def borrowing those." Molly clacked across the faded wood floor in towering platform booties. "If it's okay."

"Of course." I jumped up to hug her. "Whenever you want." I didn't let go right away. Maybe I was holding on too long. But I was so relieved to be friends again, there wasn't enough room in my brain to care.

Mols wriggled away, a mischievous grin playing over her rosy lips. "So?" A few wisps of platinum hair slipped from beneath a cropped hoodie.

"So, sit." I slapped the seat next to me.

"First you have to guess what's different about me."

"Ummm . . ." I reviewed her from head to toe. I'd seen the hoodie before, and the black leather skinnies were a definite rerun. I'd watched her buy the yellow RUCKUS tee at the showcase Friday night. It was a consolation prize for being the girlfriend of the dude who bombed onstage, she'd told me when we got back to my house.

"Kacey! Guess!"

"Did your shirt have that stain on it when you bought it?" The old Kacey would have informed Mols that wearing a (dirty) rival band's T-shirt to school made her a subpar rock 'n' roll girlfriend. The new, slightly-less-honest-but-more-aware-of-people's-feelings Kacey ran her tongue over her braces to give her mouth something else to do.

"Not a stain." Molly perched on the edge of the sofa. Her voice dropped to a whisper, and she leaned close enough for me to catch a whiff of gingerbread body butter. "It's the signature of the lead guy in Ruckus. He's in ninth, and his name is Phoenix. Which is so weird, because you know how my grandparents live close to Phoenix and it's, like, my fave place ever?"

"You said staying in the desert for spring break was like being trapped in a huge litter box." I squinted through a fresh set of contacts at the chicken scratch above her left boob. Why were we talking about some strange kid in ninth when Molly had the coolest, most talented guy in seventh by her side?

"You're not guessing." Impatiently, Mols wound a lock of hair around her index finger and yanked.

"Your hair iiiissss . . ." I bit the inside of my cheek. When I was Channel M's star reporter, I never worried about saying the wrong thing. I missed being a reporter. Or maybe I just missed having a reason to give people the straight story without having to feel bad about it. ". . . blonder?"

"Wrong!" She smacked an imaginary game-show buzzer on the coffee table, then whipped off her hoodie, revealing an angled, shoulder-length bob.

"You cut it all off!" I squealed. "Ohmygod, it looks so much healthier without those stringy exten—" I gulped. "You look so good!"

"Really? You think so?"

I grinned. "For real! What made you do it?"

"I'm starting fresh," Molly proclaimed.

I adjusted the feathered head wrap holding my long auburn waves in place. The piece was fashioned from a costume mask our friend Liv Parillo's grandmother had worn to a masquerade ball a zillion years ago. It was the latest item in LivItUp, Liv's brand-new line of upscale repurposed accessories. "Starting fresh from what?"

"Well . . ." Molly scanned each of the vintage-school-desks-turned-tables in the tiny bakery. The tip of her nose and her cheeks were tinged with pink, and not from the early-morning chill.

"What? Tell me!" I scooted close enough for our knees to touch.

"I broke up with Z last night."

The words took my breath away. I felt like I was back

in the dunking booth at last year's Channel M fund-raiser, the split second after I hit the icy water.

Okay, so it was my producer, Carlos, who'd actually agreed to the dunking booth. But I *imagined* that it probably felt exactly like this.

Molly blinked. "Hello? Earth to Kacey!"

"Ohmygod!" I coughed, my mind spinning with questions. Why would anyone ever dump Zander? Was he okay? What did this mean for us? *Was* there an "us"? Since Molly had asked me to quit Gravity in the first place, I'd been beyond nervous to tell her that I'd rejoined the band *before* I knew about the split. Did this make my news better, or worse?

"What did he—why did you—are you okay?" I asked.

"Aww, Kace. You're the best. I'm fine." She squeezed my arm reassuringly. "It's like I texted Z last night. We just don't have that much in common, you know?"

I nodded. That much was definitely true.

"Plus, I'm Molly Knight. I can't be the girl who dated that loser who sucked onstage."

"Did you tell him that?"

"I would have, but then this hilarious commercial came on and I forgot. Anyway, you're gonna love Phoenix. We have so much in common!"

"Like what?" I wanted to focus 100 percent on Molly,

but a voice in the back of my head kept ordering me to confess that I'd rejoined Gravity. Now that she'd broken up with Zander, she wouldn't care. Right?

"We're both super mature, and we both love how he's in ninth."

"He sounds great. Really. I'm happy for you." *Tell her.*

"I *knew* you would be. Only there's something I kind of need advice on." Molly tugged at the leather choker around her neck.

"About your new boy? Shoot," I said graciously. Boys were the one and only area where Molly's expertise outshone mine. This had to be killing her.

"Okay." She took a deep breath. "Phoenix likes girls who have a thing. You know, like designing is Liv's thing, and being smart is Nessa's thing. And journalism is your thing."

Used to be my thing.

"But since I quit skating lessons, I don't have a thing anymore." Molly lowered her head. "Do you think I should go back to gymnastics? I'm kind of over tight ponytails and glitter hair spray."

"So's the rest of the world. But not to worry." I borrowed the soothing, low tone that sounded so reassuring when Dr. Phil, our school shrink, used it. "You're good at a ton of other things."

"Like what?" Her white-blond lashes fluttered skeptically.

"Like . . ." I reached for my hot chocolate and took a long sip, thinking hard. "Like you always put together amazing outfits. And out of all the girls I know, you're the best at talking to boys. You don't get nervous or anything."

"I guess."

"Most of all, you're an amazing friend. I was just thinking how glad I am that we're friends again."

"Me, too," she said quickly. "Things weren't the same when we weren't talking. And"—she pulled a brown throw pillow into her lap and squeezed it—"I'm really sorry about how mean I was to you."

"Same." I wanted to hug her again. "Okay. So we've got outfits, boy-talking, and friendship. What else do you like?"

"Parties, for sure. I had a killer time at my b-day party. Everybody did." A horrified look flashed across her face. "Until you bit it, obv."

"Obv." My teeth ached at the memory. "Okay. Parties!" I settled back into the couch cushions and thought for a few seconds. "What if you were a party planner, or something? You could plan special events at Marquette! Like fund-raisers and dances and stuff."

Molly's head snapped toward me. Her delicate features

locked into a deadly serious expression. "Yes. Party planner. *Yes.*"

"Actually, I heard the student council was looking for someone to head the Party Planning Committee for the spring dance. I bet I could get Paige to approve your app by the end of the day!"

Molly's nose scrunched in disapproval. "Paige Greene has to approve me?" She and Paige, my old fifth-grade BFF, got along almost as well as my six-year-old sister, Ella, and I had during her *I know you are, but what am I?* phase.

"Well, she *is* seventh-grade class president. But it's just a formality," I assured her.

She pretended to weigh her option. Singular.

"Okay, I'll do it!" Mols reached over and hugged me.

"Yay! I really think this is a great idea," I said into her shoulder. *You know what else is a great idea? Telling your best friend the truth! Say it! "I. Rejoined. Gravity."* My mouth tasted dry and stale, like I'd been sucking on mothballs.

"Me, too. Thanks, Ka—" Suddenly, Molly jerked away. "Wait. You never said if you thought it was a good idea to break up with Zander." Her eyebrows shot up in panic.

"I—uh—" I hadn't had time to process. For that, I'd need at least a couple of hours alone in my room. And a good, soul-searching-themed playlist. I channeled Dr. Phil again. "Do *you* think it was a good idea to break up with Zander?"

Molly's cornflower-blue eyes flitted anxiously across my face. "I dunno. I guess. I mean, we really didn't have much in common. Plus, I heard he was into some other girl while we were dating."

My blood ran cold. "What? Who?"

"Ridic, right?" Molly half coughed, half laughed. "Z was totally into me when we were dating. *I* was the one who broke up with *him*, remember?" A tiny vein in her forehead throbbed.

"Yeah. I remember." I crossed my arms over my black dolman-sleeve top, suddenly aware of a draft in the bakery. "So, did you hear who it was?"

"Please. If I knew who it was, we wouldn't be having this conversation. I'd be out kicking her a—"

"OHMYGOD. I just had the most amazing idea." I cut her off before she could give me the gory play-by-play. "What if I rejoined Gravity, and then I could get the inside scoop on whether he was into someone else while you guys were together?" I reached for my hot chocolate mug again, afraid to steal a glance at her expression.

"You mean, like, you'd be a spy? Just for me?"

"Mmmm." I chugged the rest of my hot chocolate with

complete disregard for the third-degree throat burns I was inflicting on myself. And the lie I was inflicting on her. But if I'd learned anything in the past few weeks, it was that sometimes the truth wasn't the best option.

"Yes! Do it! That's totally brilliant."

"Mmmmm." I kept my mug between us. "Okay. Great. I'll talk to Zander after school."

Molly fell back into the sofa, a dreamy look on her face. "Perf." Then she sat up again. "But wait. You can't just find out whether he was into some girl *before*. You have to find out if he's into anyone *now*. He can't date anybody for at least a year after me. It's the rule. Girl Code."

Girl Code? "But aren't you and Phoenix—"

"That's different. I was the one who did the breaking up. I'm allowed to date."

"Oh." I squeezed my mug so hard I was sure tiny hairline cracks were forming in the painted ceramic lip. "Okay." The rule was insane. But the look on her face told me she couldn't have been more serious.

"So that's it, then. You'll get the dirt and report back to me. And if *any* girl even *thinks* about liking him—"

I bent over and reached for my messenger bag with numb, trembling fingers.

"—that girl will be in major trouble. She has *no* idea what I can do when I'm pissed," Molly finished.

"Got it," I said weakly.

But Molly was wrong. That girl had a pretty good idea of what Molly Knight was capable of. And that girl wasn't looking for that kind of trouble.

Not again.

CAUGHT BETWEEN A ROCK STAR
AND A HARD PLACE
Monday, 3:27 P.M.

"I'm telling you. It's my hidden talent," Zander insisted that afternoon after school. "Bet you five bucks." His steely gray eyes ignited at the prospect of a challenge, and the royal-blue streak in his long bangs flashed under the spotlights above us.

"I don't knowwww," I teased, shedding my black suede trench. I took a seat across from him, a steaming latte already at my place. We'd decided to meet at the café next to Vinyl Destination, the coolest record store in Chicago's Andersonville neighborhood. Actually, I'd decided on the café. Zander had suggested Sugar Daddy, but the possibility of running into Molly and the girls during my first "spy session" with Zander made my hair crimp eighties-music-video-style. Fortunately, my chosen hangout was dark and empty, except for the skinny dude slouched behind the dark wooden coffee bar. "I'd have to see it to believe it."

"Any song. Any voice or accent." Zander angled his chair so his back was to the empty stage—the same stage where he'd lost his mojo at the showcase Friday night.

"Without laughing."

"Without laughing." He popped the collar on the plaid button-down he wore over a faded HARD ROCK LIFE T-shirt, homage to his old band in Seattle.

"You're on. Five bucks." I yanked up my sleeves and planted my elbows on the round black table between us. "Um, 'Go Your Own Way.' As . . . Kermit the Frog."

He winced. The Fleetwood Mac tune was the same song he'd bombed with Friday night. "Nice song choice."

"You gotta try it again sometime, right? This way, it'll be the song you sang when you lost five bucks. Not the song you sang when—"

"Okay, okay. Don't remind me!" He disappeared beneath the table and popped up a few seconds later, holding a familiar acoustic guitar. "You could at least give me a hard one."

He'd tried to give me that guitar a week ago, when we were sitting around the Millennium Park skating rink. My insides had been colder than the wintry air as I'd told him

I had to quit Gravity to reclaim my lead in Marquette's production of *Guys and Dolls*. It had been a seriously inconvenient time to figure out that I had feelings for him. And an even worse time for him to flip out, take back his guitar, and refuse to speak to me for a few days.

The sound of Zander's fingers plucking the strings drew me back to the present. *"Loving you . . . isn't the right thing to do."* His Kermit was so dead-on, it was freaky. And I know a good Kermit when I hear one. Ella was Miss Piggy for Halloween two years ago. In preparation for the role, she'd forced me to watch every Muppet movie ever made.

I giggled, settling back into my chair and lifting my latte in a toast. The steam beneath the white plastic lid tickled my nose and sent a warm, tingly feeling through my body. "Just don't laugh! Don't do it!"

Zander's jaw pulsed as he tried to keep it together. This was too easy.

I glanced around the café to be sure we were still alone.

"If I could," I chimed in with my best Miss Piggy. *"Maybe I'd give you my woooorld."*

Zander's face cracked into a grin.

"You lose!" I smacked the table triumphantly. "Five bucks, Jarvis. Cough it up."

"That wasn't a laugh! I'm not laughing," he protested,

biting his lip so hard his forehead crinkled in pain. "And you cheated!"

"Hey." I lifted my hands in surrender. "All's fair in lo—" I swallowed the rest of the word before it escaped. Everything *wasn't* fair in love and war. At least not according to Molly. *Girl Code*, I repeated to myself silently. *Girl Code. Girl Code.*

"You okay?" Zander pressed his palm over the strings, silencing his guitar. His cheeks looked suddenly rosy under the fluorescent lights.

"Yeah. Yeah. Sure," I said, too quickly. "I mean, uh—I actually wanted to ask you the same thing."

"I'm good." He toyed with the leather cuff bracelet on his wrist. "How come?"

"Because of the breakup?" Either Zander was playing cool to mask his devastation, or he honestly didn't care. For the record, I was a staunch supporter of Option B.

"Oh. That. No, I'm fine." He pushed back his chair and stretched out his legs. Instead of his usual skinny jeans, he was wearing a pair of regular jeans, the wash so dark they had to be new. "It's . . . whatever. It's probably a good thing." His blue bangs flopped over his eyes.

"Yeah. A good thing." I drummed my fingers on the table. *A good thing.* Good because he and Molly were polar opposites? Good because he was into somebody else, somebody who just happened to be sitting across from him this VERY SECOND?

I had no idea why girls were always getting such a bad rap. Boys were way more confusing.

"So I've got a surprise for you," he said. "Two, actually."

"Yeah?" My throat was suddenly dry. I took another sip of my latté.

"Well, the first one's not really a surprise. I just wanted to give you this. Again." He lifted the guitar in his lap, nodding for me to take it.

"Zander. Are you sure?" Tentatively, I took it, tracing the circular opening in the instrument's glossy blond body. "But you learned how to play on this thing. Don't you want to keep it?"

"Guitars are meant to played," he insisted. "It's a thank-you for Friday night. And a welcome-back-to-Gravity present."

The guitar smelled like Zander—freshly polished wood, leather, and pure perfection. "Thanks." I squeezed the fret board tight.

"I can teach you to play," he offered. "Maybe you could play for Gravity, even."

I snorted. "In like a decade."

"You gotta start somewhere." Zander cracked his knuckles and interlaced his fingers behind his head.

"Bring it to rehearsal tomorrow. I'll teach you a couple of chords."

"'Kay." Waves of excitement and nerves reverberated through me in a rhythm all their own. I hadn't seen the other members of Gravity—Nelson Lund, Kevin Cho, and The Beat—since Friday night. And I still had no idea how they felt about me rejoining the band.

"Hey."

I looked up. Zander was smiling.

"It's gonna be awesome," he assured me. "We're all pumped that you're back."

How did he read my mind like that? I let my eyes lock with his for a quarter beat, until a tiny voice in the back of my head whispered: *Girl Code*. Reluctantly, I refocused on the guitar.

"Good. Well, I gotta go." He jumped up. "I'm supposed to watch my sister while our parents go to this art thing tonight."

"Okay," I said, hoping the disappointment in my voice wasn't obvious. "See you tomorrow?"

"Deal," Zander said in his Kermit voice. He lifted his palm for a high five, and I clasped it with mine. His palm was soft, electric. *GirlCodeGirlCodeGirlCode*. "Later." He headed for the door.

"Oh! Wait! What about my second surprise?" I called.

He turned around, flashing a coy smile. "If I *told* you, it wouldn't be a surprise. You'll find out tomorrow at rehearsal. You're gonna love it." He waved and disappeared through the doorway.

"Yeah," I murmured, cradling the guitar in my lap. Its shiny surface reflected my flushed cheeks and green eyes. As a general rule, I was not a fan of surprises. Surprises were the off-air equivalent of breaking news. Like my dad telling me he was leaving for good. Or like Ella admitting that she'd mixed Mom's facial hair removal cream in my shampoo *after* I'd already lathered, rinsed, and repeated.

But this was different. This was Zander. And if he was excited about it, then it was going to rock.

CURSE THE CODE
Monday, 9:02 P.M.

That night, Mom, Ella, and I sat around the kitchen table in our breakfast nook. A stack of my textbooks, plus Ella's weekly folder and a list of spelling words, was piled in front of Dad's old chair. After four years, you'd think we would have gotten rid of his place mat. But I never liked the way the table looked with three mats—lopsided, like it could topple over at any second.

"Great broadcast, Mom," I said over a mouthful of room-temperature Greek takeout. Ella and I always watched the five- and six-o'clock Channel 5 newscasts when we could. Even though Mom had been the solo evening anchor for over a year, seeing her on air never got old. Lately, though, it had made me a little . . . something. Not jealous, exactly. More like nostalgic for the *Simon Says* days.

"You think so?" Mom pulled her shoulder-length strawberry hair away from her face and secured it with one of Ella's purple glitter claws.

"Totally. I liked the piece on the school board scandal."

"Me, too." Ella yawned into her stuffed grape leaves. Her dark red curls were still damp and matted from the bath, and she smelled like baby shampoo and hotel lotion. "And the commercials."

"Thanks, girls." The tiny smile lines around Mom's jewel-green eyes deepened under the extra layers of foundation she wore for work. "And thanks for taking care of dinner, baby." She reached over to squeeze my arm and left her hand there.

"Ha! Baby." Ella snorted. She lunged for the pink curly-straw peeking out of her cup. I steadied the cup as she slurped her chocolate milk.

"No problem," I said. "I signed her folder and we finished her spelling words. Oh, and I have a permission slip for you to sign. It's for our Marine Bio field trip to Shedd Aquarium on Monday."

"You got it." Mom nodded. "Now run upstairs and brush your teeth," she told Ella. "I'll be up in a second."

"But—" Ella looked back and forth between Mom and me, like she was considering making a scene. In the end, another big yawn won out.

"Night, Ell Bell." I leaned over to give her a squeeze.

"Don't let the bedbugs bite!" She planted a breathy chocolate kiss on my jaw, and I lifted her off the chair and lowered her to the floor. A few seconds later I heard the slow thud of her galoshes on the stairs.

"Really, Kace." Mom sighed. "I'm sorry you had to take care of everything tonight. We lost one of our best producers last week, and the station's new owner wants to—"

"Mom." I cut her off. "Really. I don't mind." It was the truth. Sure, Ella could be a major pain. Like last week, when she used my brand-new crackle nail polish to "decorate" her math homework. But for the most part, hanging out with her didn't kill me.

"I know you don't. It's just . . ." Mom's voice trailed off. "So tell me about your day."

"It was good." I smashed a giant piece of feta on my plate with a plastic fork, eyeing the teal digits on the microwave clock. After school I'd texted Paige to come over tonight so we could quote, *strategize*, end quote, about the home stretch of her presidential campaign. I'd thrown in a P.S. about Zander and Molly's breakup, like it was totally an afterthought.

"Just good?" The lilt in her voice told me Mom's reporter instincts were kicking in. I'd have to do better than "good" if I wanted to leave the table before midnight. "Something on your mind?"

"I—" There was a sharp knock from the other side of the kitchen.

"Ella Simon, those teeth better be sparkling," Mom warned.

"It's just me." Paige appeared in the doorway and flashed a toothy smile. "But I did floss this morning."

"You pass inspection, Paige." Mom laughed. "Come on in."

"Doesn't she look amazing, Mom?" I said brightly, grateful for the interruption. Paige's short dark bob gleamed beneath the kitchen lights, and she actually looked kind of stylish in the black cigarette pants and black silk tee I'd let her borrow. Beneath her slanted bangs, her glasses added a nice, executive branch–chic touch. I congratulated myself on Paige's mini makeover.

"Always." Mom nodded. I could feel her gaze on me.

"So what's up, Paige?" I widened my eyes meaningfully. *You have top secret campaign business that can't wait. We have to go up to my room. Right. Now.*

But my telepathic vibes sailed straight over Paige's head.

"Uh, you texted me." She took Ella's seat and slid a stuffed green three-ring binder on the table. "Only ten days till the election, Sterling," she told Mom, plucking half a stuffed grape leaf from Ella's plate and popping it in her mouth. "Just thought you should know. As an informed member of the media and all."

Mom tapped her temple with her index finger. "I consider myself briefed," she said. "Now if you'll excuse me, all that quiet upstairs is disconcerting." She pushed back her chair and headed for the stairwell. "You girls can work till ten. And Kacey, make sure you watch Paige get home safely."

"She lives next door," I muttered, rolling my eyes.

"I mean it," Mom instructed. Ever since she started taking coffee breaks with Channel 5's new crime reporter, she'd been paranoid about kidnapping and identity theft.

In my room on the third floor, Paige and I kicked off our shoes and stretched out on our backs on my pink-and-black plaid duvet. I stared at the glow-in-the-dark solar system sprinkled across the slanted attic ceiling. The flatscreen across from my bed was muted, and the crisp scent of lavender drifted from the pillar candle Liv had given me last Christmas to cleanse my chi. Photos of Gravity (mostly Zander) and vintage album covers I'd bought at Vinyl Destination were pinned to the three bulletin-board walls that surrounded my bed. The chalkboard wall behind my bed was filled with song lyrics and the names of bands I'd recently discovered.

"Do we really need to work on the campaign?" Paige

asked the Big Dipper. "I've been rehearsing my speech all night. Maybe we could talk about something else."

"Liiike—" I cut my eyes at her, fighting a smile.

"Oh, I dunno." Paige whacked me with a furry pink pillow. "Like how a certain friend of yours just broke up with another friend of yours, who is so *obviously* more than just a friend where you're concerned?" She blew her bangs out of her eyes, and they fluttered back to her forehead in an inverted V.

"Ohhhh, thaaat." I flipped onto my side. The words bubbled up inside of me until I couldn't hold them in any longer. "HesaidhehadasurpriseformeandI'mgonnaloveit!"

"What? When?" Paige shrieked, scrambling to her knees on the bed.

"Girls!" Mom called from downstairs.

"Sorrryyyy," we yelled back.

"Tell me everything," Paige said in a low voice. Her cocoa-colored eyes were double their usual size.

"There's not much to tell." I sat up. "We were hanging out, and he gave me his old guitar and then he said he had a surprise for me, but I'd have to wait until rehearsal tomorrow."

"Ahhhh! Kay-cey!" Paige shoved me so hard, I toppled back onto a mound of pillows and stuffed animals. "He gave you his *guitar*? That's huge! He's totally gonna tell you he's into you!"

"You think?" I closed my eyes and let myself picture the scene. It would be after an awesome jam session with the band. The other guys would have already left the loft. And it would be just Zander and me, draped casually on the leather couch in his loft's living area. Something slow would be playing, like Death Cab's latest single. Zander and I would be humming along, and suddenly our eyes would meet.

Kacey, he'd say. *I—*

GirlCodeGirlCodeGirlCode.

Right on cue, my cell buzzed on the bedside table, forcing me back to my non-loft.

MOLLY: DID U TELL PAIGE I'M PLANNING THE DANCE?

MOLLY: ANY DIRT FROM THE SPY SESH W/Z?

"Ohmygod. Is that Zander?" Paige bounced in place on the bed.

"Just Molly." With a pang of guilt, I hit IGNORE and stuffed the phone under my pillow.

Paige made a gagging sound.

"Paaaige," I groaned. "By the way, has anybody signed up to head the Party Planning Committee for the dance?"

"No." Paige looked confused for a second; then her face lit up. "Wait. Do you and Zander want to do it?"

"Molly wants to. Is that cool?"

"Ugh, but fine, whatever. Can we get back to the point?"

I picked at the flaking eggplant polish on my big toe. "Have you ever heard of the Girl Code?"

Paige fiddled with the iPod dock on my desk, settling on a new single from Levi Stone, an up-and-coming singer-songwriter whose recent feature on MTV had propelled him to superstardom almost overnight. I'd heard on the news that he had a Chicago tour date next week. "You mean like, *Never run for office if your best friend already said she wanted to?*"

I rolled my eyes. "No. I mean like, *Thou shalt not crush on another girl's ex-boyfriend for one whole year?*" I said, half hoping the opening notes of Levi's single, "You're So Right, We're So Wrong," would drown me out.

"Huh?" Paige's fringy bob whipped around indignantly. "Did Molly tell you that?"

"No! I mean, she wasn't talking about *me*, specifically. She was just saying that no other girl can date Zander for at least a year." Saying the words out loud made me realize just how insane they sounded. But did it matter? Wouldn't a good friend stay away from Molly's ex no matter what? Even if they'd only dated for a matter of days?

Paige squinted through her lenses like she was trying

to figure out a math problem. "I can't—that doesn't even—I—" She stopped and took a measured breath. "Didn't you say she was dating some other guy already?"

I nodded.

"And since when do you take orders from Molly Knight?"

"I *don't*," I protested, irritation pricking my voice. She obviously didn't get it. My friendship with Mols was still so fragile, the slightest problem could send it crashing down for good. "Forget it." I karate-chopped a decorative pillow and face-planted into the picked silk.

"No. Wait." Paige took a running leap and dove next to me on the bed. "Sorry. I love that you're trying to be a good friend. It's just that Molly and Zander should never have been together in the first place—they only went out because you lied about her being into Acoustic Rebellion. And *you* and Zander are, like—"

"I *knooooow*," I wailed into my pillow. "Don't say it."

"—*perfect* for each other! And I just think he's too great for you to let him get away. I mean, what if you wait a whole year and some *other* girl starts to like him and then *they* start dating?"

I flopped onto my back. Paige was right: Zander and I *were* perfect for each other. A much better match than my recent ex-crush, Quinn Wilder, had been.

"I think I'm gonna throw up," I groaned. Although from excitement or worry, I couldn't quite tell.

"Ew." Paige crabwalked backward to the other side of the bed. "Need I remind you that the borrowed top I'm wearing—*your* top—is silk?"

I ignored her. "What do you think Zander's surprise is?"

"That he likes you," Paige said matter-of-factly.

A broad smile broke over my face.

"And seriously, Kace. I think it's okay for you to like him back. Can't you just be honest with Molly?"

I snuggled into a sea of pillows and plush, suddenly completely exhausted. Half of me was giddy at the possibility that Zander liked me back. The other half was worried that even thinking about Zander was a terrible violation of my friendship with Mols. If she knew how I felt, she'd never forgive me. It was like my brain was at war with itself. Fifty-fifty.

Although I knew that the next time I saw Zander, or heard him play, it would be more like sixty-forty, in favor of Zander.

Okay. Seventy-thirty.

Seventy-five–twenty-five, tops.

All's fair in love and war. The words from that afternoon came back to me, fighting for space in my mind.

IF A WHALE LEAVES THE DOCK AT 8 A.M., TRAVELING 12 MILES PER HOUR, THEN WHAT IS THE THEME OF THE SPRING DANCE?
Tuesday, 10:40 A.M.

The next morning, my Giddy-Over-Zander-to-Guilty-Over-Molly ratios were still fluctuating wildly. As I sat in third-period Marine Bio, failing to focus on the pop quiz I was probably bombing, a just-chased-a-double-shot-of-espresso-with-an-extra-large-hot-chocolate sensation sloshed around in the pit of my stomach.

I turned around and checked the clock at the back of the classroom. More than four hours until rehearsal. More than four hours until Zander's big reveal.

Torture.

"Question number six," droned our teacher Miss Finnster—or Spinster Finnster, as she'd been known since the dawn of time—from her desk at the front. Next to her were giant yellowed mason jars inhabited by pickled sea creatures as old and wrinkled as she was.

Paige and I sat at a scuffed black lab table at the back of the room. Molly and Liv sat to my right, and Nessa Beckett was camped out at the far end of our row. My ex-crush, Quinn Wilder, and his friends Jake Fields and Aaron Peterman sat in the row ahead of us, while Zander slouched in the second row. His head bobbed in time to the ticking clock by the door.

As we waited for Finnster to continue, I looked over at Nessa, the overachiever of our group. Her slick, dark pixie cut gleamed with confidence, and her spring-green cowl-neck sweater accentuated her flawless dark skin. Stacked spiral notebooks bordered her paper like a barbed-wire fence around a prison yard. She stared down at her quiz without blinking.

After a full minute of silence, Jilly Lindstrom lifted her hand in the first row. "Um . . . Spin—Miss Finnster?" she chirped. "Is there a . . . question six?"

The folds of Finnster's neck were tucked into her chunky knit cardigan, making her look like a resting turtle. Her eyelids were so wrinkled that it was hard to tell if they were closed, but the gentle snore that escaped her nostrils was a dead giveaway.

"OMG," Molly hissed. "She's totes napping. No fair." Technically she didn't have to whisper. It was a well-known fact that Finnster was legally deaf in one ear. During a fire drill last year, she'd woken from a nap after all the kids had evacuated, thought school was out, and gone home for the weekend. It was a Tuesday.

"At least her spirit hasn't crossed over to the other side." Liv twirled her jet-black ringlets into a messy bun on top of her head and secured them with a cotton ikat-print head wrap she'd made from one of her Italian grandma's old-lady skirts. "Yet."

"Shhhh." Nessa glared at us from her pop-quiz fortress.

Twirling one of the vintage brass button earrings Liv had given me as a make-up gift, I tore a fresh page out of my notebook and scribbled a quick note to Molly.

Guess who's the new Party Planning Committee chair for the dance next Friday??

A.) You, B.) You, or C.) YOU, BABY!

P.S. You're welcome, Madame Chairperson.

Molly squealed, and Finnster let out a loud snort, jerking upright in her seat. "Question six," she trilled, not missing a beat. "How many blowholes does a baleen whale have?"

"Blowhole." Quinn snickered, then fist-bumped Jake

Fields. Ugh. Why had I ever crushed on him? I refocused on Zander, who was now tapping out a rhythm on the edge of his desk.

"A.) One, B.) Two, C.) Three, or D.) Four."

"You got me the job?" Molly leaned in and squeezed me in a side hug. "You're the best."

I wrote *B* on my quiz and hugged her back. "Now you can tell Phoenix you totally have a thing."

Molly breathed a grateful sigh.

"And the last question. How long can a sperm whale stay underwater?" Finnster trilled the *r* on *sperm*, which made everyone, Zander included, burst out laughing.

"Well! I'm glad to see that you all have so much enthusiasm for marine biology." Finnster scrunched her face in pleasure, looking the way Nessa's pug puppy, Chunk, did just after he relieved himself on the entrance hall rug. "I hope you'll show this degree of interest on Monday's field trip to Shedd Aquarium."

"If I was in charge around here, we'd take a trip to Wrigley Field." Quinn raked a tanned hand authoritatively through his sandy hair. "Every Friday."

Jake hooted his approval. Aaron Peterman balled up a piece of paper and pitched it to Quinn, who whacked at it with his pencil.

"If *he* was in charge around here, the average IQ

in student government would take a nosedive," Paige muttered under her breath. Then she looked at me. "No offense."

"I'd just gotten braces and glasses, which is tantamount to being traumatized. I can't be held responsible for my crushes." I poked the brackets on my front teeth with my tongue.

"You should run for eighth-grade president, bro," Jake suggested as everyone passed their quizzes to the end of their row. "Like, for real."

"Please. Can he even spell 'executive branch'?" Paige's neck was turning bright red above the collar of the frumpy, faded black cardigan I'd advised against.

"He'll forget about it by lunch," I reassured her.

"For the remainder of class, we'll be discussing Echinoidea, more commonly known as sea urchins." Finnster rubbed her veiny hands together and turned toward the board, sketching out a detailed diagram.

Translation: *Enjoy your free period, boys and girls.*

As the guys in the third row divided into teams for paper football, Nessa slid her belongings down the row and rejoined our group.

"So. Breaking news." I let my eyes flicker over each of my best friends. "Molly's gonna head up the Party Planning Committee for the spring dance!" Under the table, I squeezed Paige's arm, begging her not to pull a presidential power play. "It's official!"

"Thanks to Kacey." Molly's cheekbones flushed a shade almost identical to that of her slinky peach pullover.

"*You're welcome!*" Paige coughed.

"Ew." Molly glared at Paige, then lifted the hem of her sweater and dabbed at her cheek in slo-mo. "Cover your mouth!"

"Oh, *please.*" Matching Molly's dramatic flair, Paige rolled her eyes in a full circle. "Come to think of it, I'm not sure I want you planning the dance. As president of the seventh grade, it's my duty to—"

"To what?" Molly sneered. But she tucked and retucked her hair behind her ears and kept glancing at me nervously. "Change out the good stuff in the vending machines for rabbit food? Act like you're smarter than everybody else?"

"Time!" Quinn paused the football game in the third row and turned around in his seat. "Catfight."

"Girls!" I hissed, gripping Molly's wrist with one hand and Paige's with the other. "Chill out."

I had never been friends with both girls at the exact same time before. It was great for me, but they were acting more territorial than my old pet ferret, Oprah Winfurry, when Ella brought home a guinea pig and insisted they were going to get married. Mom said there was only room for one diva in Oprah's cage, so Enrique Piglesias had to go back to the pet store.

"I'm just saying," Paige huffed. "If I wanted to veto her appointment, I totally could. She doesn't just automatically get to plan the dance."

Quinn perked up again. "You guys are planning the dance?" He looked at me when he said it. "Cool. Can there be, like, no chaperones?"

"Ask Molly." I shrugged. "She's in charge."

Molly's face flushed like she was about to explode with power. "I'll think about it," she said, with forced nonchalance. Milliseconds later, her right eye started to twitch.

"Sick." Quinn gave me a hair toss and turned around again.

Molly yanked her notebook out of her backpack and flipped to a new page. "Okay. So who's gonna do what for the committee? Liv, you'll be my creative consultant. And Nessa? You'll be in charge of lists and things. Okay?" She started scribbling furiously with her purple glitter pen. "And Kace—"

"Wait. *Lists and things*?" Nessa tightened her cognac leather corset belt two notches.

"It'll look good on your transcript," I offered. "Like you're a team player."

"Deal." Nessa fished around her bag and unearthed an electronic organizer.

"Okay, so we have to come up with a theme first," Liv started. "What about—"

"No. Wait!" Molly slapped the table with her palm, then swiveled her stool toward me. "Kace? Are *you* in?" Her Burt's Bees–waxed lower lip protruded slightly. "Pretty please? I really feel like this is my calling, like, in life. And I can't do it if you won't—"

"I'm in, I'm in." I squeezed her hand. "Whatever you need." In the second row, Zander ducked to fish something out of his backpack. His blue streak lulled me into a comatose state for just a second.

"Awesome." Molly settled back in her chair and gave her hair a satisfied shake. Maybe it was the new cut, but her face-framing layers made her seem way older than she had over the weekend. I wondered if it had anything to do with Phoenix from ninth. "So now all we have to do is decide who we're taking to the dance. Me first. I'm taking the person I like more than I've liked anybody else, ever—"

"Yourself?" Paige sulked.

"—my BOYFRIEND, Phoenix." Mols straightened up a little in her chair, probably so the word *boyfriend* would find its way to the second row. But if he heard her, Zander didn't look up. I swallowed the stampede of butterflies in my throat.

"Ummm . . ." Liv twirled the ends of her scarf and lowered her voice to a whisper. "There's this cute guy from my early-morning meditation class."

"Maybe I'll bring that French exchange student I told you guys about? Mattieu?" Nessa's long, dark lashes fluttered. "Not that I need a guy to validate me."

"Definitely not," I said. With her shrink mom and professor dad, Nessa had been all over the world. But despite hanging with boys in at least six different time zones, she had even less boy experience than I did. Only Molly, Liv, and I knew she'd never even come close to kissing a boy. That was because her super-strict parents set her curfew at 8 P.M. According to Molly, most boys didn't even get warmed up until eight thirty.

Suddenly, I realized that all the girls were staring at me.

"Kacey?" Nessa's almond-shaped eyes were wide, hopeful. Begging me to take back the spotlight. "Who's the lucky dude?"

All the girls glanced meaningfully at the back of Quinn's head.

Well, all the girls with the exception of Paige, who pinched me under the table. Hard.

"Ow!" I squeaked, slapping her hand away. Half the class turned to look at me. This time, Zander did look up and smile. His eyes were like mercury: a silvery gray color that was different every time you looked. Even if you looked as often as humanly possible.

"Well?" Molly hissed excitedly. "Who's it gonna be?"

"I'll figure it out," I murmured, without taking my eyes off of Zander. And I would.

Eventually.

—

LOFTY FEELINGS
Tuesday, 3:45 P.M.

I stood on the street corner outside Zander's loft fifteen minutes before rehearsal was supposed to start, my breath shallow in my chest. I'd been to Zander's block tons of times. *This is just an ordinary rehearsal,* I told myself, adjusting the guitar strap that crossed my chest. *Nothing is different.*

"Let me in!" Rapping on the metal door made my knuckles sting. "It's arctic out here!"

"It's open!" Zander's voice was barely audible over the shriek of jazz music coming from inside the loft.

I hip-bumped my way through the door, almost tripping over Hendrix, Zander's salt-and-pepper mutt. Hendrix bristled and took a few wary steps back. Even the dog didn't think my being here was a good idea.

"Easy," I murmured, trying to remember whether it was dogs or cats that could smell impending disaster. "It's gonna be fine."

"What's up, Miss Simon?" Zander yelled over the music. He was stretched out on a brand-new pool table. His right foot dangled several inches above the painted concrete floor, twitching in awkward rhythm to the erratic trumpet squeals emanating from the speakers. Nelson Lund, Gravity's keyboardist, was twirling a cue stick like a martial arts weapon. The Beat was filming Nelson with his handheld camcorder. And Kevin, our bassist, was watching from the kitchen table.

I stabbed the POWER button on the stereo by the door, plunging the loft into silence. "How can you listen to that stuff? It sounds like Ella throwing a marathon tantrum. Only more off-key," I said, eyeing the rest of the guys with surprise. Did Zander really want to give me my "surprise" with an audience?

Zander *tsk*ed at the forty-foot ceiling. "That's like saying Ella could paint a Jackson Pollock just by flinging finger paint at a canvas."

"You said it. Not me." I rested my new guitar against the wall, stuffed my hands in my pockets, and perched on the arm of the brown leather sofa in the living area. The spacious, open loft looked exactly the same as it had the last time I'd been here: Two spiral staircases led to sleeping spaces, and exposed metal pipes lined the ceiling like modern industrial sculpture. The smooth concrete was painted different colors to distinguish the kitchen from the living area from the dining room. There was a small breakfast nook in the back corner, where several stools and a mic stand sat in anticipation of Gravity's reunion.

Only one thing felt different: Seventy-five percent of the band was blatantly ignoring me.

"Um, guys? Hello?"

The Beat briefly swung his camcorder toward me, then refocused on Nelson.

"That's dude for *Welcome back*, in case you missed it." Zander sat up and hopped off the pool table, feet hitting the concrete with a slap. "You guys want a snack before we get started?"

On the copper dining table, his phone started to vibrate. Kevin reached for it, but Zander practically sprinted the few feet from the pool table to the dining area.

"Got it." He checked the screen, then stuffed his phone in the back pocket of his jeans. "Text."

"Who was it, bro?" The Beat asked as we moved to the kitchen. Kevin buried his head in the pantry and Nelson whipped open the door to the fridge.

"Nothing. Nobody." Zander reached for the box of

Cocoa Puffs on the marble-topped island and tore it open.

The guys exchanged glances, but nobody looked at me.

"HEY. GUYS. I'M RIGHT HERE," I shouted, the ball of nervous energy in my stomach suddenly unraveling into full-on anger. "The least you could do is say hi."

"Okay. You wanna talk?" Kevin hoisted himself onto the island. The cuffs of his gray jeans were so frayed they looked like cowboy fringe. "Why don't you tell us if you're back for good, or if we should get you an understudy just in case?"

I balked. His words stung, mostly because deep down, I knew he had a right to be worried. I *had* bailed on the band once before, when Molly had made me choose between music and my friends.

"I'm in," I said emphatically, taking a seat on one of the backless silver bar stools. "For good."

Kevin just shrugged.

"Give her a break, Cho. She said she's in." Zander nodded his blue streak at me in encouragement.

"Yeah. Girl deserves mad points for saving us at the showcase," The Beat piped up in my defense. "If she hadn't taken over lead vocals, we'd probably still be stalling up there."

"True, but—" A question mark lingered in Nelson's voice.

"I *saved* you because band members have each other's backs. Which is why I would never bail on you guys again." I wiped a thin layer of sweat from my temples. It felt like someone had turned up the heat in the loft for the sole purpose of making me squirm.

"I'm just saying, you left once before." Kevin shook his head, unconvinced. "What's gonna stop you from bolting again?"

"I *said* I'm not gonna bolt, and I'm not gonna bolt," I snapped, whipping my head in Zander's direction. "Can we change the subject, please?"

Right on cue, the loft's front door swung open, and a red rolling suitcase toppled through the doorway. Behind it was a girl about our age wearing shiny over-the-knee black wedge boots, distressed gray jeans, and a mesh sweater that hinted at a neon-yellow bra underneath. Her glinting jet-black hair was swept into a messy side braid, and a black-studded wrap encircled her head. Two hot-pink plastic skulls dotted her earlobes.

The girl kicked the door closed with the heel of her boot and headed for the kitchen without a second's hesitation. She moved with the unhurried confidence of a guy, but her hips were all girl. High school girl, specifically.

"Heyyy!" Zander practically tackled the hot intruder in a giant bear hug, lifting her in the air and twirling her around. Her laugh echoed in the loft. I stared stupidly, feeling like I was watching one of those cologne commercials that promised a rock-star life for those willing to smell like wood chips.

Zander turned back to us and said, "Surprise!"

My stomach bottomed out. *Surprise?* This strange, gorgeous girl was my surprise?

I should have trusted my instincts. I *knew* I hated surprises.

Who *was* this girl? Desperate, I looked to the guys for clues. But Kevin was staring like he'd never seen her before either. His mouth was slightly open and his eyes were clouded. It was the same expression I'd seen on plenty of guys' faces when Molly wore her leather miniskirt to school.

The worst part was, I couldn't blame him. The girl was objectively, scientifically gorgeous. Her skin was a deeper olive than Liv's; her eyes a light, grayish green. And her lips . . .

. . . were way too close to Zander's neck.

"You made it!" Zander said.

"Of course I *made* it," she said breathlessly when Zander let her down. Her hair floated in perfect, wispy layers around her heart-shaped face. "What'd you think, I wouldn't be able to tear myself away from Seattle?"

Seattle?

"Wasn't sure." Zander grinned, and then the two of them just stood there, staring at each other with these lame, goofy smiles on their faces. I ran my tongue over my braces, feeling the beginnings of a cold sore on the inside of my right cheek.

Behind me, The Beat coughed.

"Oh, right." Zander shook his head, like he'd completely forgotten about us. "This is Nelson, Kevin, and The Beat. From Gravity."

"Hey," the guys managed.

She waved hello, her clear pink bangle bracelets clacking together. "Aaand . . . this must be your new girl?" The girl narrowed her kohl-lined eyes at me. The liner extended past the outer corner of her eyes and slightly upward, giving an exotic twist to her features.

"You must be jet-lagged," I said sweetly. "*You're* the new girl. *I'm* the lead singer. Kacey."

"*Mrow.*" Kevin made a catfight noise in my ear. I elbowed him in the gut, but even I was surprised at the edge in my voice. I sounded like the old Kacey. Not the newer, more secure version of myself—the one who wasn't even supposed to be into Zander because of the Girl Code.

"Kacey." The girl smiled to herself like my name was some joke the rest of us couldn't possibly understand.

"Oh. I get it. It's, like, supposed to be retro. Kacey. Cute."

My face felt hot. "And you aaaare . . ." Resolving to be nice, I unearthed my best fake Simon Smile, which I hadn't used since I'd retired from Channel M.

"Stevie," she said smoothly, locking her gaze with mine. "The lead singer from Hard Rock Life."

The *and your worst nightmare* part was implied.

SIXTH SENSE SAYS . . .
Tuesday, 4:34 P.M.

I didn't know how much rehearsal time we'd wasted by the time I found myself sitting cross-legged on the floor in Zander's living area, wedged between Nelson and The Beat, a B.B. King record crackling in the background. Stevie sat on the couch between Zander and Kevin, her boots kicked off on the floor like she owned the place.

"And then I told the sound guy—" Stevie dissolved into laughter. "You tell it," she gasped at Zander.

"Okay. Wait. No. You tell it. It was your guitar." Zander's toes curled around the ropy lip of the couch cushion.

"No, *you* tell it!" Stevie opened the second of two bags of Swedish Fish she'd unearthed from her suitcase. The relentless crinkle of the cellophane made my left eye twitch.

"No, *you*—"

"Will one of you just tell it?" I blurted, lurching forward. My funny bone slammed into the cold marble edge of the coffee table, and I chomped down on my tongue.

"Ohmygod, are you okay?" Even a mouthful of Swedish Fish couldn't mask Stevie's new round of laughter.

"I'm fine," I snapped. At least the radiating pain in my elbow provided a momentary distraction from my migraine and eye twitch.

"Okay, okay. I'll tell it," Zander decided. "So then she tells the sound guy—"

"*I SAID, IT WAS SUPPOSED TO BE AN E FLAT!*" the two yelled at the same time.

The Beat leaned forward and slapped Stevie five, and Nelson grinned. Even Kevin stopped drooling over Stevie long enough to crack a smile. Clearly, I was the only one in the group with a functional sixth sense. And that sixth sense was screaming that Stevie from Seattle was trouble with a capital GET OUT.

I was suddenly furious with Zander, but I couldn't decide why. To be fair, I had a million reasons to choose from. How he'd let some random chick waltz into the loft and take over rehearsal. How two seconds after Stevie arrived he'd put out the best kind of fancy Whole Foods almonds, when he *knew* it would take an hour of flossing to excavate them from my braces.

"So how long have you been in the band?" Stevie focused her cat-eyed gaze on me. "Zander's been talking about Gravity since the school year started, but he never mentioned you by name." She yanked up her sleeves, revealing a leather cuff bracelet identical to Zander's.

"Um, a couple of weeks," I said distractedly, unable to take my eyes off that stupid bracelet.

"Then she went on a little hiatus." Kevin's dark eyes flashed.

"I was—I had a lot going on," I said, glaring at Kevin.

Stevie shot a warning glance at Zander. "Commitment issues?"

"That's not it. I—" Wait. Why did I feel like I had to explain myself? *She* was the outsider. *I* was Kacey. Elisabeth. Simon! I sat up straight and visualized myself in the Channel M studios, sitting at my anchor desk and prepping for an interview with a hostile source. I was in charge. This was *my* show.

"So, Stevie. What is it, exactly, that you're doing here?" Keeping my tone journalistically neutral was taking every ounce of my strength. "And how long did you say you were gonna be in town?"

"I didn't." Stevie shrugged. "But a couple of weeks, I guess."

"Her dad's interviewing for a job as a prof with U of

C," Zander added proudly. "Gabe. You guys'll love him."

"Cool." Nelson cracked his neck on one side, then the other. "I bet they're putting you guys up in a sick hotel, huh?"

"Actually, we're staying here." Stevie curled her feet underneath her and sank back into the sofa cushions, a few inches closer to Zander than before. "Our parents are old friends, so Vann and Lily invited us to crash at the loft."

Vann and Lily? I'd never even heard Zander's parents' names, let alone met them. "Wait. You're staying here. At the loft."

"Yep." She nodded smugly.

There were so many things wrong with that arrangement, I'd already lost count. For one thing, the loft was basically one giant room. Which meant that no matter *where* Stevie slept for the next two weeks, she and Zander would be sleeping in the same room.

"Oh, and we thought it would be cool if she came to school with me," Zander was saying. "If they decide to move here, she'd be going to Marquette anyway, so . . ."

Move here? "Don't you have homework?" I interrupted, half curious and half desperate. "Like, from your actual school?" I couldn't even process the part about a possible move. I would rather let Ella tighten my braces with a corkscrew than matriculate with Stevie.

"We're on spring break for two weeks. My school is year-round, so we get longer vacations." She popped the last of the Swedish Fish into her mouth. Kevin watched her toss them back with a look of dazed admiration.

"So, Kacey, you can introduce her around, right? Like to"—Zander shifted uncomfortably—"your friends?"

"Totally," I said through a tight smile. "I'm sure Molly would *love* that."

"Whatever. I doubt your little friends would be my kind of people, anyway." Stevie shrugged at me. "No offense."

My throat closed up. "Obviously," I mumbled.

Stevie hopped to her feet. "So, let's hear you guys jam."

The boys scrambled after her into the breakfast nook while I trailed reluctantly behind. I couldn't decide which was worse—being stuck here with Stevie or the knowledge that as soon as rehearsal ended, Zander and Stevie would be alone. In an empty loft.

"Hey, Goose." Stevie climbed onto the island in the kitchen and drew her knees to her chest. "Does this place kind of remind you of—"

"I was just about to say." Zander laughed as he tuned his guitar and Nelson tried a few notes on the keyboard.

"About to say what?" I adjusted my mic stand, even though the height was fine.

Zander pulled his stand closer to mine. I looked smugly

at Stevie, but she was picking at a thread in the cuff of her jeans.

"Before we got Hard Rock Life together, I was thinking about just doing a solo thing," he explained.

"But I kept trying to convince him to team up," Stevie added from her perch. "I knew a couple of good musicians, but nobody plays guitar like this one, you know?"

"Duh," I said into the mic. My voice boomed across the loft.

Zander rolled his eyes at the compliment. "Anyway, I was gonna call myself One-Sided Truce."

"That's the worst. Name. Ever," I informed him.

"That's what I told him." Stevie laughed.

"I was eleven," Zander protested. "Anyway, I'd booked my first gig at this bookstore on the waterfront. Two stories, a cool loft setup kind of like this one. I was pumped. Put an ad in the paper, on Facebook, everything. I even had some flyers printed, and Stevie offered to post them around town. But when I got to the gig, no one was there."

"How come?" The Beat asked.

"Funny you should ask." Stevie drummed her fingers together mischievously. "It seems there had been a little . . . *typo* on all the publicity materials."

Zander groaned. "Instead of saying 'One-Sided Truce,' the promo stuff read—"

"'—One-Legged Goose,'" Stevie finished proudly, with a slight bow at the waist. "Obviously, nobody showed up, because who wants to see that?"

The Beat tapped the cymbals as the guys burst out laughing.

"Dude. You got played!" Kevin roared.

"And from then on, he was Goose," Stevie said.

Skinny Jeans was a way funnier nickname, but whatever.

"I think that was my best prank ever," Stevie mused. "Definitely top three."

"And she's pulled some good ones," Zander said.

"He wouldn't speak to me for, like, three days. Finally I told him, 'Give this group thing a shot. We'll play one show, and if you want to go solo after that, you can.'" Stevie lifted her arms in a sweeping, dramatic gesture. "And the rest is history."

"Actually, I probably wouldn't have started Gravity if I hadn't loved HRL so much, you know?"

"You're welcome." Stevie winked at me.

I blinked back. "Is story time over? I'm ready to play."

"Atta girl." Zander grinned, strumming the intro to a song he'd written several years before. He'd played it for me last week, and it was the perfect song: romantic and smack-dab in the middle of my range. By the time I was done with the first verse, Stevie would run crying back to the West Coast.

My lips parted, and I took a slow, easy breath.

"Hold up. Hold up." Stevie lifted her hands in the time-out symbol.

The microphone amplified my sharp inhale.

"What?" I whipped my head toward Zander, but he suddenly seemed fascinated with his nail beds.

"Oh. I was just wondering where your guitar is." Stevie's voice was saccharine, the same tone Molly used with Paige. Only amplified.

"I don't play," I mumbled. "Yet. I'm—"

"She's gonna learn," Zander said lamely.

"You play?" The Beat rapped a drumstick in triple-time on his thigh. "Let's hear it!"

"But—"

The sound of the guys' cheers cut me off.

Stevie slid off the counter. Zander handed her his guitar—the prized guitar he never let anybody touch—and she let loose.

"Oh, I've got this feeling. Like I'm spinning, dancing, reeling." Her voice was low and easy, uninhibited and powerful at the same time. She stared directly at Zander as she rocked out. It was as if everyone but him had disappeared. "And it happens every time he looks at me. And I can't breathe. He sets me free."

Stevie shifted her gaze to me. She smiled innocently, but I saw through the hardness in her stare. Her look told me to watch my back.

I gritted my teeth and matched her smile. My sixth sense *had* been wrong. Stevie from Seattle wasn't as bad as I'd thought.

She was worse.

SMELLS LIKE TEEN RIVAL
Tuesday, 8:30 P.M.

"I'm upstaiiiirs!" Paige shouted down the narrow stair-well of the Greenes' townhouse when Ella and I stepped through the front door later that night.

I wiped my feet on the blue color-blocked jute rug in the entryway, motioning for Ella to do the same. Paige's townhouse had the same layout as ours, with a kitchen, half bath, and living area on the first floor, two bedrooms and bathrooms on the second, and an attic on the third. But their house had always seemed much bigger to me. It was probably the clean, low lines of the Greenes' minimal-ist décor—and the lack of finger paintings and traced-hand turkey drawings on their stainless steel refrigerator.

When we got to the second floor, Paige popped out of the first door to the right. Her bob was pulled into tiny sprouts that barely passed for pigtails, and her dad's gigantic NYU LAW sweatshirt almost obscured her green-and-yellow striped boxers.

"Hey, El! Didn't know you were coming, too."

"Mom had a late interview," I explained, then mouthed, *Sorry.*

"Thank you for us coming over, Paige." Ella beamed. I gave her a thumbs-up.

"Uh, my pleasure." Paige tousled Ella's curls, then gave me a curious, crooked smile. A dab of white zit cream dotted her upper lip. "Everything okay?"

"'Course," I said, shaking my head violently when Ella wasn't looking.

"Got it. Come on in."

If the rest of the Greenes' house was an image out of a West Elm catalog, Paige's room was a "before" shot on one of those *Help, I'm a hoarder* shows. Teetering piles of history books, presidential biographies, and rubber-banded campaign posters lay at the foot of the low platform bed. Shoes and clothes, all black, littered the hardwood floor, and Paige's pistachio duvet was draped over the bamboo papasan chair by the window. The large silver magnet board above the bed was papered with pictures, a crumpled program from the *Guys and Dolls* show I'd just starred in, and sticky notes Paige had written to herself. The computer desk in the corner was home to highlighters, an open box of granola, and an impressive haul of GO GREENE campaign buttons.

"Nessa would have a field day with this place, psychologically speaking." I stepped over Paige's hair-dryer, which was plugged into the wall by the door, and cleared a space on the bed.

Paige shrugged. "Mom says as long as she doesn't have to look at it, I can keep it however I want. So what's up?"

"It's . . . hard to explain." I eyed Ella, wishing she were still at an age when I could say whatever I wanted in front of her. These days, everything I said went straight to Mom. Verbatim.

Paige nodded her understanding. "Hey, El," she said enthusiastically. "Wanna listen to this cool new song I downloaded on my iPod?" She pulled headphones from her desk drawer.

"Kacey has those, too!" Ella reached for them.

"Nothing she shouldn't be listening to," I warned.

"Please. What kind of an influence do you think I am?" Gently, Paige slipped the earbuds into Ella's ears and fiddled with the dial. Then she led her to the papasan chair and tucked her in beneath the wilted duvet. "Okay. Go."

I took a deep breath. "So this afternoon I had rehearsal

at the loft. And I got there early for the surprise, you know?"

"Riiiight." Paige squinted, collapsing next to me on the bed.

"*¿Dónde está la biblioteca?*" Ella chirped from the papasan chair. "Where is the library?"

"So we're about to get started and . . . this girl walks in." I told her everything there was to tell about Stevie, from the perfect smile to the takeover attempt at the end of rehearsal.

"*Goose?*" Paige said skeptically when I'd finished. Her brows disappeared beneath her bangs.

"Lame, right?" I fell onto my back. "What am I gonna do? She can't move here! She'll steal Gravity, and Zander . . . I have to talk to Zander. Explain that Stevie is—"

"Is what?" Paige looked at me like I was nuts. "Cramping your style? You can't bad-mouth Stevie. If she's his best friend—"

"*I'm* his best friend, Paige!" I snapped, sitting up again. "Me. Not. Her."

"Okay. I know," Paige said softly, in the same tone Mom used when she was trying to appease Ella mid-tantrum.

"*¿Quieres un café?* Would you like some coffee?"

Paige tightened her pigtails and looked me straight in

the eye. "I just think this is one of those times when honesty isn't the best policy, Kace."

I made a gagging sound.

"And just because Stevie's here doesn't mean you and Zander aren't still good—*best*—friends, you know?" She pursed her lips. "Did they used to date or something?"

"I—I don't know. Maybe not." I sounded weak, even to myself. "It's just that I'm trying to get things back to normal with the guys. They don't trust me as it is. And having Stevie here isn't gonna help." I dug a stuffed duck out from under my thigh and pitched it across the room. Suddenly, the bedroom felt stifling.

"Just promise me you won't talk to Zander, Kace. It's not the right thing to do." Paige lifted her pinky finger, swear-style, but I shook my head.

"Give me another option, then, Madame President. Something that'll prove that I'm back with Gravity for good, and there's no room for chicks from Seattle."

"I thought you'd never ask," Paige said coyly. "Sometimes I think you forget about the strings I can pull as seventh-grade president."

"Paige. You getting me backstage passes to the Debate Club finals is so not gonna fix this."

Paige sniffed, poking at the zit cream on her face. "I'm going to pretend I didn't hear that."

"Spill!"

"Okay. So Molly *thinks* she's running the dance, but she's totally just a puppet. Guess who the faculty advisor for middle school social events is this semester?" Her shoulders inched toward her ears, which they always did when she was excited or stressed. "Dr. Phil!"

"Ohmygod. Dr. Phil." My stomach flip-flopped at the mention of Dr. Philippa Meyers, Marquette's hippie-chick school shrink. She'd been called in to mediate when I'd been ousted as the lead in the school musical due to my braces-induced lisp. "Why would you say that name to me?"

"But think about it! She'll be in charge of all major decisions," Paige said.

"Point, please."

"Decisions like, oh, I dunno . . . the evening's entertain—"

"THE BAND!" I leapt up and grabbed Paige by the shoulders. "I could get Gravity a gig playing the dance, and they'd know I was in it for good! There's no way Stevie could compete with that!"

"EXACTLY!" Paige shrieked.

"You're the best." I threw my arms around her and squeezed.

"Hey, Paige?"

We jumped at the sound of Ella's voice. The white ear-buds were draped around her neck, halter-style.

"I want to watch TV," she whimpered. Her lower lip trembled, which I recognized as the international six-year-old sign for TANTRUM AHEAD: 3 MINUTES.

"Okay, okay." I jumped off the bed and hurried over to the jumbo TV set Paige had gotten at our neighborhood garage sale last year. It hailed from the early nineties and was missing the VOLUME-DOWN button, which meant that everybody on Paige's TV was screaming, all the time.

I punched the POWER button and held it for the required five seconds. A scene in a hospital room slowly flickered onto the screen. A young female doctor in a lab coat was yelling at the camera.

"This is an extremely rare, flesh-eating fungus. There are currently fewer than fifty documented cases in the world."

"Gross." I jabbed at the CHANNEL button, but the logo in the bottom right corner of the screen stayed put.

"It's broken." Paige shrugged. "I only get the Surgery Channel now."

The screen cut to an image of a woman with a disintegrated face.

"Monster!" Ella screamed and threw her arms around me.

"Great." I groaned, petting Ella's curls with one hand and turning the TV off with the other. "Now she's gonna have nightmares for weeks!"

"Oops. Sorry, El." Paige winced.

My phone buzzed in my jacket pocket. "Hold on."

MOM: HOME FROM THE STUDIO. WHERE ARE YOU GIRLS???
TEXT IN 30 SECONDS OR I CALL NANCY GRACE.

"We have to go," I said. "Ella?"

But Ella's eyes were wide, unblinking. *"Monster,"* she whispered again.

"Uh-oh." Paige bit her lower lip.

"She'll be fine. So you'll set up the meeting?"

"First thing tomorrow."

I gave Paige a quick hug, then led Ella down the stairs and outside. We cut across the crunchy grass and ducked through the hole in the picket fence that led to our property. I grinned, the brackets in my braces turning cold. This was the perfect solution. I'd get Gravity a rockin' gig and lock down my place in the band in the process. Once Stevie realized there wasn't room for her here, she'd slink back to Seattle, where she belonged.

A BIG STARFISH IN A LITTLE POND
Wednesday, 10:05 A.M.

"We'll have a brief lecture this morning, followed by a lab activity," Spinster Finnster wheezed in third-period Marine Bio the next morning. She whacked her chest with a closed fist and reached for the can of chocolate Ensure Plus on her desk. "You may take this time to choose a lab partner." She lifted a skeletal finger. "A reminder to all students: If you haven't turned in your permission slips for Monday's field trip to the aquarium, you must do so by the end of the week."

I swiveled to the right and pinned Molly's hand to the lab table. "You're mine, Knight," I sang. I was dying to tell Molly that I'd already secured an amazing musical talent for the dance—namely, me—but I'd decided to hold off until the meeting Paige had gotten me with Dr. Phil. Just, you know, in case.

"Kacey! Oww!" Molly smiled through her whine. "Okaaay."

Liv and Nessa exchanged meaningful glances, leaving Paige as the fifth wheel.

In the row ahead of us, Quinn glanced over his shoulder. "Hey, Molly. Want to pair up?"

"She's taken," I informed him.

Molly shrugged at Quinn.

"You can be in our group, too, Paige," I said, nodding at her.

"Kacey." Molly narrowed her eyes at me. "We're supposed to pair off. If she's in our group, it'll make the group . . . *odd*."

Paige leaned over me and slow-clapped. "I had no idea you knew your numbers!"

I tuned them out and searched the room for Zander. His usual seat was empty, and I hadn't seen him all morning. With any luck, Stevie had suffered a tragic El-related accident on the way to school.

"What were you up to last night?" I asked Molly. "You never wrote back to my text about dance planning."

"Sorry. I was FaceTimeing with the BF till bedtime. I was telling him about my new extracurric. And my mom said it was time to turn off the lights. He didn't have to yet, since he's fourteen—"

"You mentioned." Nessa pulled a pink sticky note from her backpack and started sponging bits of lint from her structured velvet blazer.

"So I just put the phone next to me on the pillow." Molly's eyes glinted with naughty pride.

"All night long?" Liv asked incredulously. Then she flicked a dark curl over her shoulder. "I mean, no big deal."

"Well, until, like, three A.M.," Mols admitted, yanking the sleeves of her silvery tunic over her wrists. "Then I had to pee, and I didn't want him to hear me flush."

"All right, students. I assume you've all chosen your lab partners?" Finnster rasped. "Let's get started."

Paige bent over her notebook, pen poised for action.

"So. How're the spy sessions going with you-know-who?" Molly whispered as Finnster embarked on what promised to be a brutal lecture on starfish.

"Good! You know. Fine." I gnawed at my lower lip. I hated not telling her about Stevie. But what was I supposed to say? *There's this too-cool-for-school chick who might be trying to steal my band and the boy I have a crush on? You know, your ex-boyfriend?*

"Did you find out if he likes another girl?" Her voice dropped even lower, and she inched her stool closer to mine.

"Not yet." I tugged at the end of my ponytail, jiggling my leg at top speed.

"Restless Leg Syndrome," Nessa diagnosed sympathetically, looking down at my thigh. "I saw the commercial." Molly went silent. I couldn't even look at her, for fear I'd give something away.

"Kacey. What's going on?"

"I—um . . ." Molly had never been the most perceptive knife in the drawer, so the fact that she was picking up on my vibes meant I was sending out some pretty strong signals.

"You know something, don't you?" She bounced in her seat. "About Zander. Tell me."

I sighed. "Yesterday at rehearsal, one of Zander's friends from Seattle showed up. She's visiting for a couple of weeks."

"Like, a *girl*friend? Do you think he likes her?"

"I don't know yet," I said truthfully. "But we'll have plenty of time to find out. She'll be at school for the next couple of weeks. She might even move here."

Molly's forehead wrinkled like a boxer puppy's.

"That's all I know, though. But you've got Phoenix and everything now, so you probably don't even care, right?"

"Yeah. Right." Molly pursed her lips into a thin, pensive line. Her lashes fluttered slightly, the way they always did when she felt torn about something. During a trip to the mall last year, she'd been so undecided about a one-shoulder top that the salesgirl had asked if she was having a seizure.

The door inched open at the front of the class, and Zander ducked inside. "Um, Ms. Finnster? Sorry I'm late, but I was just in the office. I, uh, have a guest." He produced a folded pink slip from the back pocket of his jeans.

"Quite all right, Mr. Jarvis." Finnster frowned through her bifocals at the note.

Zander opened the door a little wider, making room for Stevie to strut across the threshold. The room went silent, and Quinn, Jake, and Aaron snapped to attention. In a sleek black moto jacket, low-slung army-green cargos rolled up at the ankle, and round-toed rose-gold snakeskin pumps, she looked like the cover model for a *Chicago Public School Girls: Cool Chicks Edition* calendar.

"This is my friend Stevie from back home," Zander announced, half to Finnster and half to the class. "She'll be here for a couple of weeks."

"What's up," Stevie said coolly, stuffing her hands in her pockets. Her moto jacket lifted, revealing a momentary flash of belly ring.

Molly slapped my thigh. She'd spent all summer trying to get her parents to agree to a belly ring. When they said no, she ran away to my house for an entire long weekend.

"Class, let's all say hello to Mr. Jarvis's sister, Sheila," Finnster prompted.

"Hiiii, Sheila," we droned.

The clacking of Stevie's heels on the linoleum floor was the only sound as Zander and Stevie took the empty seats next to Paige. Being this close to Stevie made my skin itch.

"*What* is everybody staring at?" Molly said into my ear. "She's not that hot. Right?" Sweat was starting to make her temples shine, and her eyeliner was smudged at the corners. Even her hair looked deflated. The very idea that she might not be the hottest girl in the grade seemed to be sucking the life out of her.

"Well . . ." Liv stared while Stevie consulted her iPhone.

Quinn whipped around and winked. "If you need a lab partner, Sheila, I'd be more than happy to volunteer."

"It's *Stevie*, moron," Stevie said without looking up.

"Ooooooh," the guys hooted. Jake and Aaron elbowed each other.

"Feisty," observed Quinn approvingly.

"That's offensive to women," Nessa announced.

Molly shushed her, then flicked her hair to get Stevie's attention. "Hey! New girl."

Stevie sighed dramatically and looked up. "Yes, B-list Barbie?"

"Whoa." Paige pushed back her stool. Nobody talked to Molly like that, no matter how cool her shoes were. And even Paige knew it.

Nessa and Liv gasped.

Molly opened her mouth, but nothing came out. Not even air. I'd never seen this kind of horror in my best friend's face. Not even last semester, when she had an allergic reaction to her mom's plumping gloss and had to come to school looking like a Real Housewife with a botched lip job.

"Mols?" I whispered, trying to catch her eye. "Molly? Are you okay?"

"Now that you all have partners, let's move ahead with our laboratory exercise." Finnster reached for her walker. "You will all find safety goggles and gloves in the drawers under your tables."

The snap of latex gloves brought Molly back to life. She turned toward me. "Kacey." Her breathing was labored. "I can't even—I don't—"

"Don't worry, Mols." I grabbed her hand and squeezed reassuringly. "She's going down."

SHRINK RAPT
Wednesday, 12:02 P.M.

Just two minutes after the lunch bell, I stood outside Philippa Meyers, Psy.D.'s office, hand poised to knock.

"Girls?" Dr. Phil's soothing voice sounded from behind the door, along with the prolonged notes of some kind of chanting music.

I jumped back. She had a freaky way of sensing when someone was loitering outside her office. I wondered if she could also sense that I'd run out of clean underwear this morning and was wearing bikini bottoms beneath my hot-pink tights.

"Kacey?" Paige nudged me forward, and we stepped inside the lemongrass-scented office.

"Kacey Simon." Sitting at her desk by the window, Dr. Phil popped a handful of raw almonds into her mouth.

"And our esteemed seventh-grade president."

Paige bowed her head ceremoniously.

"Oh, please." I plopped onto the couch with a *huff*. Just being in this office put me in a bad mood. The lavender walls clashed with the mustard-yellow armchair, and the trickling stone fountain made me need to pee.

"I'm glad to see you girls." Dr. Phil rose, her gray-and-black maxi skirt floating around her ankles as she settled into her armchair. She propped a pair of green, fabric-soled flats on the coffee table. "Paige mentioned you have some feedback about the dance, although I believe I heard another student was chairing the planning committee."

"Yes, Molly Knight." I perched so close to the edge of the couch I was almost falling off. I refused to get comfortable. If you weren't careful, you could end up curled in a ball, sobbing about how your little sister had more finger paintings on the refrigerator door than you'd ever had as a kid, and seriously, *didn't* . . . [sniff] *your mom know* . . . [sniff] *how that made you feel?*

"But Kacey's handling some of the more important . . . details." Paige wedged herself between me and the couch arm.

"Right. Like . . . the music. I know who we should hire to play the dance." I held my breath. The busted couch springs squeaked beneath me with Paige's excitement.

"Oh, good. I'm glad you have some ideas. I actually have a list of school-approved DJs somewhere around here . . ." Dr. Phil rummaged through one of six piles of paperwork at the foot of her chair, tossing an old *Trib* out of the way and frowning at a Pottery Barn catalog. "If I can get my hands on it, you girls can take it back to the planning committee and decide at your next . . ." Her voice trailed off. "Has anybody seen a green Post-It?"

"Actually, you don't have to worry about the Post-It," I said graciously. "I think it would be really cool if we hired a band, and—" I stopped short as Dr. Phil's gold-coin earrings swung from side to side.

"I'm afraid a live band won't work." Dr. Phil tapped the diamond nose stud in her nostril, probably worried she'd lost it along with the green Post-It. "It's school policy. With a DJ, we can approve the song list ahead of time. A band is just a little more . . . unpredictable."

"Wait. What?" I scooted even further toward the edge of the couch. "But—so you're saying a live band isn't even an option?"

"I'll tell you what that is." I'd momentarily forgotten about Paige, until she unleashed her outrage just inches away. "It's *censorship*. It's Marquette being the Man, flexing its Man muscles, and stomping on the People for no reason."

Dr. Phil's rosy lips twitched. "With its Man muscles?" she asked.

"No. With its Man foot," Paige huffed. "Just . . . whatever. It doesn't matter. My point is that this is unfair."

"I have to say, I—" Dr. Phil lifted her brows in my direction. "Off the record?"

I nodded. *Maybe.*

"I agree with you. It's your dance, and as long as the music is appropriate for middle school, I think you *should* be able to choose."

"Great!" My heartbeat returned to normal and I stood up. "Then it's settled. Thanks for your time."

"Unfortunately, I don't make the rules."

I dropped again.

"I'm sorry, girls, but there truly is nothing I can do. I'm relatively new here, and I just don't have much pull." The shrink shook her head, sending locks of short dark hair across her forehead. "But I'll catch up with you as soon as I find that DJ list. Deal?"

Deal? My entire body tensed. Clearly, Dr. Phil had no idea what was at stake here. My band. My best friend. My future. No way was I going to stink of incense for the rest of the day without getting what I wanted.

I stared straight at Dr. Phil. Direct eye contact was one of her most powerful school-shrink weapons, but she wasn't the only one who could stare a girl down. "Paige is right. This isn't fair. A band can get their songs preapproved, too! And the band we want to hire is a student band! From Marquette! So we'll be promoting extracurricular activities . . . and being . . . well-rounded, and stuff."

Dr. Phil opened her mouth, probably to protest, but I kept going. "You guys are always saying you want to support your students. By hiring a student band, you're encouraging kids to get involved! And haven't you seen those public service announcements? People who don't get involved in their school wind up, like, outcasts, and on drugs and stuff. Then they drop out of school. Which means the entire administration would be out of a job. So—"

"Whoa. Whoa." Dr. Phil cut me off. "Slow down. I'm going to need a little more information first, okay? Tell me a more about this band."

"It's called Gravity, and a bunch of seventh-grade boys are in it."

"And Kacey," Paige added.

"Right. And me. But we're really, really good. And we just want to show a little school spirit by playing the dance." She didn't argue, so I bit my lip and went in for the big sell. "It's just that after all the trauma with my braces and glasses and lisp and everything, I just . . .

I've been feeling like I don't really have a purpose, you know?"

Paige stifled a snort, forcing a fake cough.

"And I think playing the dance would make me feel . . ." Was a sniffle or an eye dab overkill? I settled on a medium-length shuddery sigh. ". . . whole again."

Aaand, scene.

Dr. Phil looked me straight in the eye and . . . *slow-clapped.*

My jaw dropped. "Hey! Aren't you supposed to just sit there and listen?"

"*Abort, abort,*" Paige muttered.

"I'm sorry, Kacey." Dr. Phil smiled, shaking her head. "I thought you deserved credit for a truly inspired performance."

"But I'm serious!" My voice cracked—for real this time. "It really would make me feel better. And I swear: We're really, really good."

"It's true," added Paige. "She's not just being an ego-maniac, although I could see how you would think that."

I kicked her swiftly in the shins.

Dr. Phil rubbed her chin, her expression suddenly serious. "You understand the position I'm in, though, don't you? I can't go to the principal and make a case for you without ever having heard—"

"Here! Just listen for a few seconds, okay?" I clawed at my Channel 5 messenger bag. My fingers were slick with sweat, but I managed to grab my phone. A text notification popped up on the screen.

ZANDER: U COMIN' TO REHEARSAL THIS PM?

I hit IGNORE and scrolled through my list of Gravity MP3s. I found my favorite: a duet Zander and I had done of an Aerosmith song.

I pressed the PLAY button, turned up the volume as loud as I could, and held my breath.

The sound of Zander's guitar emanated from the speakers, followed by our harmony. Zander and I were more in sync than the nerdy all-dude a cappella group that practiced in the hall during lunch. Unlike the Do-Re-Migos, we sounded cool. Smooth. Professional, even.

Dr. Phil's head listed to one side, and she bobbed her head along with the beat. "Wow," she said, sounding surprised.

"Wow, as in, we can play the dance?"

"Wow, as in, this is pretty good. And I'm a huge Aerosmith fan, so I'm tough to impress." There was still a note of hesitation in her voice. "But you guys are talented."

When the song came to an end, a heavy silence settled over the room. Something was holding Dr. Phil back, and if I didn't figure out what it was, I was done. Out of luck. Over. Kap—

"We'll do it for free," I blurted. "The money you were gonna use to hire a DJ can go back into the seventh-grade budget. So we're getting involved *and* giving back."

Dr. Phil shook her head slowly, tiny almost-dimples surfacing in her cheeks. "Kacey Simon, you drive a hard bargain."

"And?"

"Okay. And I'll talk to the principal."

"You rock." I grabbed Paige's hand and whisked her out of the office before Dr. Phil could change her mind.

THESE HALLS AREN'T BIG
ENOUGH FOR THE BOTH OF US
Wednesday, 3:09 P.M.

That afternoon when the girls and I congregated at my locker, Molly was still fuming over Stevie's diss.

"I can't even believe she talked to me like that in front of everybody." She kicked the vent on the locker next to mine, leaving a jagged scrape on the toe of her brand-new equestrian-style boots. "Ugh!" She flung herself against the painted locker door. "Now Sheila owes me a new pair of boots *plus* an apology."

"It's Ste—" The murderous squint in Molly's eye made me reconsider. "Never mind." I refocused on my combination lock, twisting the dial until I heard a *click*. Despite the usual post-bell free-for-all whirling around us, I'd never felt more at peace. I'd invited the girls over for our very first Party Planning Committee meeting. I was hoping

I'd be able to deliver the good news that I'd booked a band—my band—but I still hadn't heard back from Dr. Phil. The waiting was forcing my Restless Leg Syndrome into overdrive.

"I can't figure Stevie out." Liv crossed one vegan oxford thoughtfully over the other. "She seemed so confident—"

"Egotistical," I corrected.

"—and *centered*. But in a mean way, kind of."

I loved that Liv always tried to see the good in people. But finding the good in Stevie would require a high-powered microscope. That is, if there was any good to be found.

"There's a word for people like her." Nessa shuffled the pack of neon-orange flash cards she'd made during study hall. "Narcissist."

"Agreed." It was a given that the girls would back me up. But it still felt good to know that they were on my side 100 percent again.

"I don't get it. Why would Z like a girl like that, anyway?" Molly looked more lost, hopeless, and scared than when she'd accidentally been enrolled in Honors Algebra. "Why would any guy?"

"Mols!" Liv said reproachfully. "To be fair, we don't actually know her, like, as a human being."

"Hey, Kacey? Kace!"

I turned and saw Zander and Stevie, speedwalking down Hemingway, the seventh-grade hall, Zander's blue streak darting through the crowd like a tiny tropical fish swimming upstream. Molly whipped her hair over her shoulder with gale-strength force and glared at Stevie, who was wearing a black camisole under an open-weave crocheted top.

"He is *not* about to rub that girl in my face," Molly grumbled under her breath. "If Phoenix weren't busy being in high school right now, I'd—"

"Good. I found you. You've been tough to hunt down lately, you know that?" Zander puffed, nudging my locker door closed. "So'd you get my text?"

"Sorry. I've been MIA with my new BF." Molly pinched a piece of hair between her index finger and thumb, and pretended to inspect her ends.

"Oh. I, uh, was talking to Kacey." Zander's shoulders twitched. "But that's . . . good. Good for you." He glanced up again and nodded at Nessa and Liv. "Hey. You guys remember Stevie, right?"

"Hey." A single head nod, nothing more. Good girls.

Stevie's cobalt-winged eyes cut accusingly to me. "He's texted you a million times." She cocked her head to one side. "It's like, I hear you *saying* you're committed to the band. But I'm just not *seeing* it."

Zander elbowed her.

I pressed my lips together to contain the primal scream fighting to get out. I wanted to put her in her place right here, right now. Tell her I'd booked a major gig for the band. But I'd promised myself I wouldn't mention talking to Dr. Phil until I officially had the green light. There would be nothing more horrifying than admitting failure like that in front of Stevie.

"So . . . are you coming to rehearsal, then?" Zander asked hopefully. "We're starting an hour late 'cause I have to take my sister over to a friend's house."

"Sorry." Molly squeezed my arm. "She's with us this afternoon."

"You are?" There was a thin metallic edge to Zander's voice.

"It's just one afternoon. I have to take care of something." I felt the sharp sting of anger traveling through my shoulders and back. What right did Zander have to judge me when he was the one who'd ruined practice the other day with his West Coast import?

Zander stuffed his hands in his pockets and looked down. "Gotcha."

"No worries. You girls can hit the mall or whatever it is you do around here." Stevie unzipped her slouchy emerald messenger bag and produced yet another bag of

Swedish Fish. "Besides, I wanted to play Goose a couple of songs I wrote on the plane. They're duets. You'd be bored."

I froze in front of my locker, my tongue thick in my mouth. *Say something! Don't let her do this!* But something about Stevie left me paralyzed, unable to form the words to tell her off. And before I could move, she'd hooked her elbow through Zander's and led him back down the hallway.

Thirty minutes later, the girls and I were tucked safely away in my bedroom, where there was virtually no chance of any contact with Zander or She Who Was Ruining My Life. Just to be sure, I powered off my phone and stuffed it under my pillow.

"And seriously? That eyeliner made her look like a parrot or something," Nessa cracked. "She's obviously compensating for something." She turned back to the chalkboard wall and cleared the patch of board next to my bed, dragging an eraser in careful, even strokes from ceiling to floor.

"Tacky Wanna Cracker?" Molly's head popped out of the photo booth, where she was taking self-portraits in my still-tagged silk fuchsia minidress. "This is super cute. Can I wear it to the dance?"

"Yeah, if I don't." I sat cross-legged on the bed, hugging a throw pillow that smelled like Ella.

"Girls. Focus." Liv was doing a headstand on the wall opposite my bed. In one smooth move, she kicked her bare feet to the floor and whipped her body upright. Her face was flushed with determination. "I did *not* like the way that girl talked to us. Especially you, Kacey."

I hugged a pillow to my chest. "I know. And she's here for two whole weeks! Possibly forever!"

"If we can figure out what makes her tick, we'll know exactly what it'll take to keep her in her place." Nessa crossed the room and pulled a fresh box of colored chalk from my desk drawer. She selected a yellow piece and returned to the board. "Like, what are her insecurities? Her fears?" She wrote WEAKNESSES in all caps and underlined it three times.

"That's the thing! It's like she doesn't *have* any," I complained. "Have you guys seen the way she is around school? One day in a brand-new school and she's acting like she runs the place!"

"Her wardrobe is obviously not her weakness," Liv mused appreciatively. "She's got killer style."

Molly and I both glared at her. "Thanks."

"I bet she doesn't have any girlfriends." Molly plopped next to me on the bed. "She's always super nice to Zander, but she's been mean to us from the start. It's like she's threatened by girls, or doesn't know how to be friends with them, or something."

The rest of us were stunned into momentary silence.

"What?" Molly breathed.

"That's actually . . . pretty insightful." Nessa frowned, writing INSECURE AROUND OTHER GIRLS on the board. "What else?"

"If she's insecure about other girls, we could get every girl in the grade to freeze her out." Liv's brow knitted together. "Remember, like we did to Fiona Schiller when she almost got valedictorian last year?"

"It wasn't fair!" Nessa blurted. "She wasn't even taking any honors classes, and I was taking three!" The chalk snapped between her fingers.

"We know, Ness," I said soothingly. "But we can't do a freeze-out again. It's too mean."

Nessa and Fiona Schiller had been neck and neck for the valedictorian spot all year long. Losing the title would have sent Nessa into a full-blown meltdown. So the week before finals, I ordered every other girl in sixth to give Fiona the silent treatment. With the exception of Paige and Fiona's best friend, Jenny Hu, the grade had complied. Fiona had been so devastated that she hadn't even bothered to get out of bed on the day of her last final. I winced. Not one of my prouder moments, and definitely not an option. Even with Gravity and my relationship with Zander at stake. Zander would never forgive me.

Molly sighed. "Plus, if she only cares about guys, it might not even bother her."

"Ugh. True," Liv conceded.

"This sucks." I massaged my throbbing temple. It was like there was nothing we could do to convince Stevie from Seattle to make an early departure. She was untouchable.

And then my phone buzzed with a text.

DR. PHIL: UR ON. GO GET 'EM.

"Ohmygod. Guys!" I sat up on my bed, momentarily recharged. I'd done it! "I booked Gravity for the dance!"

"You what?" Molly's voice was pinched, her face pink. "Without asking me?"

"I did it *for* you," I said quickly, recalculating my approach and tamping a celebratory squeal—at least until I got Molly onboard. "We needed a band, right? And if Gravity's playing the dance, we'll need more rehearsal time. Which means more time for me to keep an eye on Zander, like I promised."

"And more time for you to get the inside scoop on

Stevie," Nessa added. "So we can figure out her weak spots. Psychologically speaking."

I sent her silent *Thank you* vibes. "I didn't want to say anything until I knew for sure. They've never hired a live band before."

"Okaaaay." Molly tucked her blunt blond bob behind her ear. "If you really think you can get some good intel. I want Stevie out of Chicags ASAP."

"You and me both." A fresh wave of determination washed over me as I took in my friends' pleading expressions. Marquette was our school, and Gravity was my band.

I glanced at the clock. It was 4:30 P.M. "If I hurry, I can make it to rehearsal before they get started and give them the good news." I leapt off the bed and jammed my feet into the closest pair of sneakers I could find.

"Woo-hoo!" Molly hooted. "Go get her!"

"Now?" Nessa laughed. "You're going over there *now*?"

"You know of a better time?" I reached for my messenger bag and skidded down the steps as my girls cheered me on.

Stevie was about to find out just how committed I could get.

WE INTERRUPT THIS REGULARLY SCHEDULED
REHEARSAL FOR SOME BREAKING NEWS
Wednesday, 4:56 P.M.

"I thought you were hanging with Molly." In the loft's bright, modern kitchen, Zander flicked asymmetrical blobs of cookie dough onto a greased baking sheet. The muffled beat of Nicki Minaj pumped from one of the lofted bedrooms, a change from Zander's usual old-school favorites.

"Well, now I'm here." My chest heaving from my sprint from the El, I breathed through my mouth to avoid the acrid aroma of too-strong coffee. The rest of the band hadn't gotten there yet, which should have made me happy. On any other day, I would have jumped at the chance for some alone time with Zander. But things felt different now. The smells, the sounds . . . everything had changed when Stevie had waltzed through the loft door.

"Good." Zander flung the next spoonful of dough extra hard. "It would've sucked if you blew us off." He didn't add *again*, but we both knew he was thinking it.

I heard the *clang clang clang* of heels on metal and looked up to see Stevie, winding her way down the spiral staircase.

"Perfect timing," I muttered under my breath.

Stevie looked surprised. "So you decided to grace us with your presence. Was the mall closed?"

Before I could respond, she wedged herself between Zander and me and swiped a glob of cookie dough from the bowl with her finger. "Mmm. Coconut chocolate chip. My fave." She looked up at me and fluttered her lashes. "He used to make these for me all the time in Seattle."

I stretched my lips over my braces and glared. She'd scrubbed her face free of makeup, and she looked even more amazing than usual. Her dark hair tumbled in perfect waves over her shoulders, and her skin glistened under the kitchen lights. Suddenly the gloss, mascara, and light peach blush I'd stolen from Mom's makeup drawer on my way out seemed like overkill.

"Hey, you want some coffee before we start? It's French press." Zander slid the tray of cookies into the oven. "Stevie brought my favorite kind from back home."

"Yup. He loves it. Except that one time . . ." Stevie

burst out laughing and leaned close to Zander. Too close for friends. "You remember?"

"Totally." Zander chuckled. "This one Christmas, she told me she'd bought a bunch of this really expensive coffee, already ground," he explained. "She said I had to have a super-developed palate, or whatever, to appreciate it. Except when I put it in the press—"

"It was dirt!" Stevie cackled. "And he drank, like, half a cup before he admitted it tasted like—"

"Dirt," Zander chimed in sheepishly. "Worst prank ever."

"Hey hey hey!" The Beat burst through the doorway, followed by Nelson and Kevin. The Beat was toting a handheld camcorder, the red light blinking.

I strode out of the kitchen and into the main room. The longer I kept my secret, the longer Stevie got to spend under the mistaken impression that she had the upper hand. "What's up, guys?"

Beat trained his camera in Stevie's direction, with his finger jammed on what I could only assume was the ZOOM button. Kevin and Nelson were slumped on the couch. None of them had the decency to pretend to notice me.

"Hey!" I waved my palm windshield-wiper-style in front of The Beat's lens. "Focus. *Someone* has a little breaking news she wants to share, unless Stevie just standing there is more interesting."

"Prob'ly," Stevie yelled from the kitchen.

"Oh. Uh, sorry. Hey." Through his platinum buzz cut, I could see The Beat's scalp flush. He swung the camera toward me.

"Can I get everybody in here, please?" I called, flashing my Simon Smile as Zander and Stevie joined the group. Announcing my big news to The Beat's camcorder didn't feel quite the same as doing a broadcast in the Channel M studio, but it was something. Having all eyes on me and knowing my position in Gravity was about to change made me feel like myself again. Like the totally confident, in-charge Kacey Simon I'd always been.

"Somebody's a tad dramatic," Stevie said, but I caught the worry in her tone. I wished Molly and the girls were here to witness this.

"I've got news."

"*We'llsee*," coughed Stevie.

I turned my back on her and faced the guys. The Beat's red blinking light cheered me on. "I thought it was time to take Gravity to the next level, so I got us a gig . . . playing the dance next Friday!"

"NO WAY!" The Beat pitched his camera onto the couch and high-fived me so hard, it brought tears to my eyes.

"Are you for real?" The wrinkle between Zander's eyes disappeared, and all traces of weirdness between us evaporated. "Is that where you were earlier? Booking us for the dance?" He left Stevie in his wake and pulled me in for a hug. His studded leather cuff bracelet was digging into my arm, and I could smell a hint of something earthy. Patchouli. I hadn't felt this happy in weeks. "You're the best."

"Welcome." I let myself look into his eyes for a second as I pulled away.

"So, like, a whole set? We're not just opening for somebody?" Nelson's light eyes were huge, and he slung his ratty gray sleeve around my shoulder.

"Nope. It's all us." I locked eyes with Stevie on the word *us*. She looked away. "Two straight hours of Gravity." I turned to find Kevin, who was squinting pensively at the floor.

"Cho?" I prompted him, feeling a flurry of nerves in my stomach. He *would* be the one to hold out. If he couldn't get excited about this, he and Stevie deserved each other.

"A middle school dance? I mean, it's pretty—"

"Mainstream?" I cut him off. "Meaning, a bunch of people will actually *see* us?"

"Oooh. She totally called you out, dude," The Beat yelled.

"Do kids actually *go* to lame school dances in this town?" Stevie crossed her arms over her neon-purple silk tank and lifted her nose in the air, looking like Ella did pre-tantrum. But the boys were too busy loving me to notice her.

"Yeah. Kids who actually *go* to our school actually *go* to the dances," I informed her. "But since that doesn't include you, you can feel free to stay home."

"I guess it'd be good exposure." Kevin managed a small nod, then another. "You did good, Mainstream." He clapped me on the back, which was the normal-person equivalent of a passionate make-out session.

I let the boys' pumped chatter flood my brain, the first number on my comeback soundtrack. And Stevie's slumped shoulders and pinched mouth were the album's cover art.

After ten more minutes of celebrating the gig—and, to be fair, me—Zander clapped his hands. "So, are we gonna start rehearsing or what?"

"Let's do it!" The Beat unearthed his drumsticks and rapped a quick rhythm on his thigh as we took our usual places in the breakfast nook. Stevie dragged a chair from the dining room, situating it directly in front of Zander's mic. I was too high on popularity and patchouli to care.

Let her pull out all the stops. Let her look desperate.

"So, where do you want to start?" I asked Zander, wrapping my hands around my mic stand. It felt like I was cradling pure gold.

"Well, we probably need to figure out what songs we're gonna use for the set. How long did you say we're supposed to play?"

"Um . . ." I ran my tongue over my braces. "The dance is two hours, so maybe an hour and a half? And we have to submit our song list to Dr. Phil beforehand."

"Two *hours*?" Zander's face was pale.

"What's wrong?" I asked, confused.

"We don't have an hour and a half's worth of songs." He scratched the back of his head. "We maybe have an hour, tops."

"Crap." Kevin flicked at a string on his bass. "You're right."

Stevie crossed her legs smugly.

"Okay. Okay. This isn't a problem. We can pull together another half hour!" I swallowed to keep my throat from closing. "We'll just have to rehearse a little more, that's all. Do some covers."

"You sure?" Zander raised an eyebrow. "How're we gonna learn that much new material by next Friday? And didn't you say we had to submit a song list?"

"Ambitious," Stevie agreed. I hated the way she said— well, pretty much everything. She always had that tiny smirk like life was a hilarious joke she and Zander shared over fancy coffee.

The Beat backed me up. "We should at least give it a shot. What about some of those Death Cab covers we always talked about doing?"

"I've got sheet music in my bag." Nelson played a doomed-sounding chord on his keyboard.

"Hold up. Depends on whether our lead wants to sing Death Cab." Zander looked to me. "They sing in a pretty high key most of the time."

Stevie sucked in a breath. "Yeah, that could be a problem for Kacey."

"That's not what I was saying." Zander shot her a dirty look.

My throat constricted, and my eyes started to burn. How had this gone so wrong so fast?

"Death Cab's fine." I stared at the tiny holes in the head of my mic.

"Y'know . . ." Stevie's head listed to one side thoughtfully. "There is another way around this. Zander and I could play some of Hard Rock Life's old stuff."

Instead of dignifying her offer with a response, I indulged a brief fantasy in which I rushed her with my mic stand as a weapon, gladiator-style. The look of visceral horror on Dream Stevie's face was enough to keep me sane for the next six seconds or so. Until Zander said . . .

"That's actually not a bad idea. We could use the time we have to polish, instead of all of us learning all new stuff. Whadda you guys think?"

"Awesome," Nelson said.

"Good call." Kevin nodded.

The Beat rapped his agreement on the drums.

That left me. And as much as I wanted to scream and yell and personally drag Stevie back to Seattle, I had no choice. If I pushed back, I'd look petty, like I cared more about keeping Stevie out of the spotlight than I cared about the band.

"Yeah. Sure," I managed. "Whatever you want."

"Cool." Stevie jumped up and slithered past me to The Beat. "One has a rockin' drum solo. It's pretty easy. I could teach it to you, if you want." She sat on the edge of The Beat's stool. His face turned bloodred as she snagged his drumsticks and rapped out a beat, bobbing her head to the music. "It's got killer vocals, too. Wanna hear?"

"Yeahhh!" the guys cheered.

"You mind?" Stevie jumped up and nudged me out of the way, leaving me off to the side and without a mic of my own. I was too shocked to even breathe.

"Can I get a high C?" she purred into the mic.

My. Mic.

I watched helplessly as she turned toward Zander. They gazed at each other as she sang. I didn't even need my contacts—or my coke-bottle glasses, which were at home, tucked in my desk drawer—to see the connection between them, tight and unbreakable. With no room at all for me.

AND FOR DESSERT, AN AWKWARD
HEART-TO-HEART WITH THE PARENTAL UNIT
Friday, 8:27 P.M.

After treating Ella and me to antipasto and house-made gnocchi at a new Italian restaurant in Lakeview, Mom suggested we take our hot chocolates to go. We strolled side by side along the west edge of Lincoln Park, walking south toward our townhouse.

"Everything okay?" Mom asked. "You seem a little distant tonight."

"I'm fine. I just have a lot on my mind, with the band and school and stuff." Steam rose from the tiny slit in my to-go lid, mingling with the bite of early spring.

Mom draped her arm around my shoulders and pulled me in close. The rich scent of her olive leather gloves reminded me of Zander. "If it all feels like too much, you can always—"

"I know, I know. Don't worry, school is my first priority. It's fine. I can handle them both."

"Want to race?" Ella huffed, poking at the condensation cloud her hot breath made in the biting, early-spring air.

"Too full." I groaned, painfully aware of the way the metal button on my jeans dug into my stomach. "But you go."

"Okay! Readddddyy . . . !" Ella skipped ahead at breakneck speed, almost knocking down an elderly couple hobbling in the opposite direction.

"Carefully, my love!" Mom winced. She gave the old couple an apologetic nod when they passed. "I had fun with you girls tonight. It's been a while since the three of us had a girls' night."

"Yeah."

Mom sighed. "It's my fault. I've been spending too much time at the studio and not enough time at home with you girls."

"Mom. It's okay," I protested, slipping my arm around her waist. "It's your job. We get it."

"It's not okay," she said quietly. "I mean, yes. It is my job, and I love it because I'm good at it and because it provides for our family. But if I keep this pace up much longer, I'm going to burn out. And then I won't be any good to anybody."

We fell silent, listening to the rhythmic scrape of our boots against the sidewalk. I hated when her voice sounded thin and brittle, like it was about to crack.

"Ella and I are fine, Mom," I insisted. "Really. We're just worried about you. You should do something relaxing every now and then. Take a day off."

"News doesn't take time off, sweet girl. You know that." Mom stopped and cupped her hands around her mouth. "Stop at the corner, missy!" she called to Ella, who was barreling toward Belden Avenue. "Don't make me count to five!"

Dutifully, Ella froze on the corner.

"Actually," Mom started, "I did take a little break last night after the broadcast."

"Uh-huh?" I said, tilting my steaming cup to my lips.

"Well . . . I . . ." She stuffed her hands in her coat pocket. "I . . . took a little coffee break. With a new . . . friend."

I inhaled and regretted it immediately. Scalding hot liquid burned my tongue and the roof of my mouth. "You what?" I sputtered, sucking hot chocolate down the wrong pipe. I doubled over in a coughing fit, my eyes filling with tears.

"Kacey!" Mom rubbed my back in circles. "One sip at a time."

I straightened up. "Was it a *date*?" I hissed. "Why didn't you tell me?"

"Your phone was off," Mom protested with a nervous laugh. "And you were asleep by the time I got home. Besides, it wasn't a real date. Just coffee, with the source I had the interview with on Tuesday night."

"Mooom! Kaaaacey! Hurry up!" Ella yelled from the corner.

"Are you gonna tell her?" I asked quietly.

"If it turns into something, then I will. I promise." Mom stopped and grasped me by the shoulders. "Are you okay with this?" she asked. Her eyes widened in earnest. They were green with flecks of gold. "I know I haven't done much dating since your dad left."

"Yeah, no, it's fine. It's just . . . I'm just surprised, that's all." My singed tongue tingled at the words.

"I know. I sort of sprang this on you." She ran her hand through her shoulder-length auburn hair. "But I didn't want to keep secrets."

"Are you going out with him again?"

"I think so. He asked if I was free tomorrow night."

"Where are you going to go?"

"I don't know," she said thoughtfully. "We might do one of those horse-and-carriage rides. He's new in town, so—"

"Okay, okay." I waved her away. "I don't need all the sordid details." The thought of Mom snuggled up with some dude underneath a blanket that smelled like horse pee made my stomach churn. I chucked my hot chocolate into a trash can at the curb.

"Sorry. No more date talk." We reached the corner, and she bent down to squeeze Ella. "Excellent listening, lovebug," she said. "Remember, we never cross the street alone." The three of us linked hands, Ella in the middle, and hurried toward our block as the wind started to pick up. Mom glanced over Ella's head. "It's been four years, Kacey. That's a long time, you know."

"I know." I smiled back, for Mom.

When we got home, we found Paige on the front stoop, shivering in her oversized coat.

"What're you doing here?" I released Ella's hand and hurried up the steps.

"I'm spending the night, remember? I mean, if that's okay with you, Sterling." She lifted a yellow nylon duffel bag from behind one of Mom's empty stone flowerpots.

"Of course, sweetie." Mom fiddled with the key in the lock. "Next time just let yourself in with the key under that pot. It's freezing out here." She bumped the door open with her hip and we followed.

"Can I play with Kacey and Paige, Mom?" Ella did a

running leap over a pile of dress-up clothes in the foyer. "Since I was such a good listener?"

Mom wriggled out of her winter coat and hung it on the rack by the door. "It's bath time for you, little one." She shot me a meaningful glance. After twelve years of those looks, I'd gotten decent at reading them. This one was the oft-used *Get upstairs before your sister throws a fit.*

"'Night, girly." I planted a quick kiss on the top of Ella's head and another on Mom's cheek. "Love you."

"'Night, Sterling!" Paige yelled over her shoulder as we sprinted up the stairs.

When we got to my room, Paige slammed the door and deflated against it.

"You totally forgot I was spending the night," she huffed, whipping a black infinity scarf over her head and flinging it Frisbee-style onto my unmade bed. "Don't . . . even . . . deny it."

"In my *defense*, Paige, I was kind of busy listening to *my mother* tell me about her *date* last night." I stretched my arms out and trust-fell onto the bed.

"Wait. A date?" Paige took a running leap and flopped next to me. "STERLING SIMON WENT ON A DATE?"

"Yep."

"Intense."

We stared at the ceiling for a while. I wished there

was a tiny switch I could flip in my brain, like the one on Ella's sound machine, to fill my head with white noise and squeeze everything else out. I was glad Paige was the one spending the night. Molly would have fired questions at me all night, forcing me to think about things I wanted to ignore.

"Okay." Paige sat up and presented me with two closed fists, like she was about to do a magic trick. She lifted the left fist. "In *this* hand, I've got: 'How COULD she? She's the WORST. MOTHER. EVER.'" Then she raised the right fist. "And in *this* hand, we've got: 'It's about time! Your mom's a total fox. How'd she meet him? What's his name? I'M. SO. PUMPED.'" With a tiny smile, she scooted closer to me on the bed. "Pick one. Whichever one you want."

"Ugh. Maybe a little of both." I knocked her fists with mine and tried to smile. "Also, don't ever call my mom a fox again. That's creepy."

"She totally is, though." Paige giggled, shoving her glasses up the bridge of her nose. "I bet old guys check her out all the time, right?"

"Get out."

"I can't. We have campaign stuff to work on," she said lightly. She slid off the bed and sat at my computer desk, jiggling the pink wireless mouse until the flatscreen monitor came to life.

Paige typed *GoGreene.com* into the web browser. "We should check the results of my new PrezPoll. You've taken it, right?"

"Uhhhh–" *PrezPoll?*

"KACEY!"

"Sorry! I'll take it now!" I straightened up on the bed.

"If your mother hadn't just gone on a date . . ." Paige huffed. "Question one. *My life as a student at Marquette has improved drastically during Prez Paige's tenure.* Strongly Agree, Agree, Neutral, Disag–"

"Strongly agree," I said generously.

"Stronglyyyy agreeee." She clicked the mouse. "Oooh! It says one hundred percent of respondents answered 'Strongly Agree'!" She whirled around in my desk chair, the frayed ends of her bob bouncing with excitement.

"How many people took the poll?"

She turned around again. "Oh. Including you? Two." Her shoulders slumped.

"Okay," I said brusquely. "Enough. We both need some serious stress relief." Stashed under my bed was a turquoise shoebox Ella had bedazzled with giant plastic jewels for my eleventh birthday.

"Whatcha got there?" Paige peered over my shoulder as I opened the lid.

"Take your pick." I'd stocked the box with everything

from the vials of tea tree oil Liv gave as stocking stuffers last Christmas to the cooling gel eye mask I'd nabbed from Nessa's finals-week study kit.

"Ooh." Paige palmed a slim white tube containing a clarifying seaweed mask. Mom had gotten it at some fancy hotel she'd stayed in while on assignment in New York City. "I could use some clarifying."

"Same. Maybe it'll scrub that whole dating conversation from my memory."

After lighting a few fresh cotton–scented pillar candles, I clicked on the Mellow Mix on my iPod. A slow Levi Stone track filled the room. I kicked off my boots and changed into a fluffy white robe. Paige took her glasses off and slipped on a worn navy-blue sweatshirt that was about seven sizes too big. Probably her dad's.

"Did you hear Levi's coming to Chicago soon?" Paige asked. "Next week, I think."

"Yeah. But my mom would never let me go to a concert on a school night." I tucked Paige's hair behind her ears and smoothed the thick army-green mask over her skin, patting it all the way to her lashes and over the dark spots beneath her eyes. Then I did her neck. There wasn't a patch of pale skin in sight. When I finished with Paige, I pulled my hair into a high ponytail and did my own mask.

"Lemme see," Paige said. We hurried to the full-length

mirror on the back of my closet door. "Ew! We look like aliens or something!" she squeaked.

"That's the price of beauty." I consulted the back of the tube. "We're supposed to leave it on for twenty minutes. Wanna do manicures?"

But Paige couldn't take her eyes off her reflection. She leaned into the mirror, inspecting her face from every angle. "I should go out and get myself a date for the dance right now."

I chomped down on the inside of my cheek. I hadn't thought about the date thing in days. Did playing the dance mean I'd have an excuse not to bring one? Did it mean that Zander wouldn't be able to ask Stevie? I didn't think I could handle watching them slow-dance during one of our breaks.

I smoothed a clump of mask paste beneath my eye so there were no cracks or bubbles. "Do you have a date yet?"

"No." Paige looked away from the mirror. "Guys are intimidated by a woman in power. And it's like, all eyes are on me leading up to the election, and not all guys are cut out for the spotlight."

"For sure," I said quickly. "But still, you should think about going with somebody. If you want." I gave her bob a playful yank. "'Cause you *do* look hot. In fact . . ." In one swift move, I steamrolled her into the photo booth and yanked the velvet curtain closed. "We should document this momentous occasion!"

"Kacey! I'll kill you!" she screamed, her skinny legs thrashing behind the curtain. "I'm seriously gonna strangle you with your bathrobe belt. Lemme out!"

"Say cheeeeeese." I giggled, keeping her inside the booth with one hand and punching the green button on the inside wall with the other. The flashbulb popped four times. "You're on *Candid Camera!*"

COFFEE AND CONSPIRACY
Saturday, 11:35 A.M.

By the time Paige left to meet her parents for brunch the next morning, my pores were completely clear, but my mind was more clogged than Mom's top secret junk closet. I was at a total loss for how to take Stevie down without making Zander mad at me forever. So I called in the troops for an emergency brunch meeting.

"Now this is brain food," Nessa said as the girls and I settled into a circle on my bedroom floor, divvying up scrambled eggs, maple-glazed sausages, and fresh fruit. "Give me five minutes and I'll give you a foolproof plan."

"Sayonara, Stevie." Molly yawned into her breakfast burrito.

"I just want to say that I can think just as clearly

without stuffing my body with animal products." Liv dug into her vegan tofu scramble and stabbed a wad of egg substitute with her fork.

"Mmmmm," Nessa teased, waving a hunk of sausage under Liv's nose. "Wilbur, maybe? Or Babe?" She scrunched up her nose and oinked.

"Ewwww! Get that poor thing away from me!" Liv shrieked, kicking at Nessa with her bare feet.

"Girls! Focus," I ordered. "Stevie's getting worse, and I refuse to take it anymore." I gave them a quick rundown of rehearsal the day before. "How could Zander let her take over the gig *I* got without even noticing what she was doing? It's like whenever he's around her, he goes blind. She has this weird power over him."

"I knew a girl like her once, back in elementary school," Liv said. "She did all this mean stuff to m–to, um, the girls in the class. And the guys didn't even notice. They were too busy checking her out to care."

"Guys check me out all the time." Molly's eyes cut anxiously to me.

"This is so not the same thing." I patted the leather knee patch on her black skinnies. "Stevie's, like, evil. You're just hot."

Relieved, Mols went back to her burrito.

"We have to teach her a lesson. Show her she can't get away with this. This is *my* band and *our* school." I hadn't touched my bagel, but I still felt nauseated. "We have to come up with something so good, she'll be dying to hop the next flight to Seattle."

"Breathe, Kace. Let's review what we know," Nessa said soothingly. "So like Mols said, she obviously doesn't have any girlfriends."

"And I don't think she cares." I sighed as Liv started to braid my bedhead tangles.

"So what *does* she care about?" Nessa rolled her eyes, like the very thought was ludicrous.

"Zander. Music. Completely upstaging me. Laughing about these stupid pranks she's supposedly famous for." I couldn't sit still any longer. I jumped up and started pacing. "I swear, if I have to listen to one more prank story, I'm gonna wig out."

"And remember that time she called me 'B-list Barbie'?" Molly's shrill voice drilled into my eardrums. "Raise your hand if you think there's *anything* B-list about me." She glared at each of us.

"Obviously, there isn't. She's insane." *And so is Zander for not realizing how awful she is.*

"At least we'll get a day off on Monday," Nessa

reminded us. "She probably can't come on the field trip to the aquarium if she's not a student."

"Whatever. Zander'll bring her anyway. Not like Finnster would even notice." I glared at a picture of a barefoot Zander on my bulletin board, then papered it over with a shot of Ella in her Miss Piggy Halloween costume.

"Ugh. She'll probably bring those disgusting Swedish Fish," Liv moaned. "Which, by the way, have enough food coloring in them to—"

"WAIT." A flash of genius smacked me so hard, it almost knocked me over. *Prank. Aquarium. Swedish Fish.* "I've got it!"

The girls leaned toward me, holding their breath. Nessa whipped out a crisp yellow legal pad and a new pen, writing down my words as I outlined the plan for my friends, detail by detail.

Operation: Shedding Stevie

- **Objective:** Create (and pull off) prank during Shedd Aquarium field trip that can be traced back to Stevie. Get her banned from Marquette grounds (and possibly Chicago) before the dance on Friday (and possibly sooner).

NEEDED / RESPONSIBLE?

1. Glitter markers, pens, puff paint / Liv & Nessa (Kacey can steal from Ella's art stash if necessary)
2. Swedish Fish stash / Molly (Kacey can steal from Ella's candy stash if necessary)
3. Field trip itinerary / Kacey
4. List of potential diversions to distract Spinster Finnster / Kacey
5. Cell phone (Note: Stevie can't recognize the number) / Liv
6. Victory dance, to be rocked out at a later date and separate location / Kacey (and everyone)

KACEY'S LIST OF POTENTIAL DIVERSIONS

- **Option A:** Slip sea anemone in Finnster's old-lady handbag while she's not looking. Then complain of scratchy throat and ask if she has a hard candy. She will, because she's old. Sit back. Enjoy.
- **Option B:** Fake sighting of escaped poisonous water snake. (Note: Scream like I screamed when Ella slipped Oprah Winfurry and Enrique Piglesias under my covers to "snuggle me good morning.")

- **Option C:** Scribble Molly's face with (washable?*) black marker and claim she got squirted with octopus ink.

    ***Note:** Permanent marker would probs be more believable.

- **Option D:** "Borrow" starfish from aquatic petting zoo area. Nestle securely in TBD Student's hair. (Possibly Jilly Lindstrom? Her mop's so frizzy it would be easy to slip it in there unnoticed.) Point out starfish. Sit back. Enjoy.

When we finished, we looked at one another, our eyes glowing. It was so simple. So perfect. And there was no way it could ever be traced back to us.

SHEDDING STEVIE
Monday, 9:16 A.M.

"Attention, Marine Biology students." Spinster Finnster's labored breath rattled over the bus speakers like the soundtrack to a geriatric slasher flick. "We will be arriving at Shedd Aquarium in just a few moments, and we will then make our way to the Oceanarium for the dolphin show." Mic feedback screeched as she mentioned something about being good ambassadors to the outside world. Everybody groaned, and the volume on the bus resumed its Wrigley-Field-on-game-day level.

"Okay, girls. Are we ready?" I tapped a caffeinated rhythm on the ripped leather seatback in front of me. I might have been a nervous, jittery wreck on the inside, but on the outside, I had it together. My jade jersey boat-neck dress was innocent enough, but the black fishnets and laceless black ankle boots added an appropriate hint of "bad girl on a mission."

"Born ready," Nessa assured me with a nod.

"Good." The girls and I had staked a claim on the four seats in the back row. Paige sat one row ahead of us, but luckily she had occupied herself handing out baggies of pistachios with the slogan *Go Nuts for Paige Greene* on them. Quinn and Aaron Peterman were tossing a Nerf football in the aisle while Jake Fields called the plays.

And Zander and Stevie were smashed against each other in one of the middle rows, sharing a single set of iPod buds. He'd hardly acknowledged me all morning. All I'd gotten was a nod, the kind you give your old-lady next-door neighbor Mrs. Weitzman so you won't have to stop and talk to her about cat arthritis.

"She deserves this. What goes around comes around, right?" Liv crossed her legs into lotus pose and closed her eyes.

"Right." I tightened my high ponytail and checked for bumps in the smudged window. Beyond my reflection, Michigan Avenue landmarks raced by. Pritzker Pavilion, where Molly and Zander had gone on their first (and only) date. The Millennium Park skating rink, where I'd told Zander I had to quit the band.

"Aaaand he's going long, and it's—gooooooood!" In the

fifth row, Jake jumped to his feet as Quinn jogged backward and pawed the football from the air, almost tripping over the mountain of backpacks in the aisle.

"Wilder!" I snapped, glaring at my former crush. "Watch it."

Quinn turned and whipped his thick, dirty blond locks out of his eyes. A few weeks ago, that hair toss would have made my knees buckle. Now it just made me want to give him a haircut.

"Sorrrrry, Simon." He grinned and released the football in an effortless throw. It sailed toward the front of the bus.

I rolled my eyes and refocused on the girls. "Mols. You've got all the supplies, right?"

Molly stared straight ahead, her strawberry-glossed lips slightly parted. "Did you guys see that throw?"

"Molly. Focus." I snapped my fingers just inches from her nose. "Supplies."

"Got 'em." She lifted a generic-looking backpack that used to belong to her half-brother, Nate, before he went to college. It was black, plain, and totally boring. In other words, inconspicuous. "Everything's here."

"Okay. Okay." I glanced nervously at each of the girls. "Thank you guys for helping out." This plan *had* to work. If it didn't . . . the thought alone was enough to make me want to cry. Or stuff Quinn Wilder's football down Stevie's throat.

"Obv." Molly looped arms with me and rested her head on my shoulder. "She's toast, Kace."

"Oh. Am I interrupting anything?"

I looked up to see Paige standing in the aisle, squinting suspiciously through her foggy lenses.

"Apart from a perfectly nice bus ride?" Molly studied her nail beds.

"Uh, no. 'Course not." I elbowed Mols and crossed my legs. There was no way Paige would let us go through with our plan if she found out about it. "How's it going with the pistachios?"

"Pretty good." Paige gripped the tops of the seats on both sides of the aisle and leaned in, like she was doing a push-up.

"Awesome," I said encouragingly. Paige's wide-eyed innocence, the way she was so concerned about winning and being so *good* at the same time, made me feel a little guilty about what I was about to do. But then I caught another glimpse of Stevie resting her head on Zander's shoulder. Moment over.

The Oceanarium was an expansive pavilion with high ceilings and spotlights positioned over the turquoise waters of the tank. Silver stadium-style bleachers curved halfway around the tank, facing a wall of windows overlooking Lake Michigan.

"Come along, students, the show will begin in a few moments." Finnster led the class to our seats in the top three rows of the bleachers, past a few retirees and fanny-pack-wearing tourists. Trainers in wet suits were perched on the fake rocks edging the tank. "Please take out your class journals, and be sure to make note of your observations during the show." Finnster crossed her legs, revealing the ankles of her bunchy tan support stockings.

"Come on." Molly grabbed my hand and dragged me to the seats next to Quinn, Aaron, and Jake in the second row. Nessa and Liv slipped in behind me, and Paige sat next to Jilly Lindstrom on the top row. Stevie led Zander to the very end of the row, away from the rest of the class.

"You know what would actually make this show cool?" Quinn started up again. "If they put hungry sharks in the tank, too."

"Quinn!" Molly shrieked, her face a combination of disgust and curiosity. "That's inhumane," she informed him with a sultry flick of her bangs. "Don't you ever read the side of the tuna fish can?"

"Bloodbath." Jake punched Quinn's shoulder. "Epic."

"I'm for real, dudes," Quinn insisted. "If I planned these trips, man—"

"Only you don't, Quinn." Paige ran a hand through her bob, making her bangs stick out in a million directions. "The student council makes the big decisions, while you're busy playing paper football. So let it. Go."

If I hadn't been so preoccupied, I would have been semi-impressed with Paige.

Quinn's jaw tensed. "I could do a way better job than those losers."

"Those *losers*," Paige said slowly, "do more for this school than you ever have."

"What, like getting rid of all the good vending machines and planning lame field trips?" Quinn shot back. "Nice work."

Everyone stopped talking and stared at Paige and Quinn.

"OMG. This is even better than dolphins." Liv's lemon tea–scented breath was hot on my ear.

"Whatever. I wouldn't expect you to get it, Wilder." Paige's voice started to waver.

"Gimme a break. I get it. And to prove I get it? *I*"—he turned around to face the rest of the class—"am running for eighth-grade class president."

"Duuuude!" Jake and Aaron started punching Quinn.

Molly golf-clapped. And Paige looked like she wanted to take a running leap into the dolphin tank. On Finnster's other side, Imran Bhatt, Paige's main competition for president, buried his face in his hands. Everyone else pulled out their phones. Quinn's nomination would be trending on Twitter before the first dolphin backflip.

"Students!" Finnster clapped. "Quiet, please!"

At least I thought that was what she was saying. I couldn't actually hear her. But I did see Nessa beam me a look that said: *No diversion necessary.*

"You ready?" I whispered to Molly, stealing one last glance at Zander and Stevie. Zander was laughing and fiddling with the leather cuff bracelet on Stevie's wrist. The same way he used to fiddle with mine.

"Let's do this." Molly's voice was thick with determination.

I composed a quick text to Stevie on Liv's phone. I had to get her away from Zander so she wouldn't have an alibi.

HINT HINT. U HAVE A HUUGE TEAR IN THE BACK OF UR PANTS.

Stevie looked down at her phone and stiffened, then rushed out of the bleachers toward the ladies' room, covering her butt with her slouchy messenger bag.

JUST ADD WATER
Monday, 10:24 A.M.

We had to hustle through a dingy stairwell to get to the penguin tank, the next stop on Finnster's itinerary. Slowly, we crept down the metal steps in the near dark. The stench of dead fish hung heavy in the air and pinpricks of salty sweat rose along the neckline of my dress. Every nerve in my body was on high alert.

"*Dun dun DAH-dun, dun dun DAH-dun.*" Behind me, Molly hummed the theme to *Mission: Impossible*. Nessa snickered.

Halfway down the stairs, I stopped and turned to face my troops. "Remember, if we run into a security guard—"

"Ohmygosh, Officer! We're soooo lost and just want to, you know, learn? Can you help us find our teacher?" Molly widened her eyes innocently, then triple-blinked.

"You've *got* to be kidding me." Nessa groaned.

"I can cry on cue if you want." Molly pinched her thigh, and her face twisted in pain.

"Mols!" Liv swatted Molly's hand away. "Quit it."

"That's okay. No crying necessary," I said. "Let's just stick with the plan."

The door at the bottom of the stairwell was jammed. I had to hip-bump it three times before it released, revealing a dim, cavelike room. Behind floor-to-ceiling glass, at least forty penguins hopped from fake iceberg to fake iceberg, dove into clear blue water, and blinked their beady little eyes at us. The light from the tank wove blue ribbons on the wall behind us. The room was completely deserted. No witnesses.

"Perfect." I wiped beads of sweat from my forehead and squinted at the girls. "Let's get to work. Mols? Supplies?"

Molly knelt next to her black backpack and pulled out two giant bags of Swedish Fish, a boa, and three glow-in-the-dark rubber duckies.

Nessa wrung her hands. "I can't believe we're about to do this! Wait. What if we get caught? What if—"

I grabbed her wrist and squeezed reassuringly. "We won't. I swear."

"This isn't gonna hurt the penguins, is it?" Liv pinched

her lower lip. The turquoise glow emanating from the tank lit her worried frown.

"GIRLS!" My voice bounced off the damp walls. Even the penguins stopped and stared. "Everything's gonna be fine. We want Stevie out of our lives, right?"

"Right," the girls chorused.

"Then we have to do something so big that she'll really get in trouble. And this is it." I hoped my friends couldn't hear the thunderous beat of my heart. Of *course* the plan would go off without a hitch. Stevie would be out of the picture, and I'd have Zander and the band to myself again. But if anything went wrong, we'd be in major trouble. Grounded-for-LIFE kind of trouble.

"Kacey's right." Molly nodded, locking her eyes with mine.

I grinned back. "Thanks, girl. Okay. Nessa, you take the supplies into the tank. And Liv, you take care of the glass. Molly, stand watch by the door. I'll supervise. Ready? Break!"

The girls dispersed. Liv dug a handful of glitter pens and puff-paint markers from Molly's backpack and started scribbling on the glass. Molly flattened her body against the wall next to the door, cop-style. And Nessa scooped up the candy, boa, and rubber duckies and headed for the door next to the tank. She gripped the handle and rattled.

"Um, Kacey? It's . . . locked."

My heart stopped mid-beat. "What?"

"It's locked," she said again. "I can't . . . we can't get in."

The sweat on the back of my neck turned to ice. "No. Nonononono. This is *not* happening right now." I hurried to the door and tried the handle. Definitely locked.

"Okay. I can figure this out. I just have to think. Think, Kacey." I raked my hands through my hair, my fingers catching on the jeweled hairpin that held my bangs in place.

"Aha." Nessa plucked the pin from my fingers, slid it into the lock, and jiggled.

"You are brilliant!" I peered over her shoulder as she twisted the pin. Finally, we heard a small pop.

"Is it just me, or do you totally feel like we're in a Russian spy flick right now?" Nessa turned the handle and opened the door. "Like, with subtitles and every-thing?"

"*Da*," I said in a Russian accent, flicking at the boa around her neck. "Now get to it."

She giggled and disappeared behind the door. A few seconds later, Liv shrieked.

"Nessa! Ahhh!"

"What? Lemme see!" I hurried to the front of the tank and peered through the glass. On the other side, Nessa was flinging handfuls of red Swedish Fish into the water. One of the penguins was making a nest out of the boa, and the glow-in-the-dark duckies were bobbing happily in the water. Nessa glanced up and waved, then produced a pair of tiny pink shades and placed them on the closest penguin.

"OH. MY. GOD." I doubled over in giggles. Liv and I leaned against the glass, trying desperately to catch our breath.

Nessa checked her watch and flashed five fingers.

I coughed and straightened up. "Five minutes! Five minutes."

"Help me finish up here." Liv tossed me an emerald-green glitter marker, and I started doodling feverishly on the glass. Guitars, musical notes, Seattle's space needle—anything that would point directly to Stevie. A few short minutes later, almost every square inch of the glass was graffitied with neon glitter sayings and drawings:

FREE THE PENGUINS (& THE STUDENTS)

SEATTLE ROCKS MY BOAT

HEY, MARQUETTE! HONK IF YOU'RE CORNY!

SPINSTER FINNSTER: 1,000 B.C.–????

"Awesome." I jumped at the sound of Nessa's voice behind me. "Looks amazing."

Molly waved her hands frantically and stomped her foot. "I can hear them!" she hissed frantically. "Hide!"

I snatched the backpack out of the way, and the girls and I bolted for the door, clustering behind it. My stomach was practically in my throat. What if Paige noticed I'd ducked out and started asking questions? What if someone recognized Liv's handwriting? What if Stevie—

"And here we have the peng—" Finnster's disbelieving wheeze told me she wasn't totally blind after all.

"Oh. My. Gahhhhh—" Paige's voice trailed off.

"Dude! Somebody graffitied the tank!" Aaron Peterman shouted gleefully.

The rest of the class shoved their way inside, and the girls and I slipped into the back of the crowd as if we'd never left.

Finnster clutched her chest like she was about to collapse. The class rushed the tank, snapping pictures on their cell phones and tapping the glass. Almost immediately, a SWAT team of trainers in khaki shorts appeared on the other side, chasing the increasingly aggravated birds and swiping candy from the water with giant nets.

Molly inhaled sharply when she saw the tank. Her shoulders started to shake, and her face turned bright red.

A familiar lemony scent hovered in the air next to me. Liv reached over and squeezed my hand.

"Such a shame." She *tsk*ed. "Great accessories, though."

I squeezed back and swallowed a laugh.

"Nobody messes with us," Nessa singsonged in my other ear.

. . . *and gets away with it*, I added silently.

"ATTENTION!" Finnster bellowed in a voice louder and stronger than I'd ever heard before. We shut up. The only sound in the observatory was the muffled flapping of penguin wings.

"Now. As much as I de*test* the idea that a Marquette Middle School student could be responsible for such a childish prank, it's clear that this is the case." Furious spittle leapt from her withered mouth. "I want the person or persons responsible for this to come forward immediately."

No one moved. Or breathed. Until the rustling of a cellophane bag caught Finnster's attention. The woman couldn't hear a fire drill, but apparently a candy bag was a different story.

"Ms. Jarvis?" Since nobody had bothered to inform Finnster that Stevie and Zander weren't siblings, she'd been calling Stevie by Zander's last name for days. It made me want to hurl. "Please step forward."

At the edge of the crowd, Stevie froze with her hand in her back pocket. Her elbow jutted out at an awkward angle.

"I, uh—yeah? Yes?" Stevie looked like she wanted to move but couldn't, like she was playing her own personal, doomed game of freeze tag.

Tag. You're out.

"Kindly remove your hand from your pocket."

For a few agonizing seconds, Stevie just stood there. Her eyes were twice their normal size, and her cheeks were the same pink as Molly's old bang streak. She didn't look confident, or cool, or even snarky, the way she'd looked 24-7 since she got to Chicago. Instead, she looked young and confused. Out of control.

Good. Now she knew how it felt.

"Ms. Jarvis."

Slowly, Stevie pulled her hand from her pocket. Peeking out from her fist was a crumpled piece of plastic. I held my breath.

"Open your fist, please."

I could almost see the air leaking from Stevie's body as she complied. Inside the bag in her hand was a lone red gummy fish, identical to the fish in the tank.

"Okay. I know . . . But I . . . I didn't do this!" Stevie sputtered, looking to Zander for help. He took two steps away from her. "This isn't my fault!"

Liv made a peace sign. Or maybe it was a V for *victory*.

"No way." Somebody snickered in the back. Finnster's

glare silenced the uneasy murmurs bubbling to the surface.

"Somebody set me up," Stevie insisted, her voice getting stronger. Now instead of looking scared, she looked pissed. "I swear." She scanned the crowd, and her gaze came to a screeching halt when she found me. The tiny hairs on the back of my neck stood up.

"Yeah," Jake Fields said sarcastically. "It's a conspiracy."

"Come with me, Ms. Jarvis." Finnster's steely tone chilled the room.

"But—"

"Now. We're going to discuss this with aquarium security. The rest of you will remain in this room until you are instructed otherwise," she informed us.

"Wait," I whispered to Nessa. "Security?"

Nessa shushed me with a sharp exhale. "It's fine. Remember. She deserves it."

Head down, Stevie followed Finnster toward the glowing red EXIT sign over the door, her chunky plastic bracelets clinking together like a prisoner's cuffs.

TSUNAMI
Monday, 10:46 A.M.

Back in my reporting days, nothing would have made me giddier than witnessing a scene like this firsthand. The story had everything—scandal, intrigue, a fall from grace—but I felt none of the usual excitement. Instead, the dead-fish smell combined with the wet, hot air overtook me, making the room start to sway. What if Stevie got in serious trouble? Worse, what if she ratted me out? I should have agreed to a freeze-out. Those were just as effective, sans the possibility of jail time.

Molly leaned next to me, knocking my knee with hers. I swallowed the lump in my throat and tried to smile.

"Hate to break it to you, Jarvis." Quinn shuffled over to Zander, who was standing off to the side and glaring at the exit. Quinn slung his arm over Zander's shoulders. "But your sister's a total whack job."

Zander borderline shoved Quinn, who stumbled back with a look of surprise on his face. "She's not my sister."

"Could he be any more emo?" Molly checked the reflection of her wide, satisfied smile in the glass, coming nose-to-nose with a heavyset trainer wielding a trash bag and some yellow rubber kitchen gloves. "At least now we can get back to planning the dance. Committee meeting tomorrow morning in The Square, okay?"

"Hey. Kacey." Zander's voice was strained. "Can I talk to you for a sec?" He nodded toward the stairwell, then disappeared through the exit door.

I froze, my eyes darting from Liv to Nessa to Molly. Did he *know*? I wanted one of my friends to say something reassuring, at least give me a look that said I'd be fine. But their eyes were wide. Unblinking. Petrified.

I considered bolting, but the stairwell was my only way out. And Zander was waiting.

Holding my head high, I strode through the door. I had starred in *Guys and Dolls*. I could totally pull off "innocent girl who definitely did not just frame someone for penguin vandalism." That was, until I tripped over the first step and went down, palms first.

"Hey! Whoa!" Zander reached out to steady me. He

was sitting on the third step with his back against the wall. "You okay?"

"I—sorry. I'm fine. Just a couple of scrapes." *I'm sorry for everything,* I thought as Zander cradled my hands in his, inspecting my injuries. *For possibly getting your friend, girlfriend, whatever she is arrested, even though objectively, she has the worst personality ever. For almost bailing on rehearsal.*

"You're bleeding a little. Here." Zander shrugged off his yellow hoodie and dabbed my wounds with the sleeve.

"That was stupid of you," I blurted, tears springing to my eyes for no reason. I felt like a kid, like Ella when she fell in front of my mom or me. Everything was fine until somebody took an interest. "Now you've got blood all over your sweatshirt."

"So?"

I looked up at him, tried to find his eyes through the blue streak that kept slipping over his forehead. "I'm sorry Stevie got in trouble." A snot bubble hovered dangerously close to the edge of my left nostril.

He shrugged. "Whatever. It's her own fault."

"Is she your girlfriend?" I didn't realize how stupid the words sounded until it was too late to take them back.

"Huh?" Zander stopped playing nurse long enough to stare at me. "Stevie?"

It wasn't a denial.

"Oh, come on." My toes curled inside my boots. "You guys act like you're . . . like you . . ."

"We were," he said quietly after a few seconds had passed. "I mean, back in Seattle, we were."

"Oh. Okay." I fought the fresh wave of salty tears threatening to spill onto my cheeks.

"You really hate her." He said it matter-of-factly, without judgment.

"I don't—" I shuddered and took a breath. "I—"

"It's okay. I mean, it sucks. I wanted you guys to like each other. But I know she can be tough."

"You do?"

"Kace. Give me a little credit," he said ruefully. He knocked my boot with the toe of his sneakers. "She comes off pretty strong sometimes. Kind of like this other chick I know."

"Hey!"

He shrugged. "'S true."

"You ditched me." The words were out before I could take them back. "For her. Like you didn't care if I was in the band at all."

"What? No way." Zander went down a step so we were at the same level. He looked genuinely lost.

"It seemed like it," I insisted. "As long as you were with your *girlfr—*"

"She's not my girlfriend, okay?" Zander's laugh was harsh. "It didn't work out. I don't like her that way anymore." He leaned over and stared at his sneakers. "And I didn't mean to ditch you, or hang out with Stevie more, or whatever. I just wanted to give you some space."

I blinked. "Why?"

He shrugged. "Because of the breakup. With Molly? I thought hanging out with you as much as I . . . wanted to would make things weird between you and her."

As much as I wanted. My pulse raced. I couldn't even look at him. Then . . . "Wait. You know about the Girl Code?"

"I know about the Bro Code. And if one of my guys ever broke up with a girl, and then I started hanging out with her . . ." He shook his head.

"Oh."

"Yeah," Zander murmured. He rested his hand on the stairs, his fingers just inches from mine. "So, like, for example, Bro Code would totally forbid me to ask you to the dance on Friday."

My mouth went dry. "Oh," I said again.

"And Girl Code would prevent you from accepting."

Finally, I looked up at him.

"Then again, if we went, like, in *secret*, without telling anybody . . ."

His silvery eyes locked with mine, and warmth spread through my body, making my fingers and toes tingle with anticipation. Zander and me, on a date? A real (secret) date? Did that mean we were . . .

I felt myself nod. "Okay," I whispered.

"Okay." Zander leaned close. Before I could think about how I was going to keep my feelings about him secret now that I knew how he felt—

—Zander Jarvis and I were kissing.

Kissing. As in, heads tilted, noses and lips pressed together, hearts racing, toes curling. KIS. SING. Zander's lips were so soft that I barely noticing the rotting-fish stink swirling like orchestra music around us. He lifted his fingers to my cheek and lightly cupped my chin in his palm. It felt unfamiliar and completely comfortable at the exact same time. Like I was breaking in a brand-new pair of shoes with my favorite socks.

He pulled away too soon.

"But—I—"

"Okay," he whispered with a sleepy smile. And then he kissed me again.

MISSION ACCOMPLISHED
Monday, 6:30 P.M.

As I eased into a hot shower that night, I replayed the kiss on loop. The soft warmth of Zander's lips on mine, the slow tilt of his head as he moved toward me.

Before I could decide which would make a better theme song for the kiss, Ben Folds's "The Luckiest" or Christina Aguilera's "Ain't No Other Man," I heard Mom's muffled voice on the other side of the bathroom door.

"Giiiiiirls!"

"In the shoooower!" I bellowed, kicking one of Ella's battery-operated bath mermaids out of the way.

A knock sounded on the other side of the door. "Baby?"

"Mom? What are you doing home?" I turned away from the shower curtain, feeling completely exposed. Partially because Mom had an even better sixth sense than I did and could probably smell my Zander kiss a mile away. And partially because I was naked.

The door opened, and the toilet lid dropped. "Whew! Steamy in here!" Mom said. The lid creaked as she sat down. "What smells like—"

"—dead fish? That would be me." I grabbed my pouf and scrubbed hard.

"Oh, right! The field trip! How did it go?"

"Fine." I bit my lip, grateful that she couldn't see my grin.

"Good." The lid creaked again. "Listen, I'm glad you're showering. We're going out to dinner in about an hour. You know that new sushi place in Lincoln Square?"

"Can't we just order in? I'm kind of tired." All I wanted to do was wrap myself in a clean, fluffy bathrobe, eat Chinese takeout, and replay the kiss over and over. And think about whether it was too soon to text him.

"Nope!" The faux cheer in Mom's voice was enough to make me stop exfoliating. "I got a sub for the night and made special plans. So hop to it, eldest daughter of mine."

I finished showering in record time, and after throwing on an aubergine silk romper over gray fishnets, I headed for Mom's bathroom to finish getting ready.

"Kacey!" Ella dove for me the second I walked into the lilac-and-white bathroom. She was wearing black tights, a pink tutu, and a green-and-blue zigzag tankini bathing suit top over a turtleneck. There were unidentified neon-orange stains on her fingertips. Cheese puff residue, if I had to guess.

"Ahhh! This is silk!" I grabbed her wrists just in time and held her at a safe distance. "Keep. Off."

"Better yet, why don't you wash your hands, El?" Mom bent over one of the white marble pedestal sinks and pouted at the mirror, filling in her lips with a creamy, pinkish-nude gloss. She'd flatironed her normally wavy auburn hair so that it fell in a sleek, angled curtain around her shoulders.

"Whoa." I whistled as she straightened up, showing off a close-fitting black knit dress with a high neck and a semi-low V in the back. Paige was right: My mother *was* a fox. "Hot date?"

I *knew* the second the words left my mouth. "Ohmygod. No way."

"Kacey." Mom sighed. Then she turned to Ella and took her by the hands. "Ella, sweetie? I want you girls to meet a friend of mine at dinner tonight, okay? A . . . man . . . friend."

Ella's eyes became flying-saucer wide. I knew the feeling.

"MOM! I can't believe you're springing this on us,

like, half an hour before!" How had I not seen this coming? The heart-to-heart Friday night, the second date on Saturday . . . I should have been prepared. But I was too busy worrying about Zander and Stevie to focus on my mother, Chicago's newest bachelorette.

"I didn't know until a couple of hours ago." Mom glanced back and forth between Ella and me, like she wasn't sure who was more deserving of her excuses. "He called and asked if I wanted to go to dinner, and said he wanted to meet you girls, so—"

"So you just said *okay*, without asking us first, because that's what *he* wanted? Hello? I thought you were a feminist!" I huffed so hard the cilantro-scented candle on the shelf by the door went out.

Mom bit her lip to hide a smile, which made me want to pitch her jar of super-fancy eye cream at the mirror.

"I don't even like sushi." It was a lie, and everybody in the bathroom knew it. But I couldn't think of anything else to say. "And besides, I have a headache."

"Me too." Ella's lower lip trembled. "I have a headache."

Mom shot me a look. "Girls. Come here."

If I'd been wearing heels, I would have stomped across the white tiles. But since I was just in tights, I had to settle for some very stern walking. "What?"

"Sit down," Mom said softly. Her voice was equal parts authority and softness—the worst possible combination. "Okay, listen. I may not have handled this in the best way. I should have given you girls more time to prepare, or talk about it, or whatever you needed. So I apologize for the short notice."

"Whatever." I rolled my eyes to the ceiling.

"But I hope you girls know that I would never, ever ask you to meet someone unless I thought he could be an important part of my—our—lives. Can you trust that?" She crouched in front of the tub and rested a hand on both our knees. "Trust me?"

I swallowed the knot in my throat and nodded.

"And I do. I really do think he could mean a lot to me. But nothing"—her voice cracked as she squeezed our hands—"*no one* will ever mean more to me than my precious girls. Which is why I want you to be involved here. Got it?"

I got it. But I didn't have to like it.

After I'd wrestled Ella into a suitable jumper and tights and corralled her curls into a ponytail holder, the three of us hailed a cab north to Lincoln Square. We were silent the whole way, which was fine by me. I stared out the window into the dark, my gaze blurred and unfocused.

I needed a few minutes of not having to talk, or think, before we walked through the restaurant doors.

"Right here is fine, thanks." Too soon, the cab came to a stop and Mom slipped a wad of cash through the partition. We stepped onto the street just below the glowing green Lincoln Square marquee. The commercial district was bustling with twenty- and thirty-somethings carrying shopping bags and talking on cell phones. Wrought-iron streetlamps cast a buttery glow over the sidewalk. I'd been to Lincoln Square a million times, but tonight it felt like unfamiliar territory.

"They're supposed to have this incredible sashimi." Mom straightened the hem of her dress. "Do you girls remember the seafood place in Streeterville we used to go to sometimes? Well, the head chef there left to open up his own place, and this is—"

"Mom. Can you chill out, please?" I gripped her forearm with one hand and Ella's wrist with the other. Sometimes living with my family was like having two kids of my own. "It's probably not gonna be a total disaster."

"Reassuring, Kacey. Thank you." Mom ran her fingers through her hair twice in a row.

"And if it *is* a total disaster, look on the bright side," I said cheerfully. "We're never, ever doing this again."

"Do I have lipstick on my teeth?" She flashed a flawless Simon Smile at Ella and me.

I folded my arms over my chest. "What's it worth to you?"

Mom looked to Ella, who shook her head.

"Thank you. Now let's do this." She took a deep breath and pulled open the door.

The restaurant was ultramodern, with dim lighting and a smooth, dark wooden floor. The tables were low to the ground, looking like square platform beds bordered by overstuffed silk floor cushions. Diners sat cross-legged on the pillows, chopsticks poised over bowls of seaweed salad and trays of artfully arranged sushi. On any other night, I would have been impressed.

"Oh! Hey there!" Mom lifted her hand and signaled for us to follow.

I squinted hard, trying to make out the man standing next to a waterfall wall at the back of the restaurant. He was tall but solidly built, with tanned skin that set off his light blue eyes. Barefoot, in worn jeans and an army-green button-down with the top two buttons missing, he was definitely underdressed. But his longish salt-and-pepper hair and the smile lines around his eyes and mouth told me he probably didn't worry too much about things like dress codes.

He looked nothing like my father.

"Sterling." As we approached, Mystery Man rested a hand on her waist and kissed her cheek.

Easy, cowboy. I regarded him warily.

"Gabe," Mom murmured back in a voice that made me want to dry-heave. "Meet my girls, Kacey and Ella."

"A pleasure." Gabe smiled kindly, but didn't make an attempt to hug us or shake our hands. Again, fine by me.

I forced a smile back. *Gabe?* Where had I heard that name before?

"And I'd like you all to meet someone as well. Sterling? Girls? This is my daughter—" Gabe stepped aside, and I gasped.

Standing in front of me, her dark hair pulled into a side braid and her full lips pressed into a pout, was—

"—Stevie."

AFTERSHOCK
Monday, 7:34 P.M.

The next thing I knew, introductions were over. Everyone else had claimed a floor cushion: Mom and Gabe on one side of the table, and She Who Shall Not Be Named and Ella on the other. I was still standing next to the table, temporarily paralyzed. According to Nessa, this kind of thing was pretty common when a person experienced a traumatic event. Such as a ruggedly handsome stranger spawning evil, then hitting on my mother.

"Have a seat, Kacey," Gabe said.

You can't tell me what to do. I eyed the green-and-gold silk cushion at the end of the table. Fortunately, Ella had snagged the middle cushion, so all I could see of Stevie was a perfectly swooped side bang and a leather cuff bracelet. I'd never despised anyone more.

"Join us, won't you?" Mom "suggested" with a taut laugh. I recognized her *Don't-you-dare-embarrass-me-in-public* voice from a few weeks ago at the grocery store, when Ella had practically cannonballed into the bakery guy's wedding cake sample tray.

Slowly, I sank onto the cushion and sat back on my heels. Everything was a muted blur: my thoughts, the dull roar of the waterfall wall behind Mom and Gabe, the ebb and flow of conversation at the surrounding tables, the fuzzy edges of the flickering tea light flames in the center of the table. My dream afternoon had just turned into a nightmare.

"Stevie, Sterling's daughter goes to Marquette. Maybe you've seen each other in the halls?" Gabe rested his hands on his knees, palms to the ceiling. "We're staying with family friends from Seattle," he explained to Mom. "Their son goes to Marquette as well, and Stevie's been—"

"Zander," somebody croaked. Judging by the way Mom and Gabe refocused their weirded-out stares across the table, that somebody was probably me. "They're staying with Zander."

"What a small world! Kacey and Zander are in a little band together." Mom smiled. But her eyes never left me, and the tiny creases in her forehead deepened. "Right, honey?"

I decided to let the use of the word *little* slide. In times like these, a girl had to pick her battles. And mine was sitting two cushions down.

"Oh, yeah?" Gabe's wiry eyebrows lifted. "I play a little acoustic guitar myself. In fact, Stevie learned from her old man."

"Yup." The tinny anger in Stevie's voice chilled my blood. That was the tone of a girl who knew something about rogue Swedish Fish and wasn't afraid to rat me out.

"Don't worry. You're only a *little* old," Ella told Gabe graciously.

"Ella!" Mom scolded, lifting her water glass to hide her smile. "Apologize."

"No need." Gabe chuckled. "In fact, I think that's the nicest thing anybody's said to me all day." He pressed his palms together like he was about to pray, then bowed. Ella bowed back.

"Now hold on." Mom frowned playfully. "Don't I get a shot at the compliment game?"

No. No way. Was she . . . *flirting*?

"Be my guest," Gabe said coyly.

"Let's see . . ." Mom tapped her polished red nail against her bottom lip. "Okay, got it." She shifted her whole body toward Gabe, so that there were only a few inches between their noses. OMG. What if he had already *kissed* her? "You, sir, look more and more handsome every time I see you. I think Chicago agrees with you."

"*Kacey!*" Ella hissed. "*Ewwww!*"

I squeezed her hand in solidarity. Out of all the geezers in Chicago, how could Mom have picked Stevie's dad? There were old men everywhere: hogging the good seats on the El, shushing the girls and me in the movie theater during—no joke—the *credits*. But no. She had to pick this guy.

"Sorry, kids. We'll try to keep it G-rated." Gabe winked.

"Would you? That'd be ever so swell." Stevie's caustic tone made Ella scoot a little closer to me.

If I'd made a comment like that, Mom would have grounded me until I was eligible for the senior-citizen discount at Sugar Daddy. But Gabe just cocked his head slightly to one side and said, "I hear your anger. And I think we both know it's not me you're frustrated with."

Disbelieving, I ventured a glance at Stevie. She was squeezing her knees into her chest and staring straight ahead, her face pinched with rage. An involuntary sympathy pang vibrated in my chest. Not because of what I'd done to her, since she'd done way worse to me. But because she had a dad who said things like *I hear your anger*.

"Rough day?" Mom guessed gently.

"You could say that. She got in serious trouble for a prank at the aquarium today," Gabe explained, like Stevie wasn't even there. "She'll be doing a few community-service projects around school." He shook his head and pinched the braided hemp necklace around his throat. "You're pretty lucky that the aquarium's agreed to drop the matter."

"Yeah. Really lucky," Stevie said bitterly. Her words dripped with accusation. "Hey, Kacey? Why don't *you* tell what happened? I'm sure my dad would be really interested to hear your version."

My body temperature skyrocketed. This was it. Any second now, she was going to tell our parents everything. I cursed our justice system for not shipping Stevie to juvie when they had the chance.

Grabbing my silver snakeskin clutch, I shoved away from the table. "Sorry, I have to—" I rasped, stumbling to my feet and lurching past a server. "'Scuze me." Blindly, I barreled around the waterfall wall and down a long, dark wood-paneled hallway. I passed the kitchen, the clanging pots and pans sending Richter-scale-esque aftershocks through my core.

At the end of the hall there were two wooden doors, each with a circular orb featuring the glowing outline of a mermaid. The mermaid on the left was wearing a shell bra with a seaweed halter, so I made an educated guess.

A relaxation soundtrack with the occasional dolphin squeak and low whale call emanated from hidden speakers. I bent over and checked beneath each of the stalls to make sure they were empty, then collapsed onto a wide teak bench by the door, stretching out on the creamy ivory cushions. Right now, Stevie was probably telling Mom and Gabe everything.

I stared up at the glittering blue and teal mosaic tiles that swirled in a frothy pattern on the ceiling. Of course she had figured it out. I was the only one at Marquette who had a real problem with her. But she didn't have proof. She couldn't. Right?

I pulled my phone from my clutch. Six missed calls from Paige, along with a text asking why Quinn hadn't dropped out of the race yet. I deleted them and hit number one on my speed dial.

"*Heyyy, guys,*" Molly's raspy outgoing-message voice murmured in my ear. "*I'm probably out with the boyf right now, so leave me your deets, and I'll call you back whenevs.*"

"It's me." I plugged my left ear to drown out the sudden screech of a seagull. "Where are you? You *have* to call me ASAP. You will not believe what is happening to me right now, and I really need your—"

A bangled hand swooped in and grabbed my phone.

"Hey!" I scrambled to my feet.

I'm on the phone, Stevie mouthed, lifting a finger to shush me. "Um, hey. Mols? It's Stevie. Nice work today, by the way. Good luck getting away with it." She sidestepped me as I flailed wildly for the phone. "So annnnyhooo, your BFF can't come to the phone right now. She'll have to call you later." With a satisfied smirk, she raised an index finger and stabbed a button on my cell.

"Give me that, you lunatic!" I barked, ripping the phone from her grip.

A couple of girls around Ella's age shoved through the bathroom door.

"Get out!" we screeched. Eyes wide, they backed through the doorway.

"Did you know about this?" Stevie snapped. "Your mom and my dad?"

"Of course not! Why would you ask that?"

Stevie's laugh echoed from the tiles. "Why? Um, let's see. You set me up, and now I have to spend the week as Marquette's student janitor. Your flirt of a mother is, like, *seducing* my dad—"

"OH! PLEEEEEASE!" I smacked the wall with my palm. "You know it's your *Survivor*-host-wannabe father who's seducing my mother. Who, by the way? IS A TOTAL FOX. Your dad should *be* so lucky!"

Stevie stalked to the other side of the bathroom, the heels of her cowboy boots clacking against the floor.

"Just so we're clear? This is one hundred percent your fault," I informed her, wiping the sweat from my hairline.

"Oh, really? How's that?" She leaned against the wall between two stall doors, staring me down.

"If you hadn't come here in the first place—"

"Then what?" she challenged, pointing a finger at me. "Then you wouldn't be so desperate to keep your spot in the band that you had to sabotage me?"

My heart rate sped up again. "Nooo. Then our parents wouldn't have met, and I'd be eating Chinese in bed right now, two whole time zones away from you."

"Well, it's too late now, isn't it?"

BAAAAH-OOOOHHH. What could only be classified as a massive whale fart erupted over the speakers.

Stevie snorted. I pressed my fist against my mouth, dropping my head so she couldn't see my cheeks twitching.

"Okay. So seriously. Before they send your Mini-Me in here to get us." Stevie slunk across the bathroom and sat at the other end of the bench. "What are we gonna do about this?"

I rolled my eyes. "Her *name* is Ella. And I don't know. I mean, there's got to be something about your dad that would be a deal-breaker for my mom." I tilted my head back and thought. "Has he ever gotten arrested for some kind of hippie demonstration?"

"My dad's a world-renowned anthropologist. He spent six months in the Amazon, living with the Aweti tribe." I couldn't help but notice that she didn't answer the question.

"So what are you doing in Chicago? Tell him you miss the rain forest!"

"We—I—didn't get to go." Something in Stevie's tone warned me to back off. "Okay. I got it. Did your mom ever fart in the middle of a live interview?"

"EW! No!" I scooted over and slapped the leather patch on her black leggings.

"Well, then, I don't know!" she huffed. After a few seconds, she bent over and fished something out of her green canvas bag. "Here." She tilted a sandwich baggie of Swedish Fish in my direction. "You like these, right?"

I swallowed. The sight of the red gummy candies made me want to gag. But I took one anyway, because Stevie was scrutinizing my reaction the way Liv scrutinized the Sugar Daddy menu for free-trade cocoa.

I plucked a single fish from the bag. "Thanks."

"I didn't tell on you, by the way. My dad would just think I was lying, and I'd get in more trouble."

"I don't know what you're talking about," I said evenly,

but when I lifted my gummy fish, it trembled in midair. "To getting your dad away from my mom."

Stevie rolled her eyes at my lie, but lifted hers, too. "To pawning your mom off on any guy who's not related to me."

We clinked fish. "Cheers."

STEP INTO MY TORTURE CHAMBER
Tuesday, 7:28 A.M.

Less than twelve hours after being forced to stomach a deadly combination of seaweed salad and emotional anguish, I found myself in yet another dire position: curled up in Dr. Marvin Haussman, D.D.S.'s exam chair, waiting to have my braces tightened.

Frozen in the pleather lounger, I briefly considered making a run for it. It would only be a few steps to the WARNING SIGNS OF GINGIVITIS poster on the back of the office door, and I was wearing flats, so I'd be on the elevator before anyone knew I was gone. But after the sleepless night I'd just had, I wasn't sure I had the strength to bolt—or to face Mom's wrath when she figured out I'd ditched.

"So! Dr. H!" The sugary glaze on my voice was Splenda-fake. "How's the wife? Kids? I need an update, like, immediately." I crossed one blush patent oxford over the other and pressed my lips together in a closed-mouth smile. My braces were throbbing already, and he hadn't even come at me with the dreaded pliers yet.

"Fine, fine, Kacey. And your mother?" Dr. Haussman squatted on the rolling stool next to my chair and put on his paper mask. Then he reviewed the silver tray of instruments next to the exam chair. Needle-sharp anticipatory pains shot through my gums.

"She's . . . good." I turned away from the tray and squinted at the door. "She had to get to the studio early this morning." Actually, Mom had offered to come to my appointment. I'd told her that she'd have to be a pretty sick lady to watch me writhe in pain for two hours during her dinner date last night, then come back for more in the morning. Then I'd hightailed it out of the house before she could marry Stevie's dad as my punishment for sassing her.

"Tell her I said hello." The clink of metal on metal made my stomach heave. I definitely shouldn't have had that second bowl of cereal.

"Mmmhmmm." I screwed my eyes shut.

"Aaand if I could get you to turn toward me and open?"

"Mmmhmmm."

"Kacey?" I felt his thick hand on my shoulder. "Turn and open?"

"Oh. Right." I forced my eyes and jaws half-open, try-ing not to focus on the terrifying instruments he was using to prod my teeth. Was it too late to tell him I'd taken World History, that I knew all about the Geneva Conventions and could totally take him down on charges of inhumane treatment?

"MARGHHH," I cried as Doctor Death shoved what looked like a wrench into my mouth. Seconds later, electrifying pain shot through my gums. I hooked my claws into the exam chair.

"Just another minute."

I closed my eyes, blocking out my terrified reflection in his inch-thick lenses. Hadn't last night been enough torture? I'd been forced to watch Mom and Gabe feed each other with chopsticks when they thought we weren't looking. To listen to Ella sob about how she was *positive* she found Nemo in her spicy tuna roll. To ignore Stevie's suspicious glare throughout dinner.

I knew exactly what she was trying to do with that look. She was trying to make me feel guilty enough to confess. But she was the one who was trying to push me out of the band. She was the one who had to be taught a lesson.

"OW!" I stiffened again as the doc tugged and twisted the ropy metal wire weaving my brackets together. Tears sprang to my eyes.

"I know, I know," Dr. Haussman murmured sympathetically. "It hurts. But it'll get better with time. I promise."

Ugh. How could he possibly know things would get better? For one thing, he'd probably never had his mouth rearranged with a shiny new set of power tools. For another, he couldn't possibly get how I was feeling. Like I was trapped. Like if I didn't make exactly the right move at exactly the right time, I could lose my mother, my best guy friend, and my band, all at once.

And there was absolutely *no way* Dr. Marvin Haussman understood the nagging sensation ebbing and flowing in the pit of my stomach. The sensation that, if I was being honest, felt a little too much like . . . guilt. Which was ridiculous, because Stevie from Seattle was getting exactly what she deserved. You could call it justice; you could call it karma.

You could *not* call it my fault. Even though it was.

"Just a few more minutes, and then we'll be done. You're doing great." Dr. Haussman ducked out of the hot exam light, and I let my shoulders sink a few inches. Relief. Blinking into the light, I forced my aching brain to think about anything other than Stevie or Shedd Aquarium. Anything at all. Something pleasant. Something amazing.

Something like my first kiss with Zander.

A smile played over my chapped lips as I replayed the memory for the millionth time. No matter what, I still had that perfect kiss. No one could take that away; no one could ruin the moment when I'd felt Zander lean close, when I'd felt his lips brush against mine.

Unless Stevie told Zander. Unless Molly found out about the kiss before I told her. Then she'd do everything in her power to ruin my relationship with Zander. And according to Girl Code, she'd be 100 percent justified.

The churning feeling in my stomach intensified to a mini tsunami. I'd just shared an incredible kiss with the boy I liked! The boy who was a zillion times cooler, nicer, and more talented than all other boys! My soul mate. I should have been floating on air. Humming cheesy nineties love ballads under my breath. Doodling Zander's name in bubble letters in my Marine Bio notebook. Making all the single girls in my grade want to kick me, then *be* me.

Instead, I couldn't stop thinking about how every second I didn't tell Molly about my feelings for Zander was another second I was betraying her. I couldn't stop wondering whether, even though Stevie was a terrible human being, she might not have deserved what we did to her.

And I couldn't stop picturing my mother and her old-man hippie date, who, FINE! SEEMED LIKE A NICE

ENOUGH GUY! BUT THAT DIDN'T MEAN I HAD TO
BE HAPPY ABOUT HIM!

My phone buzzed in my messenger bag. I practically
flung myself from the exam chair and dug through the
bag.

"Kacey? We're not exactly finished here."

"Just a sec, Dr. H."

PAIGE: WHERE R U??? QUINN WILDER IS RUINING MY LIFE. I
NEED YOUR HELP. CALL ME.

But it was the next text that made me break into a
cold sweat.

STEVIE: MEET ME AT SUGAR DADDY TODAY AFTER SCHOOL.
3:15. WE NEED TO TALK.

I stared at the screen until the pixels blurred in front
of my eyes. My phone vibrated again.

STEVIE: P.S.: BAIL, AND I TELL FINNSTER–AND ZANDER–
EVERYTHING.

I'LL TELL YOU MINE IF YOU'LL TELL ME YOURS
Tuesday, 3:07 P.M.

"The counter by the window's open." Stevie held a green
ceramic mug in one hand and her black patent clutch in
the other, all while balancing a cupcake plate server-style
on her forearm. "Come on." She headed for the long bar
that faced Marquette's front entrance across the street.

"Nah. Let's go to that table in the back." At the Frost-It-
Yourself cupcake bar in the middle of Sugar Daddy, I swirled
a glob of birthday cake frosting over a warm chocolate cupcake, then added two heaping scoops of chocolate-covered
espresso beans for good measure. Being blackmailed required
all the sugar and caffeine I could manage.

"Fine." Stevie turned from the window. Outside, a
slight girl with blond hair identical to Molly's scampered
by. I hit the deck.

"Kacey?"

"Sorry! Lost an earring." I waited for three measures and popped up again. "Found it." I faked putting the earring back in. Good thing we did that lame section on the art of mime in Sean's theater class this semester.

"Um, good." Stevie looked at me strangely.

I mentally smacked myself on the forehead. *Of all days not to accessorize*, I thought as I shook my waves over my naked earlobes.

"Let's go." I grabbed my mug and cupcake and headed for the back corner. Other than us, there were only two other customers—a high school boy listening to his iPod with his eyes closed and a mousy-looking girl with her nose buried in a book. There was a 99 percent chance Molly and the girls wouldn't make an appearance at our hangout this afternoon, since they were shopping for decorations for the dance. But what if they took a retail break? Ditching my girls to meet up with Stevie was bad enough. But bringing her to Sugar Daddy was unacceptable. I felt like I was cheating on Molly. Again. I might as well have brought Zander for a make-out session by the cash register.

A hot, steamy make-out session.

With Zander.

"Kacey," Stevie snapped. "What's with you?"

"Nothing." I sat down.

Stevie shrugged and slid into the sparkly red seat across from me. "Whatever. It's not like we're here for pleasure. I brought you here because we have to figure out a way to break up our parents."

"First of all, *I* brought myself here." I pulled one of Nessa's mini legal pads from my back pocket and flipped to the list I'd made in study hall. "And second of all, are we just not gonna mention the part where you're black-mailing me? Not that you have anything to blackmail me *with*." I started doodling, too nervous to make eye contact.

"If you believed that, you wouldn't be here."

"Wrong." I braced myself and met her gaze. "I'm here for the same reason you are. To break up our parents."

"And because you're scared. Because you know I could get you in serious trouble," Stevie said coolly, quickly rebraiding her dark, glossy hair. "Because you're guilty."

"You're bluffing," I said, gritting my teeth. My already tender gums screamed in pain. "You've got nothing."

"Wanna try me?"

We stared at each other for a long moment. From her disgustingly long lashes to her hardened jaw, she was a fortress. This was a girl who was not going to go down without a fight. Which actually made her the perfect ally for Operation: Date Sabotage.

"Okay." I flipped to the next page on my pad so fiercely that the bright yellow paper tore in half. "We can start by brainstorming some reasons people break up. Then we could figure out a way to apply those reasons to—"

"Are you assigning *research*? Because I'm not doing that."

"Do you want them to break up or not?" I said, exasperated.

Stevie bent over her hot chocolate mug and sighed, blowing the steam directly into my face. "Keep going."

I scooped a blob of icing from my cupcake and licked my fork. The sugar rush was instantly soothing. "First question. How come your parents split up?"

"What?" Stevie's features hardened once more. "Are you *kidding* me?"

"Look. I know it sucks to talk about this kind of stuff. But if we're gonna break them up . . ."

"Fine," Stevie conceded. "So what's my last name?"

"Huh?"

"My last name. If you can tell me my last name, I'll tell you why my parents split."

"I—you never—" I cradled my mug in my hands. It burned. "I don't really see how that's relevant."

"Too bad. You were so close." She shrugged. "So, what about your folks? Your dad probably got sick of your mom's career coming first, am I right?"

A hot flash of anger ignited at my core. "That's none of your business."

"I'm just saying. That's usually how it works when one person has a high-powered job."

"Well, you're wrong." I lifted my mug and took a long sip, even though I knew it was still too hot. It scraped my throat as it went down.

"Hey, do you girls mind if I crank up some tunes?" the girl behind the counter asked, fiddling with the dial on an old-school boom box.

She paused briefly on a classic rock station. Static buzzed over the speakers, but I'd heard enough.

"NO JOURNEY!" I yelled at the exact same time as Stevie. For a second we just stared at each other, then we burst out laughing.

"Okay, okay." The girl cracked her gum and switched to the pop station.

"Goose worships Journey. I don't get it." Stevie traced the rim of her mug with her index finger, her silver dome ring glinting in the fluorescent light. "The lead singer sounds like a girl."

"Right? But what kind of musical taste can you expect from a guy who wears—"

"—skinny jeans?" Stevie's lips lifted in a smile. "I told him to burn those puppies before he moved. But did he listen?" She shook her head. "Boy's got a mind of his own."

I didn't answer. It didn't take a genius to know that she was still into Zander. Or that there wasn't room for her in my relationship—whatever it was—with Zander.

"I think maybe there was someone else," I said quietly.

"What?"

"When my dad left. I think there was some other . . . person. Woman. Whatever." I'd never had proof, but it was the only explanation that made sense. When he'd lived with us, he'd been around all the time. More than Mom, actually. He was the one who went to parent-teacher conferences. He took me to Lincoln Park to toss the Frisbee. He made peanut-butter-and-honey sandwiches for school lunch and always remembered to put them in the freezer for twenty minutes in the morning so they were perfect by lunchtime.

And then one day we were on the Ferris wheel at Navy Pier, and I was looking over Lake Michigan and holding a pouf of blue cotton candy on my tongue. And we got to the top, with the whole world just beyond the tips of our sneakers, and without even looking at me, he said he was moving to Los Angeles. He said things weren't working out with Mom and that this was "better for everyone." Just like that.

The worst thing about it was that I should have known. I was a journalist—I had instincts about these kinds of things, especially since they fought all the time after they thought we were asleep. It was the only time my sixth sense had failed me.

"Oh." At least Stevie had the sense to not say anything else, like how she was sure my dad still loved me or how she knew this girl whose parents divorced and then got back together.

"I mean, I don't know for sure. We don't talk, really. Do you talk to your mom?"

"Yeah." Stevie stared down at her untouched red velvet cupcake. "They only split a couple of years ago. Dad got that grant to go to the Amazon, and I guess he had to pick between staying with us . . ." Her jaw tensed, and she shoved the cupcake plate away. "Anyway, Mom filed for divorce the day he left."

"So how come you live with Gabe now?" I asked, tentatively taking another sip of hot chocolate.

"Mom got kind of depressed after the split. She still lives in Seattle, though, so I see her a lot. But when Dad got back, I decided to move in with him."

I tried to imagine what it would have been like if my mom had fallen apart after the divorce. After Dad left, nothing was the same anymore. His shoes weren't in the doorway. The bathroom didn't smell like his mint soap. But my mom was still there, a wonderful, reassuring constant.

The bell jangling over the door made me jump. But it was just a crowd of over-pierced twenty-somethings from the community college around the corner.

". . . 'cause he works so much. I get the apartment to myself a lot," Stevie was saying.

"Yeah. Me too." I wondered if she was lonely by herself. At least I had Ella when Mom was at work and Paige right next door. "Don't you ever get bored, though?"

Her chin dropped, releasing a shiny curtain of bangs that blocked her eyes. "When Goose was in town, he used to come over and hang out. Sometimes he'd even spend the—"

"We're supposed to be talking about our parents," I reminded her, a little too loudly.

Stevie cleared her throat. "Yeah, not anymore." She shoved back her chair. "I'm getting more frosting."

"But we're not done!" I protested. A familiar stabbing feeling in the pit of my stomach chided me for telling Stevie anything. It was the same feeling I'd gotten the morning after my first sleepover with Molly, when I'd had one too many bowls of ice cream, gotten a serious sugar rush, and accidentally blurted out that I'd never had a boyfriend.

PAIGE'S CAM-PAIN
Wednesday, 6:57 A.M.

"It looks like Marquette swallowed Quinn Wilder whole, then barfed him up again," Paige said early the next morning, her voice echoing in the deserted Square.

Grimly, Zander, Paige, and I surveyed the LET'S GET WILD(ER)! campaign posters that clung to the walls and floor. Someone had even sprayed THE WILDER, THE BETTER in shaving cream on the roof. In the forty-eight hours since he'd announced his candidacy, Quinn's beaming face and glistening hair had taken over every inch of our school.

"This sucks," Paige pronounced. She kicked a Quinn poster out of her path, revealing a crumpled Imran Bhatt ad.

"I know." My chest tightened. There were two days left before Friday's election. I didn't like to think about what Quinn's next move would be.

Paige punted a giant white beach ball with Quinn's name on it across The Square. It smacked the door to Silverstein Hall with a sickening slap and deflated. When Paige turned away, Zander grabbed my hand and squeezed. I squeezed back.

"Okay. That felt good. Now let's get to work." Paige rolled up the sleeves on her black mini shirtdress, then leaned down to tighten the laces on her suede booties. As Election Day got closer, she seemed to be suiting up for battle in much better clothes than usual.

I dug a few rolls of green crepe paper from the tote at my feet. "Zander and I will take care of the ceiling and walls. And this"—I tossed a few thick hunks of green sidewalk chalk in Paige's direction—"is courtesy of Ella."

Paige snatched the chalk out of the air and dropped to her knees. I bit my tongue as she started making sweeping emerald arcs on the floor, then crawled through them in Lurex-threaded black tights. *My* Lurex-threaded black tights.

"Let's start with the far corner," Zander suggested with a smile. His hand brushed mine in what was definitely not an accident.

"Sounds good." If anyone noticed the flush to my cheeks, I could blame it on the tropical temperatures in the glass-enclosed Square. Zander and I hadn't been alone since our kiss in the stairwell. Not that I knew what to say to him. It was times like this when I wished Molly were here. And times like this when I cursed the Girl Code.

I followed Zander to the corner of Silverstein and Addams, my heart jangling along with the lucky gold-coin earrings Liv had made me for our Secret Santa this year.

"Paige seems pretty bummed," Zander said, fiddling with the torn edge of a crepe paper roll. "You think she'll be okay?" The space between his eyes crinkled with worry.

"She'll be fine." I loved how much he cared about Paige. About all people, really. Unless those people were blackmailing pranksters with boy names. Then I did not approve. "I know Quinn, and—"

"Yeah. Spare me the details." Zander smiled, but didn't look me directly in the eye.

"Gimme a break." I shoved him lightly. Okay. Technically, I shoved him a smidge harder than lightly. "We weren't even together that long."

"Me and Stevie, either," Zander shot back.

"Okay, okay. Can we *not* talk about exes, please?" Just hearing Stevie's name made me think about Mom and Gabe, which made me want to puke. I would have to tell Zander about them soon, but I still couldn't figure out how to get the words out without dry-heaving.

"Deal," Zander agreed.

"Here. Catch." I took a few giant steps back and hurled the roll of crepe paper toward the ceiling. It sailed over one of the rusted ceiling beams, then dropped into Zander's outstretched palm.

"Niiiice!" He nodded, looking pleasantly surprised. "Good arm."

"Yeah, well." I stuffed my hands in the pockets of the cerulean knit shift dress I wore over a yellow mesh tee. "I'm not just an award-winning journalist and rockin' lead singer, you know." The minute the words left my mouth, I regretted them. Did they make me sound like the old, self-centered Kacey? Was it bragging if it was true?

But Zander just laughed. "Apparently," he said flirtatiously. He whipped the crepe paper roll across The Square. It fluttered over the center beam and made a beeline for Paige. "Heads up!"

"Ahhh!" Paige's head snapped to attention just as the crepe paper smacked her in the stomach. "Zander!"

"Sorrryyy!" we yelled in unison.

I turned back to Zander and lowered my voice to a whisper. "I'm just saying. I know Quinn, and he doesn't care about politics. He cares about basketball and his stupid friends. And being popular. That's it. He'll get bored and drop out." Sometimes I couldn't believe I'd ever crushed on Quinn, that I'd been the type of girl who cared more about my popularity than my good friends. Or my band.

"Isn't that what this election is all about anyway? Popularity?" Zander asked, frowning. "I mean, you and I know Paige has done tons for the grade, but do you really think everybody else is paying attention?"

"I don't know. Maybe you're right." I'd never admit that I had no real concept of what Paige had done as president of seventh. Apart from switching out all the good vending machine snacks for granola, at least.

"I guess we'll just have to wait and see." Something in Zander's face changed. He looked at the ground. "So, um . . . I wanted to ask you something."

"Yeah?"

"Nah. Nothing. Never mind."

"No. What?" My heart sped up in my chest. Suddenly, I could feel the electricity between us; could almost visualize gold lightning bolts shooting from my core to his.

"It's nothing. I just . . . this musician I used to like in Seattle is playing a small show in town tomorrow night. I didn't . . . do you think your mom would let you go out on a school night?"

My mouth went dry. "What, you mean like a d—what about Molly?" I pinched my thigh, hard. How stupid could I possibly be? Zander was asking me out *for real*, and all I could think to say was *What about Molly?*

"Well, we'd just be . . . hanging out. It doesn't have to be like a big thing."

BUT I WANT IT TO BE! my brain shouted. "Okay, cool. So tomorrow?"

"Yeah. Tomorrow. Seven thirty. Show starts at eight, but it'll be pretty packed. He's playing at the café next to Vinyl Destination. It's gonna be a pretty small show."

"No Stevie?"

Zander looked at me and grinned. "No Stevie."

"Hey! What are you guys whispering about over there?" Paige stood up and brushed green dust from the knees of her tights. She flung the crepe paper in our direction. Zander caught it and tossed it back. The ceiling was starting to look like an emerald spiderweb. "Flirting does not count as working."

"We were just talking about everything you did for the school." Zander caught himself a few seconds too late. "Everything you're gonna keep doing. After you win on Friday."

"Nice try," Paige said dryly. She hopped over a half-chalked GO GREENE ad and teetered toward us, looking like a baby duckling in her too-high ankle booties. "For real. Do you guys think I'm going to lose? Be honest." She leveled her eyes at me, and instantly my insides were wound tighter than one of Ella's bath toys. Was this one of those times I was supposed to lie to spare her feelings? Or did she really want truth, the whole truth, and nothing but the truth?

"I was just telling Zander that Quinn doesn't belong in politics," I said firmly, ignoring the sweat stains probably forming under my arms. "I don't think he's gonna stay in the race."

"But what if he does?" Her voice was pinched with anger.

"He won't."

"But what if he—"

"Paige." Gently, Zander cut her off. "Who budgeted more money for student-run activities this year than any other student body president?"

Paige pursed her lips together. "I did."

"Who kept the school board from censoring the *Marquette Gazette* when they wanted to kill that story on unsanitary meat storage conditions in the cafeteria?"

"I did." Paige's eyes flitted to mine. I nodded encouragingly.

"Who donated her birthday money to the Environmental Club?" Zander continued.

"Okay. How did you even know that?" I interrupted, impressed.

"For your information, donations are public record," Paige sniped.

"Hey! Whoa!" I lifted my palms and took a few steps back. "I come in peace. Before seven A.M. Give me a little credit."

Paige's shoulders slumped. "Sorry. I didn't mean—it's just that you've been kind of MIA these past few days." She stared at the ground, her chocolate fringe obscuring her eyes.

Zander looked at me and shrugged, as if to say *Girl's got a point.*

"You'd be MIA, too, if your mom was dating Stevie's dad!" I blurted.

"What?" Zander's eyebrows disappeared beneath his blue streak, and Paige's jaw dropped. "Are you serious?"

"My mom interviewed him the other day, and I think they really like each other," I said, the words coming out in a rush.

"Oh. Wow." Zander moved toward me, then rocked back on his Chucks.

"Stevie's *dad*?" Paige sounded skeptical. "Like, Stevie's *father*?"

"Paige! How many times are you gonna make me say it? My mom is dating the father of the girl I absolutely, positively cannot—" My gaze fell on Zander, his face all scrunched up like I was about to hit him. "—uh, Stevie's dad."

"Whoa. That's bad," Paige said sympathetically.

Zander caught my eye. "You doing okay?"

I shook my head. "Yeah. No. I dunno. I just . . . that's why I've been a little preoccupied lately, I guess."

I plopped down on the stone bench in the center of the courtyard and buried my face in my hands. I had stayed up past two last night, staring at my mini legal pad, and I still had no idea how to make our parents break up. I didn't even have a spark of an idea. "The other night, they took us on this family date. And apparently, we're going on another one tonight! I can't even—"

"Hey. I know. It's gotta be super weird." Zander sat next to me and slipped his hand in mine. "Your mom hasn't really dated much since your parents split, right?"

I shook my head. "Not really."

"So it would be hard for her to start dating no matter what, right? But dating Stevie's father, that makes things like a million times harder."

"Yeah." I stared at our hands intertwined in my lap. Zander didn't seem to be wondering what Paige thought about our holding hands. He wasn't defending Stevie or telling me what a seriously great guy Gabe was. He just wanted to make sure I was okay. "Exactly," I whispered.

"Is your mom happy?" Paige asked, triple-blinking at Zander's hand in mine. Then she wiped her hands on her dress, leaving two green palm prints on her thighs.

"What?" I sniffed.

"Is she happy? Like, does she seem happy when she's with him? Is she singing in the shower and stuff?"

"Yeah, I guess."

"So then that's all that matters, right? I mean, yeah, it's awkward for you and Stevie. And that sucks. But you do want your mom to be happy, right?"

I squeezed Zander's hand so hard that he winced. "Obviously, I want my mom to be happy, Paige. I just want her to be happy without Stevie's dad."

Paige was my oldest friend. The one I'd cried with when my dad left. Why wasn't she getting this? It wasn't that complicated. My Mom + Stevie's Dad = No, Thank You.

"But maybe Stevie's dad is exactly what will make her happy. And wouldn't that be amazing, if—"

"I don't want to talk about this anymore." My voice cracked, and I turned away from Paige and toward Zander. "Can we just finish up, please?"

"Totally." Zander helped me to my feet. "But if you need to talk about it, I'm, like, here. You know?"

"I know." At least I could count on one of my friends.

THE ICE IS GETTING THINNER
Wednesday, 6:35 P.M.

"Simon, we've got a problem." That night after rehearsal at the loft, Stevie and I stood side by side on a crowded southbound Red Line train. We stared into the inky Chicago night as the El stopped at Lakeview, then Lincoln Park, then River North. Further south was Chicago's Loop, the commercial district downtown where Stevie and I were meeting Mom, Ella, and Gabe for a skating date at the Millennium Park rink.

"You're going to have to be more specific." I glowered past my own reflection in the window, the city racing by just out of my reach. "I've got lots of problems right now."

After the prank at Shedd, I'd thought the administration would ban Stevie from the dance, or (preferably) school property, or (even more preferably) the Midwest.

When that didn't happen, I assumed her dad would ground her. But apparently, Gabe didn't believe in punishment. I should have known. The man wore hemp.

"Hello? I'm talking about our parents." Stevie yanked the ends of her salmon-colored scarf. "My dad has this thing he does when he's in a really good mood."

"Lemme guess. He does a little dance around the rain forest. No. Wait. He plays the bongo drums in a loincloth."

The train lurched to a stop and Stevie slammed into me, pinning me to the cold silver pole closest to the doors.

"Ow! Get off!"

"Oops. Sorry." She blinked innocently, showing off a set of turquoise-and-navy faux lashes that looked like peacock feathers. I hated how awesome they looked. "No, whenever he's in a really good mood, he hums in the shower."

"So what? A lot of people hum in the shower. I do, and trust me when I say I am *not* happy right now." The doors slid open and I hopped onto the platform, which was packed with tourists doing headcounts on their kids and comparing the maps on their iPhones with the ones on the station wall.

Stevie's hand fell heavily on my shoulder. I fought the urge to shrug it off. "Yeah, but this morning he was singing a *Marvin Gaye* song. In a really low key."

"Ewwwww!" A blast of cold air whipped my cheeks as we stepped onto State Street. "Please don't tell me which song."

"You know the one."

"Craaaaaaap." I stuffed my hands in my coat pockets and stormed south. "Can we not talk about this anymore?" I'd always loved hitting downtown at night, and I wasn't about to let Stevie or Gabe or Marvin Gaye and his sexy songs ruin the experience. The bite to the evening air, the golden storefronts glowing around us, the hustle of people on the sidewalks and the distant honking of horns: Chicago had a rhythm, a kind of music to it that made me feel alive.

"Just one more thing." Stevie fell into step beside me. "This morning at breakfast, he told me he was planning a big date for her. Something about a hot-air balloon ride."

I sucked in a breath, and the cold air pricked my lungs. "Could your dad get any cheesier? And by the way, my mom hates—" I stopped in my tracks. "That's it. I'm a freaking genius!"

"Hey! Watch it." Stevie smacked into me, almost tripping over my over-the-knee shearling-trimmed boots.

I whirled around and grabbed her by the shoulders. "Shut up and listen. We'll point out all the terrible things about our parents, in front of them. Like . . . your dad sings gross songs in the shower. And my mom always forgets to check for deodorant stains before she leaves the house. That kind of thing. Then—" I flung my arms out *ta-da* style, almost backhanding a little old lady. "Oops. Sorry. Relationship over."

"So, like, make them look bad in front of each other?" Stevie pulled her white mohair cloche low over her ears, looking deep in thought. "That'd be pretty easy, as far as your mom's concerned."

I snorted, thinking of her dad's bare feet at the restaurant. "We might not even have to do this. Your dad seems like kind of a flake, anyway. Maybe he'll forget to fill out his application for U of C or something. Then you won't be able to move."

"Or maybe he'll get the job and decide he's not interested in a lady with PIT STAINS."

"DEODORANT STAINS! At least my mom wears it. Your dad probably goes au naturel." I wrinkled my nose.

"What, like, naked?" Stevie looked confused.

"No, like . . ." I shook my head, exasperated. "Never mind."

We entered the Millennium Park rink, where bundled-up skaters wobbled across the ice. Mom, Gabe, and Ella were waiting outside the rental hut. Gabe was kneeling in front of Ella and tying the hot-pink glitter skates Mom and I had given her for her last birthday.

"Kacey! Stevie!" Ella lit up when she saw us. "Look!" She wiggled her feet, sending the laces on her skates flying. "I'm like Cinderella!"

Gabe laughed and steadied her skates. "Easy, princess."

"Gimme a break," Stevie mumbled under her breath.

I elbowed her in the side. Hard. "Back off. She's six."

"Hey, girls. We got you some skates." Mom lifted two dingy pairs of skates by the laces and smiled. Her cheeks were flushed peach from the cold, and her hair fell in fiery waves from underneath her celery-green wool cap. She looked beautiful.

Is she happy? Paige's voice from this morning floated into my brain.

"So how was school?" Gabe straightened up, then took Ella's hands and pulled her to standing. She promptly face-planted into his chest.

"Classes were good, for me." I smiled at Stevie as I kicked off my boots. "How was your community service? Feel rehabilitated?"

"Kacey Elisabeth Simon," Mom warned.

Stevie narrowed her eyes at me. "Thanks for asking, Kacey. Some moron papered the entire Square with green crepe paper. I spent, like, two hours pulling it down."

"Bummer." I shoved my feet into my skates and yanked the laces tight. "Whoever spent their precious time decorating The Square is probably really pissed at you right now."

"Oooooohhhhhhhhh." Ella slapped her palm over her mouth.

"Okay, girls." Mom sighed. "Shall we hit the ice?"

Ella screeched something that sounded vaguely like a *yes*, but mostly like an overexcited hyena.

"Stevie and I have never been skating, so your mom insisted. I hear the three of you are pros." Gabe winked at me. The salt-and-pepper scruff prickling his cheeks and chin made it beyond obvious that he hadn't shaved all day. And if he couldn't even manage proper personal hygiene, how could he hope to hold down a legit job or contribute to society? If there was one thing Mom hated more than anything, it was a slacker.

"So, Mom." I glided effortlessly on the ice, skating backward as Stevie and her dad hunched over like linebackers and clomped toward the center of the rink. "How was *your* day?"

"Great, thanks." Mom smiled nervously, looking confused at the sudden cheer in my voice. "I subbed for the morning anchor, and had a really fascinating interview with the alderman for ward—"

"So you got up super early and were, like, really productive," I summarized, sending *your turn* vibes Stevie's way. "Awesome."

"So, Dad," Stevie jumped in, right on cue. "Didn't you get up at like, ten, or something?"

I kept my eyes trained on Mom.

"Ten?" She wrinkled her nose like Gabe had just told her he was wearing dirty underwear.

Gabe's left skate shot out to one side, and he grabbed Mom's arm to steady himself. "Ooof! I got up at eight, but spent two hours meditating. I was feeling uncentered—a little like I am now, actually." He laughed and pulled Mom close. "So I took some time to quiet my mind."

Oh, please. Meditating? That was just a fancy word for sleeping with wind chimes in the background. This was too easy.

"I just love that," Mom said.

Wait. What? I nearly tripped over my own skates and had to grab the hood of Ella's puffy purple coat to keep from biting it.

"Kacey! Ow!" Ella swatted my hand away, then dropped to the ice and started making ice angels. "Look at me!"

"I think it's so refreshing to find a man who takes the time to tend to his spirit." Mom blinked up at Gabe.

"Ohmygod," I muttered under my breath. I skated in tight circles around Stevie. "*Tend to his spirit?* That was totally something your dad would say! He's rubbing off on her!"

Her eyes were wide. "This is worse than I thought."

I whipped around, skating directly toward Mom and Gabe.

"Kacey! Whoa!" Mom had to let go of Gabe's hand to let me through. He wobbled like a giant bobblehead, but didn't hit the ice. "Careful!"

"Sorry," I said lightly. Then I forced a laugh. "Hey. Mom. Remember that time you went on the air with lipstick on your teeth? And it basically looked like you had no front teeth for a whole broadcast?"

Stevie sucked in a breath. "That's pretty unattractive." She caught my eye, looking super serious. I rolled my eyes at her. Did she have to be so dramatic? If Mom hadn't figured out my endgame before, Stevie had just given us away.

But instead of threatening to ground me, or even using my middle name again, Mom just joined hands with Gabe and laughed. The kind of easy, openmouthed laugh that told me she was completely relaxed around Gabe. "I *do* remember that! I was mortified!"

Oh, no. I recognized that smile. It was the way I looked when I caught a glimpse of myself mid-Zander–thought.

Gabe leaned down and kissed her hat. "I love that you were so invested in your work, you didn't even have the mental energy to worry about your appearance."

Disgusted, I speedskated away from Mom and Gabe, while Ella screamed at Mom to watch her skate backward. What was *wrong* with my mother? She used to be so level-headed. So practical. Ever since she'd met Gabe, it was like she'd been brainwashed.

"Um, in case you didn't notice, your little plan tanked." Stevie tripped into me and grabbed my arm a few seconds later.

"Yeah. I was there." I kicked at the ice with the toe of my skate, sending a spray of fluffy white shavings in Stevie's direction.

"So? What do we do now?"

"I'm not sure there's anything we *can* do."

Stevie stopped skated entirely. "What? Why?"

"Because . . ." I glared at the ice, which was covered in grayish-white tracks from the other skaters' blades. I imagined a tiny crack at my feet getting wider and wider, until the ice parted and swallowed me whole. If only I were so lucky. "Because I think they're in love."

THE MARQUETTIAN CANDIDATE
Thursday, 12:02 P.M.

I didn't sleep at all that night. My brain and body were wound tighter than my braces. I tried everything to relax: a hot shower. A yoga relaxation DVD I'd bought last summer when Ella was going through her *But why?* phase. I'd even Skyped with Molly and the girls, spilling everything about Mom and Gabe in hopes that one of them would have an inspired idea about how to wreck their relationship.

The next day, all I had to show for my efforts was frizzy hair (thanks to two washes in one day), a slight limp (thanks to an off-balance downward-facing dog), and a cell full of pity texts (thanks to my sweet, completely unhelpful friends).

By lunchtime, I considered calling Mom and telling

her I was sick. Which wouldn't have been a total lie. But Molly was hosting a Party Planning Committee meeting in The Square. More important, my big date with Zander was that night. So I dragged myself to the overpopulated courtyard as soon as the lunch bell rang, my black silk pants billowing indignantly behind me.

Molly and the girls were already clustered in a circle around our usual stone bench. I wriggled past a herd of eighth graders shooting hoops and broke into the center of The Square. Though the green crepe paper spiderweb Zander and I had made yesterday had vanished, the Quinn Wilder posters were still everywhere. At least Stevie had had the decency to leave a few GO GREENE posters up, but Imran Bhatt's presence was virtually nonexistent.

"Hey, Kace! Over here!" Mols waved me over, all business in camel wool skinnies and a fitted leather blazer with an asymmetrical zipper. Her glistening stick-straight hair was styled with a no-nonsense center part. I'd had most of the morning to get used to her new edgy-young-professional look, but it was still more disorienting than seeing a teacher at the grocery store on a Sunday.

"Hey." I wriggled between Molly and Nessa. A poster crinkled beneath my butt, and I pulled out a neon-blue flyer that had nothing to do with school politics. It was a Levi Stone flyer, advertising his show at the Goodman

Theatre. "Did you guys know Levi Stone is playing the Goodman next Tuesday?"

Molly handed me a clear pink folder with my name on it in glitter. Liv and Nessa were already perusing matching folders. "Phoenix says he's a total hack."

I shook my head. "I think he's pretty good." I made a mental note to ask if Mom could get comp tickets from the arts and entertainment reporter at the station. Maybe for Zander and me. Maybe for our second date.

Molly shrugged and handed me a gigantic latte with my name scrawled across the side of the cup. The bench was crammed with Sugar Daddy to-go cups and vegan sandwiches from the deli down the street. "BTW, I told the girl at Sugar Daddy to give you an extra shot of espresso. You probably didn't sleep much last night," she said sympathetically.

"That's so nice, Mols." I managed a weary smile and wound my frizzed-out mane into a messy bun. "Thanks."

She beamed. "Welcome."

"Hanging in there?" Liv looped her arm through mine and rested her curls on my shoulder.

"Yeah. I guess." I closed my eyes for a second, inhaling the scent of Liz's lemongrass shampoo. It felt good to hang with my old friends instead of being forced to spend time with Stevie at rehearsal or one of our terrible Mandatory

Blended-Family Dates. And at least Mols and the girls were sympathetic to my situation. Which was more than I could say for Paige. "I just want things to go back to normal. I liked it when it was just Mom and Ella and me." *And Dad.* I shoved the last thought from my mind.

"I get it." Nessa toyed with the dark fringe grazing her brow. "It's, like, what you were used to. You didn't ask for Gabe to just swoop in like this."

"Remember when Nate came to live with us the summer before he left for college?" Molly said quietly. Nate was her half-brother from her dad's first marriage. He'd always lived with his mom in Oklahoma, but he stayed with the Knight family one summer while he took premed classes at Northwestern. I'd only met him twice. He was nice enough, but it was still weird.

"I remember you stuffed a bunch of Snoopy's hair in his pillowcase," I reminded her. Snoopy was the Knights' three-legged diabetic cat, and Nate was deathly allergic to him. "And that Nate had to go to the ER to get some kind of emergency shot."

"He stole my room!" Molly protested. "Am I not allowed to defend my territory?"

"Peace, girly. She's just kidding." Liv grinned.

"I'm just saying that situation was kind of like this one," Molly said. "I had my family, and everything was good, and then all of a sudden, things just . . . changed."

"Yeah." I reached out and squeezed her hand. I'd never really thought about what that summer must have been like for her. Knowing that she'd felt the same way I did made me feel less alone.

"Things are good now, though." Molly double-squeezed back. "He sent me an NYU hoodie for Christmas, and he's coming home this summer to intern downtown."

"Good. Okay, enough about Gabe and our crazy families. We've got a dance to plan." I took an extra-long sip of latte, feeling the caffeine shoot through my veins. I flipped my folder open and found a song request list for Gravity, a catering menu from a hip Asian-fusion bistro in Lakeview, and a checklist of tasks for the committee, arranged by the necessary completion date and time.

I blinked. It looked like Molly really *had* found her calling.

"So I'm calling this meeting to order." Molly straightened up at least two inches. "We still haven't decided on a theme to go with the decorations we picked out the other day. Plus, we have to clean up The Square. These campaign posters are killing the vibe in here."

"I can't believe Quinn is still in the race," Nessa said.

"Right?" I exclaimed.

Molly lowered her fingertips to a black-and-white

LET'S GET WILD(ER)! flyer on the ground and traced Quinn's chiseled cheekbones. "He's totes overcompensating." But her awed voice didn't quite match her words.

We all stared at Molly for a beat. Then I coughed.

"Ummm, don't we need to get on with the meeting?"

"Oh. Right. Okay. First, we need a theme idea. The floor is now open."

Liv leaned in excitedly. "I was thinking about this last night and—"

Molly shook her head vehemently. "Please address the chairperson in the proper manner, Committeeperson Parillo."

"Fine." Liv raised her hand. *"Madame Chairperson,* may I have the floor?"

"You may." Molly beamed, stealing a glance at me. I gave her a thumbs-up.

"What if we picked a cause, like global warming or cancer or something, and charged a few bucks at the door? We could donate the proceeds to charity."

"People aren't gonna pay to come to a depressing party. Besides, how do you decorate for cancer?" Molly made a fist and thumped it against her knee. "Veto. So here's what *I* was thinking. We could do a dance with a date auction, where everybody comes by themselves, and then people bid to be my date?"

"You mean, they bid to be *your*—the universal *your*—date," Nessa said dryly.

"That's what I said." Molly raised an eyebrow.

"Wait. What happened to the new boyfriend? You're not . . . you don't wanna bring . . . him?" I asked carefully.

"I mean, obv, I do." Molly's left eye twitched. "I'm just thinking that most of the dateless freaks at this school—and I'm *clearly* not talking about you guys—would rather not have to go through the humiliation of showing up alone," she explained. "And we could make a lot of money for the school this way."

"Okayyyy." I exchanged glances with Liv and Nessa.

"It was just an idea. Whatever. We can come up with another one." Molly dragged the zipper on her jacket up, down, and back up again. Down. Up. Down. Up.

"We could just do something really simple," Nessa suggested, pointing the toes of her bronze ballet flats. "Like, Marquette at Midnight, or something. We could have the dance here in The Square, under the stars. Just make everything really elegant."

"Ooh! I like that." I nudged her knee with mine. "Good one."

"Madame Chairperson!" Liv's gold-henna-inked hand thrashed in the air. "We could use those tea light votives we bought! We could hang them from the skylights to save electricity! And be romantic!"

Molly sighed and rolled her eyes. "So nobody wants to do my date auction idea?"

I bit my lip.

"Whatevs," she said drily. "All in favor of Nessa's *romantic* idea?"

"Aye!" the girls and I chorused.

"Fine." Another eye roll. "Okay, so music? Kacey?"

"Gravity's rehearsing today and tomorrow after school, so I'll take your requests and see what we can do."

"Good." Molly's gaze lingered on me a few seconds too long, but I couldn't read her expression. "So now all we have to do is get rid of these ugly campaign posters."

"Over my dead body. Didn't anybody tell you it was election week?"

I turned around to see Paige standing behind me, her arms crossed so tightly over her chest it was a wonder she could breathe.

"Hey, Paige." I rubbed my temples. "We were just kidding. Nobody's gonna take down your posters."

"Uh, yeah. I am." Molly slapped her folder closed and stood up. "They have to go. I can't throw a decent party with your mug everywhere."

"Excuse me?" Paige's face turned tomato red. "Say

that to me one more time." A few feet away, a crowd was starting to cluster.

"Okay, okay." I jumped up and grabbed Paige's hand. "You. Come on." I dragged her across the courtyard, to an empty patch of real estate outside Silverstein.

"Oww! Kacey!"

"Hey. Look at me." I pointed at Paige's eyes, then at mine. "Focus. Do you really think I'd let Molly mess with your posters the day before the election? Come on, Paige. I helped put them up!"

She stared at the ground. "I guess not. Sorry. It's just that this Quinn Wilder thing is driving me crazy." Her shoulders dropped. "And I'm sorry about your mom and Gabe. I know you're upset, and it's just that I'm just really stressed out, and—"

"I know." I pulled her in for a hug, and she sniffled into my shoulder. "It's okay. I just really don't want you to worry about Quinn, okay? I mean, it's *Quinn!*" My laugh sounded fake even to my own ears. "He can't even make it through homeroom without losing focus. There's no way he's gonna see this thing through."

Paige pulled away. "You really think so?" Her eyes said she wanted to believe me. Almost as much as I wanted to believe myself.

"Heyyyy, Marquette! Make some NOOOOOISE!"

Before I could reassure Paige, Quinn's voice boomed over the courtyard. A few seconds later, he emerged from Hemingway, holding a megaphone and wearing a T-shirt with LET'S GET WILD(ER)! printed across the chest.

The Square erupted into cheers as Quinn paraded around the perimeter. "Are you guys sick of lame field trips and even lamer vending machine snacks?"

"Yeahhhh!"

Paige croaked and grabbed my hand.

"Then I say, let's take back our student government! Starting with our snacking privileges!" Behind Quinn, Aaron and Jake whipped out Marquette gym bags and started pitching mini candy bars into the crowd. Soon, the kids in The Square were more out of control than Liv in the back room of a vintage consignment shop.

"TELL ME AGAIN HOW I SHOULDN'T WORRY ABOUT QUINN RUNNING?" Paige shouted, her eyes wild with panic.

"YOU'LL BE FINE! PROMISE!" I hit the deck to avoid getting whacked in the head with a mini Snickers.

It was a blatant lie, and we both knew it. But this was one of those times when the cold, hard truth was simply just too painful.

DRESSING IS NINE-TENTHS OF THE LAW
Thursday, 5:49 P.M.

"I'm not so sure about this!" Paige yelled over the blare of car horns and squealing tires. "Can't we go home and practice my speech?"

"Hold up." I stopped at the corner of Michigan and Chicago, standing at the edge of a crowd watching an old man beat out a staccato rhythm on an African drum. The body of the drum was long and the head was made of animal skin stretched taut. The Beat had brought something similar to rehearsal once. A *djembe*, I remembered. If Zander were here, he'd give some useless but adorable trivia about some obscure drummer he loved.

"I have to give my speech to the entire grade *tomorrow*." Paige tapped her watch impatiently. The wind whipping around the corner made her bob fly in a million different directions.

"Yup. And unless you follow my advice, we'll both be listening to Quinn Wilder's victory speech on Monday."

As we set off down Chicago Avenue, I snuck a quick glance at my watch. *Five fifty-two.* Still plenty of time to make sure Paige was suitably dressed for tomorrow's presidential rally and get to Andersonville to meet Zander for our first date.

Our. First. Date. Possibly the most beautiful words in the English language. Unless, of course, we were just "hanging out" in a way that was "no big thing."

"I don't know why I need a new outfit," Paige argued, sidestepping a half-dozen elementary school kids in back-packs, marching in dutiful single file behind two harried adults. "I have plenty of clothes at home."

"No, *I* have plenty of clothes at home. *You* have a closet full of the most depressing goth threads I've ever seen." I held up my palm before she could chide me for my honesty. "I'm sorry, but it's true. And it's also true that you need to look amazing tomorrow."

"Have you ever listened to anything I've said in the history of our friendship?" When Paige huffed, her breath clouded resentfully in front of us. I charged through it. "Politics is about ideas. Not outfits."

"If people don't like your outfits, they don't listen to your ideas! Why do you think Michelle Obama wears J.Crew twenty-four-seven-three-sixty-five? You have to be a role model, Paige. And that includes fashion."

"All the stores down here are too fancy for me. I don't have that much holiday money left, you know."

"That's why we're gooooooing . . . here." We stopped directly in front of the glass doors of Nordstrom Rack. "My mom gets sale stuff here all the time. Good stuff. Maybe we can even get you a dress for the dance, too."

Paige opened her mouth like she was about to protest. Instead, she squinted thoughtfully at our reflections in the storefront. "I *do* like Michelle Obama . . ."

"Why? Because her wardrobe is killer. Her arms are, too, but we're working on limited time here." I shoved Paige through the doors into a brightly lit white-and-chrome entrance.

We joined the bevy of chic shoppers riding the long escalators to the first floor. If we had time, maybe I'd pick up a new set of bangles for tonight. My black pants, silky mint-green top, and patent flats suddenly felt blah. Plus, Zander had already seen me in this outfit at school. That settled it. I needed a new . . . everything.

"Hey." Paige snapped her fingers in front of my face. I blinked. "Are you listening? Repeat what I just said."

"Ummm . . . something dull about politics or principles? Wait. No. You quoted a dead president." I crossed my fingers and held them up, faking excitement. "Don't keep me in suspense."

"Hilaaaaarious. What's going on in there?" She wiggled her index finger in front of my nose. "There's something you're not telling me."

I took a deep breath. Paige was my and Zander's biggest cheerleader. But what if it didn't work out? What if, halfway through the concert, Zander decided he didn't like me anymore? Sure, things seemed good now. But things could change. People could change their minds. Like my dad did. And like I was hoping to make my mom and Gabe do now.

"Are you okay?" Paige cocked her head to the side and peered into my eyes. "You don't look so good."

"I—I'm sort of hanging out with Zander tonight."

"I KNEW IT!" she shrieked, pinning me to the escalator rail. I gripped the rubber edge to steady myself. "I knew you guys were together! I totally saw you holding hands in The Square."

On the step ahead of us, a lady in bloodred lipstick and a fur pillbox hat turned around and glared.

"Paige!" I hissed. "Chill. We're not *together*." Just in time, I hopped off the escalator and out of her reach. Ahead of us stretched an endless array of outfit possibilities. Designer jeans were packed on rolling racks. Colorful cashmere scarves hung from accessory displays. And ruthless bargain hunters clawed through stacks of folded cardigans with jeweled buttons.

"You need jeans," I decided. "Like, nice jeans that say, *I'm in charge here*, but also, *I can be casual*. Agree?"

"I'm not agreeing to anything until you tell me what's going on with you and Zander." I hadn't seen Paige look this determined since first grade, when we got to our classroom on St. Patrick's Day to find all the desks overturned and green glitter everywhere. It was the work, said our teacher, Mrs. Phelps, of mischievous leprechauns. Horrified at the disrespect for school property, Paige launched a full-scale investigation to find said leprechauns, until Mrs. Phelps quietly pulled her aside and confessed.

"Can we at least talk and try on clothes at the same time? I'm supposed to meet Zander at seven thirty." I spotted a pair of gray wax-coated skinnies and tossed them over one arm. "These are a definite yes. They'll make you look taller, which will make you look more presidential."

"Okay! Whatever! Tell me everything!"

"We're just hanging out tonight at that café in Andersonville. It's not really like a *date* date. More like a friend thing. A 'no big deal' thing." Or was it a big deal? We *had* kissed. I turned away, pretending to check the price on a pair of leather fingerless gloves. "Before you freak, these are for me."

"It *so* is a date." She scoffed. "You guys just don't want to call it that. Does Molly know?"

"No." I whacked the gloves against Paige's arm. "And she's not going to know until I figure out how to tell her." I lifted my pinky finger menacingly. "Swear."

"Okay, okay." Paige latched her pinky to mine. We shook. "Like you have to worry about me gossiping with *Molly*. Please." She spotted a boxy black blazer and yanked it from the hanger. "How about this?"

"Throw on a dude's shirt and a tie with that and you could pass for Imran Bhatt." My gaze fell on a bald mannequin sporting a cropped charcoal blazer with black leather piping. "Now *this* is a blazer." I whipped it off the display, leaving the mannequin bare-boobed. "You might actually look like a girl in this one."

"Gee, thanks." Paige sniffed behind me. "Besides, I heard from one of my best sources that Imran dropped out of the race this afternoon."

"Seriously? Because of Quinn?" I held the blazer up to Paige's frame.

Paige nodded, her eyes suddenly glassy behind her

smudged lenses. "I should go back and practice my speech. What if—"

"Look. Here. Try this on," I said gently. I lifted her messenger bag over her head and helped her out of her peacoat. "You already have everything you need to beat Quinn. You have better ideas, an actual track record. This is just the finishing touch."

Paige slid into the blazer and checked out her reflection in a mirrored column.

"It's not bad." She cleaned her glasses on the hem of her black T-shirt, then took a step closer to the mirror. "It looks professional, at least."

"And the leather ups the cool factor." I draped my arm over her shoulder and brushed her bangs away from her eyes with my other hand. "Makes you much more relatable."

Paige's lips curved into a small smile. "I'll think about it."

"Give me a few lines from your speech."

"Huh? Here?"

"Why not? See if it fits with the new threads."

"Umm, okay. I'll try out the part about Quinn." Paige blinked at the mirror and buttoned the center button on the blazer, then unbuttoned it again. "My *opponent* is trying to ride the popularity wave right into office," she said disdainfully. "Sure, he's got a ton of friends, and I hear he's super fun at parties. He's promised to make our field trips more fun, and if it's up to him, we'll probably have nothing but junk food and soda in the vending machines."

"Uh, Paige? Don't we want people *not* to vote for Quinn?"

"But do you know what he doesn't have, people?" Paige planted her palm on the mirror and glared into it, her voice getting stronger. "He doesn't have experience. None. Zip. Nada. So when it comes time for you to vote on Monday, you have a choice. Do you want the candidate with years of leadership experience? Or do you–"

Just then, my cell phone buzzed. "Oops. Sorry." I checked the screen.

Stevie. Ugh.

"Kacey! You killed my flow!" Paige stomped her foot.

"I have to take this. Sorry. You're doing great! Great flow!" I lifted the phone to my ear and made a beeline for a rack of plus-sized fur coats. "Hello?" I ducked between two coats, creating a soundproof barrier.

"I got more details on this hot-air balloon date." Stevie's voice was almost a whisper. "He's doing it Friday night."

"As in tomorrow? The same night as the dance?" I whispered back.

"Yeah. *And* he went out and bought a new shirt today. *And* he shaved."

"So, basically, he's acting like a normal, hygienic person." I closed my eyes.

"He hasn't bought a new shirt since I was born. This is a problem. I think he's gonna drop the L-bomb."

My blood ran cold. "Okay. First, nobody says 'L-bomb.' And second, what do you want me to do about it? We've tried to break them up, but they're too into each other."

"Desperate times call for desperate measures. We have to figure out a way to make your mom miss the date completely. He'll think she stood him up, and he'll break it off."

"Isn't that a little harsh?" I pictured Gabe standing alone next to a hot-air balloon, weeping softly in a brand-new shirt made of wheat.

"Do you *want* them to get married?"

"Okay. She'll miss the date," I said quickly. "It's just gonna be hard to figure this out on the same night we're playing the dance."

"Kacey?" Paige's scuffed black boots shuffled impatiently on the other side of the coat curtain. "Everything okay in there?"

I pressed my hand over the receiver. "*Fine!* Everything's great."

"I found a hot dress for the dance. And one for you, too!" A teal tulle-wrapped mini bobbed next to her boots.

"Love it. I'll meet you at the dressing rooms?"

"Okaaay." After a few seconds, Paige's boots and the mini meandered off.

"Hello?" I whispered into the receiver. "I'm back."

"Yippee," Stevie muttered. "Just figure something out. We all know you're great at coming up with plans that totally ruin other people's lives."

"If I had any idea what you were talking about, I'd say you were being way too dramatic," I said sweetly. "I'll call you later."

"You better. Because I am *not* sharing a room with you."

I hung up on her and buried my face in the closest fur coat. My brain was jumbled with everyone else's problems: Paige's campaign. Mom and Gabe's fling. Stevie's fear that if we ever had to share a closet, she'd realize that my clothes were way better than hers. The poor animal that had given its fur for this ugly coat. For one night, for just a few hours, I didn't want to think about anyone else.

Well, about anyone other than Zander. And me. Together, on our very first (maybe) date.

IT'S ~~A DATE!~~
~~JUST A FRIEND THING!~~
COMPLICATED!
Thursday, 7:45 P.M.

The café was hot and more crowded than I'd ever seen it. I had to turn sideways and hold my breath just to squeeze past the bouncer who stamped my hand with a glow-in-the-dark icon of a coffee cup. The house lights were dimmed, and a spotlight haloed the empty stage at the other end of the room. The churn of the espresso machine and the sharp, intermittent squeal of the coffee grinder punctuated the steady hum of conversation.

I clutched my shopping bags close and searched the crowd for Zander, trying to distinguish one silhouette from the next. Usually, I'd just look for the kid with the bright blue hair. But almost everybody's hair was dyed some unnatural color or swept into a fauxhawk.

"Hey, aren't you the lead singer of Gravity?"

I spun around, almost knocking two cornflower-blue mugs from Zander's grip.

"Oh. Hey!" I sputtered. "Hi."

He was close enough to trigger a wave of crush-shivers that rocked my core. But I didn't take a step back. Probably because there wasn't room to step. And it didn't hurt that in the low light, his eyes were a fiery chrome color. I had to remind myself to blink. And inhale.

"I thought you might be standing me up." He grinned and handed me one of the mugs. "Careful. It's hot."

"I got it. Thanks." I slipped my fingers around the handle, but only because I was safety-conscious. Not because I wanted our hands to touch. "Sorry I'm late. I was helping Paige with some stuff for tomorrow."

"No problem. You look . . . I like that top thing." He looked over my shoulder.

I smiled into my coffee cup. "Thanks."

After helping Paige, I'd spent an extra twenty minutes picking out my new black leather camisole and boy-friend blazer. And taming my frizzy mane into a *This is intentional, I swear* messy bun. And conning the snobby salesgirl into letting me sample a non-tester perfume that smelled like buttercream frosting.

"So I guess it's standing-room only. That okay?" Zander nodded at the factory windows overlooking the street.

There was just enough room for the two of us, plus my bags. Every inch of the left side of my body was pressed against every inch of the right side of Zander's body.

Which was probably why my left hemisphere was completely numb.

"This is good." I leaned against the chilled window-panes and sipped my coffee, saying a silent thank-you that Stevie wasn't there to tell me about all the coffee she and Zander had drunk together in Seattle.

Ugh. Stevie.

For the next two hours, I didn't even want to think the name, let alone say it. I had the rest of the night to worry about her; the rest of the night to freak about keeping Mom away from Gabe and his hot-air balloon; and the rest of my life to deal with her if Operation: Date Sabotage didn't work.

"So your mom didn't mind?" Zander looked straight ahead, at the stage.

"What, about tonight? She's working, like always. Ella's with a babysitter, and I'll be back before she gets home."

I peered around the café. Groups of people had staked claim to tiny black café tables meant for two. Coffee mugs and plates with half-eaten pastries on them littered the tabletops. I wondered if anyone else in the crowd was on a date-or-maybe-just-friends-hanging-out kind of thing. And if anyone else felt as nervous and sweaty as I did.

"Looks like your guy is pretty popular." I took another sip, telling myself to relax. This was no big deal; not even a date. It was just Zander! Dyer of bangs. Wearer of skinny jeans and ripped T-shirts. Just Zander, who I hung out with all the time. "What's his deal?"

"Burton Wells. He just graduated from U-Dub. Used to play a lot of local shows around Seattle. He's a classically trained violinist, but he mixes classical music with hip-hop."

"Cool." I nodded.

"For sure." Zander's face lit up, and he turned toward me. "It's totally unique. He's got this one beat—" Zander rested his coffee mug on the windowsill and started rapping a fast beat on his thigh. "And then the violin comes in with that Mozart requiem—you know the one?"

"Um, obviously not, you loser." I giggled and set my mug next to his.

"Yeah, you do!" His hands were flying now. "Come on, Simon. Weren't you paying attention in music class? This is kid stuff! Think!" He hummed the first few bars.

"Some of us aren't music geeks!" I pointed out.

"*Duun dun dun duuuun dun,*" he hummed, his eyes

flashing with laughter. "It's in that commercial where the baby's driving the SUV!"

"Oh! Wait! The SUV baby! I know this! Ummm—"

"You got this!" He sped up the beat. "Time's running out!"

"REQUIEM IN B MINOR!" I slapped him on the shoulder.

"D minor! But good enough!" He leaned into me. His lips might have been almost touching my hair. My heart might not have been beating.

"D minor. Right. D minor." I focused on the stage and hummed the next few bars. When I sneaked a glance at Zander, he caught me. Or I caught him. Either way, one of us was staring.

I squeezed back.

Zander coughed. "So, you know how Levi Stone's playing the Goodman next week? I thought maybe Gravity could go, as like a band-bonding kind of thing."

I must have had a funny look on my face, because Zander's eyes got wide. "Or, I mean, we could just go. You and me. If you wanted. Actually, I read on this music blog that he's playing a couple of different shows around town. Supposed to get to Chicago tonight, actually. So we could go see him, like, over the weekend, and then maybe Gravity could—"

"Yeah. That sounds good. You and me. Or the whole band, if you want. Either one," I chattered. *Stop. Talking.*

"Sweet." Zander looked past my left ear and grinned.

The lights dimmed, plunging the crowd into darkness. Despite the cheers and the clinking of coffee cups, it felt like Zander and I were the only two people in the world. In the universe. I wished we could stay like that forever, our fingers so close I could almost feel his pulse.

But the lights came up just a few beats later, revealing a lanky black man with dreadlocks, holding a violin. He was wearing a light-pink collared shirt with the sleeves rolled up to his elbows, black jeans, and neon-green kicks.

"What's uuuuup, Chicaaaaaagooooooo?"

The crowd cheered, and the dude onstage lifted his violin in one hand and his bow in the other, his arms stretched out like wings.

"I'm Burton Wells, and it is an honor"—Wells lifted his instrument to his shoulder—"and a privilege to share this time, this space, and this music with you all."

"You rock, man!" shouted a girl hanging by the bar.

Wells set his bow against the violin's strings. "We're all in this together, Chicago. Let's make some magic!"

Cheers rose again as an old-school Busta Rhymes beat pumped over the speakers. The beat ran from the floor through the soles of my feet and into my body. I looked over at Zander; his eyes were closed, a smile on his lips. I closed my eyes, too, as Wells lit into a fast classical piece I didn't recognize. The sweet, high violin notes were in perfect balance with the heavy thump of the beat.

We stayed like that for song after song, our eyes closed and our fingers grazing each other's every few seconds. As the show went on, Wells's energy level rose, and I cheated and opened my eyes once to refresh my image of him. Sweat glistened on his forehead and soaked through his shirt. He kept his eyes screwed shut as he played, and his entire body seemed to move with every stroke of his bow. He was totally at peace, 100 percent absorbed in the music.

It had been too long since I'd felt that way about Gravity, or felt that way about music. Lately, I'd been so worried about Stevie and Zander and my mom and Gabe that I hadn't focused on music at all. I hadn't focused on how amazing it felt when I belted out a high note, or how exhausted and happy I was at the end of an awesome rehearsal.

"Wooooohoooooo!" The audience hooted as Wells killed the last note in a song. Chest heaving, he bowed at the waist once, then twice. Then he nodded at someone offstage, who dragged a stool and a bottle of water to the center of the spotlight.

"Thank you." Wells rested his violin carefully in its case, then unscrewed the lid of the bottle of water and chugged the whole thing in a single gulp. "Thank you." He wiped his brow with his forearm and adjusted the tiny mic on his shirt collar.

"I want to take a second to bring a fan up here on the stage."

"Ahhhhhhhhhh!" Everyone in the café shrieked with excitement.

"Hold up, people." Wells laughed and raised his palm. "I've already got somebody special in mind. This is a fan who wrote me a letter a while back. She's a student here in Chicago—Marisa Gonzales, are you and your mom in the audience tonight?"

I heard a tiny shriek and popped up on tiptoe.

"Can you see anything?" Zander tossed his bangs out of his eyes.

A few seconds later, a little girl who couldn't have been any older than eight climbed onto the stage with her mother. The girl turned to the audience and flashed a gap-toothed grin.

"Marisa Gonzales, everybody!" While the crowd cheered, Wells bent down and gave the girl a hug, then shook her mother's hand.

"Marisa wrote me a letter not too long ago to tell

me that she'd applied for a national music scholarship we set up through the Burton Wells Foundation. She said she wanted—actually, I'll let her tell you." Wells unhooked the mic from his shirt and held it out to the little girl.

"To take violin lessons and learn how to play like you. I'm your biggest fan," the girl said into the mic.

"Awwww," cooed the crowd.

"That's awesome." Wells bobbed his head like he could hear a beat no one else could hear. "And do you know what's even more awesome? We're picking a scholarship winner from every city on my tour this month. And you're the winner for Chicago! So now you'll get those violin lessons for free, for as long as you want to play."

Everybody clapped. Marisa Gonzales's jaw hit the floor. Marisa Gonzales's mother screamed.

"No fair!" I hissed to Zander. "She's, like, in elementary! There's no way she appreciates this."

"How did I not know about this scholarship thing?" Zander pouted. "I so want to learn violin right now."

"We're gonna take a little break, but I'll be back in a few." Burton crouched next to Marisa. "Will you stick around? I think we've got some folks from Channel Two who might want to interview you."

"Oh, come on," I said, a little too loudly. "I know she

can't appreciate that kind of exposure."

A purple-haired chick with a lip ring standing in front of me turned around and glared.

"Not that this isn't newsworthy," I backtracked.

My cell buzzed and I pulled it from my clutch. There were seven new texts.

STEVIE: GOT A PLAN? WE'RE RUNNING OUT OF TIME.

STEVIE: DO U KNOW WHERE Z IS?

STEVIE: SERIOUSLY, SHEDD LADY. PLAN.

STEVIE: IF THEY GET MARRIED, YOU'RE SLEEPING ON THE COUCH.

STEVIE: AND I'M GETTING THE BIG CLOSET.

STEVIE: OK. I WAS SEMI-KIDDING. BUT SERIOUSLY. DO U KNOW SOMETHING I DON'T????

STEVIE: I'LL RUN AWAY BEFORE I SHARE A ROOM WITH YOU. WE HAVE. TO BREAK. THEM UP.

"That's not your mom up there, is it?" Zander shaded his eyes with his palm as the crowd herded toward the coffee bar.

I shook my head. "No, that's the lady from Channel Two. They're Channel Five's biggest compe—" I froze. "Ohmygod."

"What? Are you okay?"

Slowly, I nodded. "Yeah." I was okay. I was better than okay. Maybe it was the music. Maybe it was my chemistry with Zander. Maybe it was Burton Wells's good vibes. But suddenly, I had the perfect plan.

WHEN LIFE IMITATES ART
Thursday, 9:20 P.M.

When I got home from the concert, the townhouse was dark. The red answering machine light was blinking on the console table by the door. I stood there for a few seconds in my coat, grinning into the darkness like a complete moron. The music, the one-on-one time with Zander—everything had been perfect. Out of habit, I reached for my cell to call Molly, then stopped myself. What was I supposed to say? I just went on a non-date-but-who-are-we-kidding-it-was-totally-a-date with your ex? Screw Girl Code, I think he's amazing?

I ditched my coat and shopping bags in the entrance hall and punched the button on the answering machine before heading up the stairs. I'd texted Stevie to meet me here, but I probably had a few minutes before she arrived.

"Hey, Kace, it's Mom. It's a little after nine, and I'm leaving the studio. I'm guessing you figured something out for dinner—I meant to leave money for pizza. Sorry. Picking Ella up on my way home. We'll be there soon. Love you."

Good, I thought as I whirled around the banister and took the second flight of stairs to my room. Mom wouldn't be home until at least 9:45. That gave me plenty of time to explain the plan to Stevie and—

"Ahhhhhh!" I screamed when I opened my door and flicked the light switch.

Stevie was bent over my desk, sifting through my record collection.

"OH. MY. GODDDDD. How did you get in here, you psycho?" I snatched the Who album she was holding and wiped the cover with the hem of my shirt. My heart was thundering in my chest. "Seriously. How did you get in here?"

With a flourish, Stevie produced a glinting silver key. "You Midwesterners are so predictable. Who actually leaves their spare key under the flowerpot?"

"You just broke into my house," I said, disbelieving. "You actually broke into my house."

She shrugged. "By the way, I only have twenty minutes. And I had to tell my dad I was emergency tutoring you as part of my community service." She kicked off her moto boots and nudged them under my desk. "So if he asks you how Slow Math is going . . . just play along."

I gritted my teeth so hard my braces started to throb. "Do you want to hear the plan, or what?" I reached over her and plucked the photo strip of Paige in her green seaweed mask from the bulletin board wall behind my desk.

Stevie eyed the photos. "Let's hear it."

"Okay. If we can pull this off, Mom will definitely have to miss the date with your dad." I stuffed the photo strip in my back pocket. "Follow me. My mom will be home in a few."

We hurried down the steps to the second floor. "Her office is back here." I opened the door next to the master bedroom and flipped the light switch.

"Huh. Not bad." Stevie clucked her approval.

"I know." Ella and I were under strict instructions not to mess around in Mom's office, so it had been a while since I'd been inside. The room was small but inviting, with textured grass-cloth walls and a rich Persian rug she'd inherited from her mother. Leather-bound books, broadcasting awards, and framed photographs lined the built-in bookcases behind her desk. The floor-to-ceiling windows on the right wall looked over the soft glow of Clark Street and, beyond that, Lincoln Park.

"Here. Check Levi Stone's website on your cell." I plopped down in the leather rolling desk chair and jiggled the mouse. "He probably has a contact e-mail on there."

"Levi Stone?" Stevie's eyebrows shot up.

I sighed. "Just do it."

"Fine. On it." Stevie hopped onto the desk, knocking over a picture of Ella and me in the tub when we were little. She didn't bother to pick it up, instead tapping away on her phone. Sighing, I straightened it myself.

"I'll take care of the actual e-mail." I found Mom's Channel 5 e-mail icon on the desktop and double-clicked.

Password?

I typed in my birthday and hit ENTER.

Invalid password.

Password?

Next, I typed in Ella's birthday.

Invalid password.

Our birthdays together. Mine first, then hers. Hers first, then mine.

Invalid password. Invalid password.

"Moooooom." I groaned. I checked the clock over the door. They could be home any second. "Come onnnnn."

"Password protected?" Stevie guessed. "My dad does the same thing with his. It's like they don't trust us or something."

"Right?" As a last resort, I tried *Murrow*. She was always quoting Edward R. Murrow, basically the most famous newscaster ever. I hit enter.

Welcome, Sterling Simon!

"Yessss." I opened a new e-mail. "Okay. Address?"

"LeviStoneRocks-at-gmail-dot-com." Stevie's heels banged against the desk. "What exactly are you doing—"

"I got it, I got it. Just give me a second." My fingers flew over the keyboard, fueled by genius and desperation. This had to work. I couldn't live in the rain forest with Stevie and Gabe. My hair could not handle that kind of humidity. "Aaaaaand, done," I announced a minute later. "Here. Check it out." I swiveled the desktop screen in her direction.

From: "Sterling Simon" <Sterling@Channel5.net>

To: "Levi Stone" <LeviStoneRocks@gmail.com>

Re: DYING CHICAGO GIRL REQUESTS LEVI STONE CONCERT BEFORE SHE CROAKS

Dear Levi,

My name is Sterling Simon. You've probably heard of me, but if not, I'm the solo evening anchor with Chicago's Channel 5 news. And believe me, your series of concerts in Chicago this week is major news here in Chi-town.

I'm writing with a favor-slash-photo-op. Here in Chicago, at our own Marquette Middle School, we're proud to boast your biggest fan, seventh-grade school president Paige Greene. Tragically, Paige is dying of infection from a terrible, rare, green flesh-eating bacterium called Verticopolus. (Don't bother looking it up on Wikipedia. It's a very technical medical term.)

It is brave Paige Greene's dying wish for you to play a concert at her next (and probably last) school dance tomorrow night. It would mean so much to her. If you're willing, Channel 5 would like to do a human interest segment on you tomorrow night on the news. Please contact me immediately to discuss this potentially huge publicity opportunity.

See you tomorrow, hopefully,
Sterling Simon

P.S. Please come.

P.P.S. If you do come, don't mention this e-mail to Paige. She's very self-conscious about her cracking green skin, poor thing.

A light went on behind Stevie's eyes as she read. When she finished, I explained every minute detail, from the spark of an idea I'd gotten at the Burton Wells concert to the bitter taste of the coffee Zander had bought me. On our (non)DATE.

"So?" I felt jittery and alive, like I'd just tossed back another giant mug of coffee. "What do you think?"

"About the plan, or about your pathetic attempt to make me jealous that you were out with Zander tonight?" Her eyes were narrow with disdain.

I met her stare with silence. It was this trick I learned from Nessa and used on my toughest interview subjects. For some reason, silence makes people uncomfortable, so all you have to do to get someone to agree with you is wait them out. Eventually, they won't be able to stand the awkwardness anymore, and they end up blurting out anything just to—

"About the PLAN, duh!" I shrieked.

Occasionally the method backfired.

Stevie took a maddeningly slow breath and leaned against the wall next to my computer desk, running her tongue over her irritatingly white teeth. "I think it doesn't suck. It might bomb, but it's the best we've got this late in the game, right?"

"It *won't* bomb." Not exactly the enthusiastic response I'd been hoping for. "And when he agrees, I'll call in an anonymous tip to the station and say he specifically requested Mom, so she'll have to cancel the date and do the interview. That's the upside to having a mom who's a workaholic."

"Okaaaay." Stevie twirled her silky black hair around a lavender-painted nail. "Oh. Don't forget to put your cell number."

"Right." I bent over the keyboard and typed: *P.P.P.S. It's easier to reach me on my cell.* Then I put my own number at the end of the letter.

"Wait." Stevie suddenly sounded worried. "So if this works, does that mean Gravity won't be playing the dance?"

"Oh." I stared at the screen until the type in the e-mail blurred together. I'd been so blinded by my need to break up Mom and Gabe, I'd completely forgotten about Gravity. About our big break tomorrow night. "We'll probably still play, right? I mean, he's a busy guy. He'll probably just come in, play a couple of songs for Paige, do the interview, and sketch out."

"Right. Yeah. I'm sure you're right." Her brows unknit.

"Okay. Now for the visual aid." I hopped up and pulled the photo strip from my back pocket. Four Paiges stared back at me in a cracked, bubbling, puke-green seaweed mask. Each picture was worse than the last.

"I don't even wanna know why you have these."

Stevie's hair brushed my shoulder as she hovered over the photo strip. "I want to look away, but I just can't."

"Right?" I cut out the picture where Paige's mouth was twisted down and she sort of looked like she was dying. I think that was right after she'd threatened to kill me. Then I laid the photo facedown on the scanner and punched the START button. I attached the file to the message, my index finger hovering anxiously over the mouse. "Are we really doing this?" I asked Stevie. Suddenly, my stomach was a rubber-band ball of nerves.

She lunged across the desk and clamped her hand over mine. Then she smashed my finger into the left mouse button.

Message sent successfully!

"Guess so," she said.

FATE IS A FOUR-LETTER WORD
Friday, 2:35 P.M.

"Is anybody, uh . . ." Zander nodded at the last seat in the second row of the auditorium, where Molly, Nessa, Liv, and I were waiting for the final bell to ring and assembly to start, along with the rest of the seventh grade. Onstage, Paige and Quinn sat behind the podium, where Sean, our American Government teacher, was making notes in his planner.

"Oh! Hey. Do you want to sit?" Hands shaking, I scooped up the heap of purses and bags we'd piled into the chair and deposited them on the floor, burying my gray round-toe boots in colorful leather rubble.

"Hey! That's a new bag!" Molly glared at Zander before tugging a shiny yellow patent tote from the pile and cradling it in her lap.

"Sorry, Mols." I exchanged a glance with Zander as he plopped into the seat next to me. After a few beats, the glance turned into a gaze. Neither of us looked away until my fingers and toes started to go numb and I was forced to break the stare for health reasons.

"So I, uh . . ." Zander eyed Molly warily, then stared into his lap. "I went to this concert last night." A hint of a smile lit his lips.

"Oh yeah?" I stared straight ahead at Sean, sitting on my hands to keep them still. I couldn't risk looking at Zander again. Nessa was only two seats away, and it was a miracle she hadn't picked up on my crush vibes already.

"Yeah. It was kind of . . . amazing. You know?"

I know. The air in the auditorium was hot and stale, but I shivered.

"Please. How would she know?" Molly scoffed. She flicked her hair over her shoulder, and her ends stung my cheek. "It's not like she was there."

My toes curled in my boots. "It's just a saying, Mols."

"You ready for the dance tonight?" I might have been imagining it, but Zander seemed to scoot a little closer. "Only one more rehearsal till showtime."

"Right. Showtime. Yeah." I braided the end of my low side ponytail, then shook it out and started over. I'd checked my cell every three minutes, on the minute, since last night. Nothing. If Levi was going to be a no-show, there wasn't any reason to come clean to Zander about the e-mail, was there?

"What's up? You're not excited?" Zander knit his brows.

"No. Totally. I am. Just nervous about Paige, I guess."

Molly snorted. "You should be. This is going to be a disaster."

"Mols, you don't have to look so happy about it." Liv rolled her eyes toward the olive jeweled headband taming her shiny curls. "This could be really humiliating."

"Traumatic, even." Nessa grabbed a few sunflower seeds from a small plastic baggie in her lap, then tilted the bag toward us. I shook my head.

"I know!" Molly said gleefully. "Seriously traumatic."

Zander glared at Molly. "You can't just—"

"Hey. Goose. Move. I need to talk to Kacey." Stevie appeared in the aisle, hands planted firmly on the waistband of her navy velvet bell-bottoms. "Now."

"Uh—" Zander looked at me, confused. "Talk to Kacey? Seriously?"

I bit my lower lip and nodded. "Sorry. It'll only take a sec." I let my knee knock against Zander's in a last-ditch attempt at contact.

"Um, okay." Zander looked back and forth between

Stevie and me a few times, then slid off his seat. The seat bottom banged against the seatback as he stomped up the aisle.

Stevie slid in next to me. "So? Any word?" she said under her breath, without looking at me.

"I know you didn't steal Zander's seat just to ask me that," I whispered back. "And no."

"Test." Sean took a step back from the mic, then thumped it with his index finger. "Test. Test."

"We hear you, dude!" somebody yelled from the back row.

"Nothing?" Stevie hissed. "Not a call or anything?"

"Don't you think I've been checking? Maybe we just have to accept that he's not going to respond." My throat closed up. How could this be happening? The plan was so perfect.

"No. I refuse." Stevie death-gripped the armrests. "He'll write back. I know it."

"Look. I hate our parents together as much as you do. But—"

Sean cleared his throat again, looking directly at me. "As you all know, we're here to give the floor to our candidates for eighth-grade class president, Ms. Paige Greene and Mr. Quinn Wilder."

"Woooo-hoooo!" The auditorium burst into applause.

In the front row, Jake Fields and Aaron Peterman jumped to their feet, doing what looked like some kind of end-zone victory dance. Onstage, Paige bowed her head, and Quinn mimed a roof-raising. Gross.

"Okay, quiet down." Sean checked his watch. "I don't have to remind you that voting in an election, even a school election, is a privilege. And I hope you'll give both your candidates the attention and careful consideration they—"

"Speech!" Aaron shouted through cupped hands. "Speech. Speech. Speech."

Soon the whole seventh grade, minus Stevie, me, and the girls, was chanting along with him.

"Hey!" Sean tapped the microphone again. "Seriously, guys. If you can't keep it together, we'll film the speeches and air them in homeroom on Monday. You can use the rest of the day for silent study hall."

That shut everyone up.

"Better. Just a reminder: I'll ask you to hold your applause until both candidates have finished their speeches. First up, we have Ms. Paige Greene."

The auditorium was dead silent.

"You can clap for the candidates." Sean sighed into the mic. "Just hold your applause until after they speak."

Paige clutched several pages of notebook paper to her

chest and strode to the mic to the tune of stilted applause. Her chin was up and her gait confident. Considering the disastrous circumstances, she looked pretty good. She'd swept her bob back in a mini ponytail and trimmed her bangs. Evenly, for once. Her usual square black frames had been replaced with a retro pair of cat-eye glasses, and the leather-piped blazer we'd picked out looked commanding but cool. Around her waist was a surprisingly stylish skinny green belt.

"Goo—good afternoon, Marquette." The rattle of Paige's notebook paper revealed her nerves. My stomach dipped, and I straightened up in my seat. "And thanks— thank you all—for your time."

"I can't believe he hasn't called," Stevie muttered under her breath. "I'm never downloading him again. Even for free."

"Good. Because that's illegal. Kind of like breaking and entering. Now shut up so I can hear." I angled my body away from Stevie. It was stupid, but watching Paige up there all alone, just a weekend away from losing everything to Quinn Wilder, suddenly made me want to bawl. She'd worked so hard and wanted this more than anything. She deserved this. And just when things were starting to look good, somebody swooped in and ruined everything. She was powerless to change it.

It was just fate. Cruel, backstabbing, nothing-she-could-do-about-it fate with a capital *F*.

"What is a leader? Well, the dictionary defines the word *leader* as, quote, *a person who has influence or authority*."

Oh, no. The dictionary opener? What happened to her old speech, the one we'd practiced so many times? Anyone who had ever spoken in front of ANYONE ELSE, EVER, knew the dictionary opener was the hallmark of a terrible speech. And from the sounds of backpacks being unzipped and the number of cell phones popping up around me, the seventh grade had officially lost interest.

"I'm Paige Greene, and I'm asking you for the chance to continue as—to still be your—" Paige faltered. The bright auditorium lights spotlighted the sheen of sweat on her skin. Right now, she looked dewy and youthful. But in five minutes, she'd be drenched and defeated. "To be your eighth-grade president leader."

President leader? This was too painful to watch. I closed my eyes and imagined myself rushing the stage, steamrolling Paige out of her misery.

"I'd like to highlight my record during my time as seventh-grade president."

"NO THANKS!" somebody yelled.

"Hey!" I shouted over the giggles, whipping around to glare at the crowd.

"Um—" Paige's voice cracked as she stared down at the podium, shuffling her papers. One floated out from the pack, and she scampered to save it, sending the other papers flying. Diving to her hands and knees, she clawed the first page from the edge of the stage.

Come on, Paige, I willed her. *You can do this.*

She stood up and brushed herself off, the light reflecting off her lenses. Her jaw tightened, then she crumpled the piece of paper into a ball and chucked it into the audience.

"Okay, people. I know you don't want to be here. But this is America. And democracy. So listen up." Even without the microphone, her voice was clear and loud. The giggles and whispers and texting sounds stopped. Stevie and the girls leaned forward a little.

"Look." Paige planted her hands on her hips and started pacing the length of the stage. "Here's a little something you might not know about me. I love politics. Like, am completely obsessed with it. I could recite all the presidents in reverse order by the time I was six. I know the preamble of the Constitution by heart. And yes. Sometimes I watch C-SPAN for fun."

I knew it. KNEW IT.

"And none of those things make me the most popular kid here, which is fine. They don't make me the best soccer player, or the prettiest girl. But they make me a really good class president. And I think I've proven that to you guys over the past year. Quinn Wilder's a great guy, but he's never even been to a student council meeting." She turned to face Wilder. "No offense."

Quinn hair-tossed his forgiveness.

I gripped the edge of my seat, reminding myself to breathe.

"It's simple," Paige continued. "If you think I've done a good job and want someone in office who really wants to be there, you should vote for me. If you're ready for a change, then okay. Maybe I'll have to get good at soccer or something."

Everybody laughed. Even Quinn cracked a small smile.

"So vote for me, Paige Greene. That's all."

"WOOOO-HOOOO!" I shrieked, leaping to my feet. The rest of the grade followed my lead and burst into riotous cheers. Confetti poured from the ceiling, and Quinn Wilder yelled, "I QUIT!" and carried Paige off the stage on his shoulders. Oh, and Oprah showed up and gave everybody in the audience a free car and some solid life advice.

Okay. So maybe that was all in my head. In reality, I whistled, and a few people clapped politely, and Paige took an awkward half-curtsy that made it look like she was about to wet her pants.

When she sat down, Quinn walked to the podium. And *that* was when everybody jumped to their feet and started screaming.

"WHAT'S UP, MARQUETTE MIDDLE?" Quinn hair-tossed and double fist-pumped, which was apparently the secret code for Queen's "We Are the Champions" to start blaring from the speakers. Paige sat stiffly in her seat, her ankles crossed and her eyes wide, looking as traumatized as a band geek held hostage at a frat party.

One more hair toss, and the music dipped to a normal volume. "Thanks, guys. Have a seat. I'm gonna keep it short and sweet, 'cause it's Friday, and I know the ladies wanna get home and start getting ready for the dance tonight, am I right?"

The *ladies?* I tasted lunch.

Molly leaned forward in her seat as Quinn slid the mic out of its holster on the podium and started slinking around the stage like a bad Vegas lounge singer. I had to admit, though, he did look pretty cute. His sandy blond hair appeared extra silky under the lights, and his dark-wash jeans and silvery-blue henley were wrinkled enough to give off a casual vibe without being sloppy. Well played, Wilder. Well. Played.

"I just have a few questions for you guys, and I want you to answer loud and clear, so I can hear you. Are you sick of having homework over winter break?"

"YEAH!" everybody yelled. Paige's already thin lips did a vanishing act.

"Do you think standardized tests blow?"

"YEAH!"

I looked over at Molly to exchange eye rolls. But her face had turned a purplish-red color.

"Ohmygod. He's amazing!" she breathed.

I blinked. Was my class actually falling for this? Was *Molly* actually falling for this?

"One last question, Marquette." Quinn's blindingly white smile gleamed in the spotlight. "Do you think seventh grade's been cool, but want eighth to be WILDER?"

"WILD-ER! WILD-ER! WILD-ER!" The thundering chants and stomping sent vibrations buzzing through the seats. For a second, I flashed back to Molly's birthday party last month. My classmates (the cool ones, anyway) had been chanting like this just before I wiped out in the middle of the skating rink. My back molars pinged at the memory.

"Then vote for me, and eighth grade will rock!" The Queen song swelled again, and Quinn ditched his mic and jogged down the steps to the audience, fist-bumping his way up the aisle.

"Can you believe him?" Molly gushed. "He's gonna be, like, the most amazing prez ever."

"The energy in here *is* kind of amazing," Liv admitted.

"He can't deliver on that stuff," Nessa said skeptically.

At least one of my friends was impervious to Quinn's empty promises.

I didn't make eye contact as Quinn passed our row. Instead, I watched Paige sit alone on stage. She held her head high, but inside she was probably crumbling. If she hadn't known it a few minutes ago, she knew it now: The election was over.

HARMONY
Friday, 3:25 P.M.

"Everything okay?" Zander asked as Stevie and I came through the loft door, dragging our heels. Between Paige's bombed speech and Levi's radio silence, this was turning into the worst day ever.

The guys were already in the breakfast nook, tuning their instruments. The Beat's camcorder sat on a tripod in the kitchen, its red light flashing.

"Yup!" I said, forcing a cheery tone into my voice as I whipped off my jacket and flung it rodeo-style onto the pool table. "Annnnyway. Who's up for a little rehearsal time?" I took my place next to Zander, and Stevie leaned against the island in the kitchen. The only way to salvage the afternoon was through a little music therapy. I wanted to lose myself in the notes like Wells had last night at the café.

Zander handed me a few pieces of sheet music. "We probably shouldn't try new stuff before tonight, but I've been kicking around a new melody and I want to give it a shot. If it goes okay, maybe we can put the recording on the website. You in?"

"Do you even have to ask?" I cupped the mic in my right hand. It fit perfectly. I smiled directly into the camera lens. It might not have been a Channel M camera, but it felt good to be back in the limelight anyway. "Let's do it."

"I want to warm you up a little first, Kace. We'll start here." Without even looking at the keyboard, Nelson played a perfect chord progression. "Can I get a *zing-ah*?"

"*Zing-ahhhhhhh.*" My voice filled the loft, from the concrete floors to the high ceilings. It was powerful, strong. It was me. "*Zing-AHHHHHHHHHH.*" Stevie looked away, pretending to be mesmerized by a photograph on the refrigerator.

"Whoa." Zander bowed his head when I was finished. "You sound amazing."

"Yeah, you do," The Beat said.

I smiled. "Not that I'd mind you guys complimenting me all night, but can we get to the music?"

"Nice, Mainstream." Kevin looked at me out of the corner of his eye. "So you're really sticking around, huh?"

I lowered my mouth to the mic. "Try and stop me."

"No way. You're on a roll." Zander's tiny head-bob in my direction asked, *You ready?*

I head-bobbed back, *Let's go.*

"And five, six, seven, eight!" The Beat rocked a slow rhythm, easing me into the song.

"Here you go," Zander said. "This is you, riiiight—"

"*Outside the world is gray and I listen.*" My voice was soft and soulful, almost a raspy whisper. "*As the minutes tick away, I'm just wishing. For the one who makes me feel like it's all gonna be okay.*"

Zander was watching me as he played. I closed my eyes. "*I don't know how she does it, it's the way she says my name. The way she sees into my soul, and how she takes away my pain. And she tells me, sweet she whispers, that it's all gonna be . . . okay.*"

I felt a longing at my core as the final notes of the song evaporated, wishing I knew everything in my own life would be okay.

"Holy—" Kevin shook his head, breaking the silence in the loft. "That was—"

"I know. I know." I tightened my grip on the mic. "Should we try it tonight?"

"For sure," Zander said. The rest of the guys murmured their agreement.

"Aaaand . . ." I zeroed in on Stevie. She nibbled her thumbnail, her brow scrunched together like she was trying to drum up the best insult possible. But then her face relaxed, and she offered the slightest hint of a smile.

"It was good. But I think I know how to make it better."

I rolled my eyes to the ceiling and sighed directly into the mic. "Of *course* you do. Enlighten us." I should have known better than to ask her opinion.

"Stevie. Come on." Zander cracked his neck. "You have to admit, it was—"

"Just hear me out. I think it feels more like a duet."

"And I'm sure you want to give it a shot?" I snapped.

She waltzed past my mic without acknowledging me. "Goose. You could do a pretty easy harmony, right? Just a few steps up, like this?" She hummed the first few bars. "Just keep it soft, so you don't overpower her. She sounds good." She signaled The Beat. "And five, six, seven, eight."

Wait. What? Zander and I stared at each other in disbelief as Stevie sashayed back to the kitchen without commandeering my mic.

"You're about to miss your cue," she called over her shoulder.

"Yeah. Okay." Zander abandoned his mic and joined me at mine. Our lips were millimeters apart. With every new measure, every note, we stayed in perfect harmony. Stevie was right—this song was a duet, and Zander and I were the perfect people to sing it. Together.

"I can feel it, dudes. Tonight is gonna be huge for us." The Beat picked up his camera after our final note faded. "Say something. I want this moment on film."

"Five bucks says this guy drops his camera before the end of the rehearsal." Kevin smirked at the lens. "No. Ten."

"I'll get in on that action," Nelson piped up.

"Say something about the *show tonight*, morons," The Beat said, swinging around wildly and nearly falling backward. Zander had to grab his arm to keep him from eating concrete.

"*So* close." Nelson laughed.

"I'll say something." Zander picked up his guitar. "*Thanks to Kacey for booking this gig,*" he sang to the camera. "*After tonight, we might make it big. Our fans'll demand that we write more jingles. They'll even ask us to record a single.*"

"Nerd alert." Stevie stuffed her hands in her pockets.

"I love it," I said, beaming at Zander over Stevie's head.

"Actually, we should start talking about putting together an album," Kevin agreed. "If we get good footage of the show tonight, maybe we could use it to get some paying gigs. Earn enough money to get a couple of hours in a recording studio."

"Totally," I said. Over on the pool table, my phone beeped in my coat pocket. I pulled it out and stopped in my tracks. There was one new voice mail from an unknown number.

I grabbed Stevie's wrist. "Can you join me outside for a second?" I muttered urgently through a Simon Smile.

Stevie slapped my hand away. "What are you doing?"

"Chick fight!" Nelson crowed.

The Beat swung his camera in her direction. "Nice. Does anybody know if this thing has a slo-mo setting?"

"Dibs on a copy," Kevin said quickly.

I crossed my arms over my chest. "You're all disgusting."

"What's going on?" Zander asked.

"Nothing. Stevie dropped a mitten outside. We need to go get it." I grabbed her hand, my heart racing with adrenaline.

The rest of the band stopped and looked at Stevie's hands. Stevie's fingerless-glove-covered hands.

"Fine. I have to talk to her." I sighed. "In private. About . . . girl problems."

"Ohhh!" Kevin and Nelson jumped back.

The Beat turned off the camera. "I'm out."

"We'll, uh, we'll be here. Whenever you're done." Even Zander looked freaked out. "Take your time."

"We'll just be a second," I yelled at the guys' backs, then dragged Stevie outside. It couldn't have been over forty degrees, but I barely felt the cold as I showed her the screen of my phone.

"Ohmygod." Stevie clutched my arm. It was the first time I'd seen her lose her cool.

"Calm down. It's probably just Mom, asking me to stop by the dry cleaner on my way home." Still, my fingers were clumsy on the keypad as I typed in my voice mail PIN.

But when I heard the voice, I nearly dropped my phone.

"Ms. Simon? My name is Mick Williams, and I'm Levi Stone's manager. Apologies for the last-minute call, but Mr. Stone wanted me to contact you regarding your message . . ."

I finished listening to the message, then blinked victoriously at Stevie.

"So . . . we did it."

"Huh?"

"We *did* it!" I grabbed her by the shoulders. "As in, Levi Stone is coming to Marquette Middle School *tonight* to dedicate a song to his number one fan. And in a few hours, Channel Five will get a call from yours truly saying

Levi specifically requested that Sterling Simon interview him at the school."

There was a silent beat. Then Stevie screamed and shoved me into the chain-link fence that bordered the sidewalk. "No. You're lying."

Gleefully, I shook my head. "Nope. He's gonna come in and dedicate a song to Paige. After he plays, Levi will give an exclusive interview to Mom. And do you know where she can't be when she's in the courtyard at Marquette?"

"On a hot-air balloon with my dad?" Her smile was all teeth.

"Bingo."

"Nice work, Simon." She held up her palm.

I slapped it. "You too."

We hurried back into the loft, a huge smile on my face. In just a few hours, Mom would get a huge opportunity, Marquette would get to see Levi Stone, and I would get my family back. Just Mom, Ella, and me. The way we were supposed to be.

A LITTLE GLOSS AND
A MAJOR POP STAR SHOULD DO IT
Friday, 5:47 P.M.

"Would you hold still? You're gonna look like a linebacker if I don't get this liquid eyeliner right." Liv sat back on her heels and inspected my makeup. Palettes of organic shadows, blushes, and glosses littered the floor at the foot of my bed. Liv's hand and the hem of her ratty I THINK, THEREFORE I AM VEGETARIAN T-shirt were smudged with shimmery swatches.

"Scalp burns aren't too hot, either. Just sit tight a second," Nessa said. Crouched behind me in a lavender lace miniskirt and long-sleeved black blouse, she wound a thick handful of my hair around a jumbo hot roller. Then she plucked a hairpin from the hem of her skirt and secured the last of my locks.

"I know, I know. I'm just excited." *And counting the*

minutes until I can call Channel 5, request Sterling Simon's presence at Marquette Middle School, and threaten to call Channel 2 if anyone else shows up in her place.

I glanced out my tiny bedroom window. Paige's townhouse was dark. She'd refused to get ready at my place as long as Molly and the girls were there, but had pinky-sworn to make an appearance at the dance, despite the fact that the rally had rendered her life "hollow and meaningless."

"What about this one?" Molly popped out of my closet in a body-hugging gray silk number with an asymmetrical hem. I'd bought it for the Channel 5 holiday party last year, but then Ella chugged half a carton of eggnog before we left and the dress never made it out of the house.

"It's yours, Madame Chairperson. Just make sure to cut the tags off."

Molly smooched the air and disappeared again.

"Are we done here, fabulous hair-and-makeup team?" I hopped up and tightened the sash on my silky bathrobe.

"Yup," Nessa and Liv chimed.

"Awesome. Thanks." On my bedside table, a Lady Gaga dance mix pumped from my iPod dock. The second I reached for the volume button, Molly reappeared in a pair of gladiator-style booties.

"Don't touch the Gaga," she warned, waving a satin

jewel-toned clutch menacingly. "*Never* touch the Gaga."

"Easy, little monster." I backed off, even though I was dying to hit PAUSE and spill my big secret about Levi Stone. But an announcement like this deserved the ultimate in perfect timing. And with Liv chasing me around with a lip brush all night and Nessa flossing for the fourteenth time, I hadn't found the right moment yet.

A knock sounded at my bedroom door, and the handle squeaked.

"Moooom!" I knew it was her because she'd always done that: knocked and then waltzed right in. I'd explained over and over that this was as pointless as Ella yelling "EXCUSE ME!" before she bulldozed her way into a conversation.

"Don't mind me; I just wanted to see you girls all dressed up." Mom leaned against the doorjamb, wearing an ivory V-neck sweater, dark-wash skinny jeans, and espresso equestrian boots. Ella wriggled past her in purple flippers and a sundress with—

Stop. Rewind. Play.

My mother. Was wearing. Skinny jeans.

"Ow ow!" Molly turned from the full-length mirror behind my closet door and gave her butt a little shake. "You look hot, Mrs. Simon! Hey, Ellie Bellie."

"Ow ow!" Ella wriggled her butt, too. "Hey."

"You think they look okay?" Mom tried to hide her smile. And failed. "You don't think they make me look too—"

"Young?" I offered. "Like you're trying too hard?"

"Lemme see!" Liv leapt out of my closet in a burnt-orange backless halter dress. The silk grazed my arm as she rushed to hug Mom. "No way. I think you look amazing."

"Agreed." Nessa paused in her meticulous pomade-to-pixie application long enough to admire my mother. "Total ten. Eleven, even."

"Well, you girls made my night. I just got them. I have a little . . . engagement tonight."

"Wooooo-hooooo!" My friends whistled.

"Get it, girl." Nessa grinned.

"Nessa! Ew." I rolled my eyes. It was weird seeing Mom look so . . . young. But the longer I watched her, the more I wondered if the jeans really had anything to do with it. Maybe it was the natural flush to her cheeks or the sparkle in her green eyes. I was used to seeing her after a long day at the studio: crow's feet, dark circles, and tired smile beneath layers of makeup.

"You guys look a lot alike tonight," Nessa observed, glancing between me and my mom. "All happy."

"Me, too! Me, too!" Ella waved her hand frantically.

"You, too," Liv said gently, tousling Ella's curls.

"I'll take that as the highest of compliments." Mom pulled Ella and me in for a quick squeeze. "Now I've got to finish getting ready." She kissed me on the forehead. "Have fun tonight, baby."

"Yeah. You, too," I muttered as the door closed again. With my next breath, I inhaled a cloud of Mom's gardenia perfume and swallowed hard. Was breaking up Mom and Gabe a huge mistake? I *wanted* my mother to be happy. I wanted her to have flushed cheeks and sparkling eyes and even skinny jeans, as long as she didn't steal mine. But couldn't she have all those things with Ella and me? Weren't we enough?

"Kacey. Is she not the cutest?" Molly was saying. She whipped her hair into a high ponytail, then let it fall and started over.

"Who?"

"Your mom, duh. I wish I could find a guy who'd take me out on dates like that."

"Ummm . . ." I shook my head, trying to rid it of Mom and Gabe. "Don't you already have that? What about . . . Detroit?"

"Phoenix."

"Right. Phoenix," I said as I slid the bronze sequined racer-back mini Paige and I had picked out at Nordstrom Rack from its hanger. Then I slipped the dress over my head and sat at my vanity, unwinding the rollers from my hair.

Molly's reflection seemed to shrink in the corner of the mirror. "We kind of . . . aren't together anymore."

"Wait. What?" I ditched the rollers and jumped up. "Are you serious? What happened?"

"I don't know, really." Mols dropped to the edge of my bed. "He just sort of stopped FaceTimeing me and stuff, so a few days ago I texted and asked him what was up, and he texted back that he was looking for somebody who was more mature."

"No way! I can't believe that guy!" Nessa whacked my duvet with an open palm. "And by the way, *mature* is code for *old*. Mommy issues."

"Oh, Mols." I knelt in front of her. "I—boys suck," I proclaimed. "He's a loser."

Liv rubbed Molly's back in wide circles, like Mom always did mine when I was sick. "He's so not worth it, sweetie."

"But how can he not like me? Guys always like me." She looked genuinely bewildered. "It's my thing."

I brushed her white-blond layers away from her eyes. "It's not your *only* thing. What about your party-planning thing?"

"I guess."

"You're right, though." I sighed semi-dramatically, realizing instantly what would make her feel better. "When you're in the room, it's like guys don't notice any other girl. Like tonight. Eeeevery girl's gonna want to talk to Levi Stone, and he probably won't notice any of us once you hit the dance floor." I let my shoulders slump.

"I know, but—" Molly blinked. "Huh?"

"Levi Stone," I said casually. "Did I not—did I forget to mention?"

"Kace. Are you okay?" Liv squinted at me like she was staring through a foggy set of contacts.

"I'm *fine*," I insisted. "But I'll be better once we get to school. To see Levi Stone. Who just agreed to play a song at the dance in exchange for an interview with my mother."

It was partly true. The part about Levi Stone playing a song was, at least.

We sat in silence for a full eight beats, while the girls studied me like we were back at Shedd and I was some exotic species of flying dolphin.

"Oh. My. God. I think she's serious!" Nessa whispered. "Levi Stone!"

"Ahhhhhhhhh!" The girls scooped me into a giant hug, hooking their arms around my neck and squeezing. The scent of vanilla, amber, and brown sugar body lotions overwhelmed me.

"How did you—I don't even—how is this possible?" Molly screeched into my neck. "This is gonna be the best dance ever! And I'm the party planner! I mean, I'll give you credit and everything, but *still*!"

"I have to redo my hair," Nessa decided.

"No time," I argued. "You guys have to finish setting up, and I'm late for sound check." I tugged at the hem of my dress. "Oh. And you can't tell *anyone*. It has to be a surprise when he shows. Swear?"

"But—" Molly looked like she was about to pee right there on my bed.

"SWEAR."

"Okaaaay."

"Good." Reaching for my bedside table, I plucked a sparkly guitar-shaped statement ring from my ring dish and slipped into a pair of sky-high black calf-hair heels. Then one last mirror check. My waves were huge, adding a sixties mod vibe to my sequined dress. For my makeup, Liv had gone with a rich, brown smoky eye, peach blush, and a hint of icy pink gloss on my lips. Everything was perfect. The only thing missing was Zander.

"Let's go, let's go!" I sang. "It's time, baby!"

"Wait! Wait." Liv crouched next to her makeup bag and

pulled out three slender green glass rings. "My grandpa helped me make them from these old natural soda bottles we found in the garage."

"Love!" I slid mine on my middle finger. It fit perfectly.

"Good. Now, it's picture time." Liv dragged us to my photo booth, and we crammed inside. Molly collapsed on my lap.

"Ow! Mols! You're bending my sequins!" I smacked her thigh.

"Everybody say 'Leeeeviiiiiiii!'" Liv instructed.

We held out our hands to the camera like we were flashing serious bling.

"Leeeeeeeeviiiiiiiiiiii!" The flashbulb exploded in a burst of gold, like fireworks signaling the beginning of a perfect night.

COUNTDOWN TO MARQUETTE AT MIDNIGHT
Friday, 7:50 P.M.

"Check. Check." Zander's voice boomed across the nearly empty courtyard. "We're Gravity, and we'll be holding it down all night. Check."

"Why don't we try a few bars of your new song?" I bounced next to him on the low black platform that extended from one corner of The Square and came to a point in the center. Molly had flirted one of the seventh-grade tech crew guys into painting Gravity's logo in silver glitter paint beneath our feet. Kevin, Nelson, and The Beat hung behind us, tuning instruments and checking amps.

"Sounds good." Zander cupped his palm over the mic. "Except you mean *our* song, right?" he said coyly.

"Obviously." I nodded, instantly grateful for the low lighting in The Square. Above us, hundreds of mercury-glass votives hung from the ceiling at different levels, casting a romantic haze over the gleaming slate floors. It was as if Zander and I were standing at the edge of the universe together.

Stevie, on the other hand, was teetering on the brink of insanity. I'd never seen her this nervous. She power-paced in front of the door to Silverstein, little jet-black wisps from her messy bun tumbling around her temples. *Let her freak out*, I thought. I'd never been more at peace. Everything was falling into place. Finally.

"Hold on just a sec. I'm a little out of tune."

While Zander plucked a single string on his Gibson, I took in Molly and the girls' handiwork. Newly planted flower beds filled The Square with the fresh, green scent of gardenia and tulips. Sleek silver tables and bar stools lined the perimeter. And a long rustic table at the back was piled high with snacks, drinks, and punch bowls. The vibe was chic romance, all the way.

"You did good, Mols," I said into my mic. "Sweet theme." Across The Square, Liv and Nessa were hanging a MARQUETTE AT MIDNIGHT banner above the refreshments, while Molly checked her lip gloss in the reflection of one of the hanging votives.

"Thanks, Kace! And, um . . ." Molly released the candle into the air and hurried to the edge of the stage. She eyed

Zander and let her voice drop so low, I could hardly hear her. "You should know that I kind of advertised our celeb musical guest on FB like an hour ago."

"*Molly KNIGHT!*" I crouched to her level, ready to throttle her with one of Zander's out-of-tune guitar strings. "Is this a joke?" I hissed. "I specifically told you not to say anything!" I turned around. None of the guys seemed to be paying attention to our powwow, but it never hurt to be sure.

"Hey, Beat. Can I hear that drum solo you were rocking the other day? From the Hard Rock Life piece?" I asked.

"Lady wants the drums, lady gets the drums," The Beat agreed. "ONE! TWO! ONE, TWO, THREE, FOUR!" He threw himself into the solo.

"What's going on?" Stevie popped up behind Molly in nude platform peep-toes and a white feather-skirted number that fluttered when she walked.

"Molly Facebooked about Levi!" I yelled over the drums. Sweat was starting to form under my sequins.

"Okay, I'm really hoping I heard that wrong." Stevie took a menacing step toward Mols, who didn't back down. "What if he doesn't show or something? Did you bleach your brain the last time you did your hair?"

"HEY! This color is *natch*."

I coughed.

"And before you freak out, you should know I didn't post his name. I just said a 'mystery celeb musical guest.' That way, people are sure to show."

"Whatever. You better hope you can deliver." Stevie yanked her bun tight. Then she grabbed my wrist and pulled me offstage. "Excuse us for a sec."

"Doors open in five. Where *is* he?" Her voice was getting more and more panicked with every second. I hadn't seen her blink in at least ten minutes, and it was starting to freak me out.

"Relax. He'll be here. His manager guy, Mick, called and said he'd show up a few minutes late so he doesn't ruin the surprise. Gravity can get started, and then we'll bring him in for his song. Easy."

"And you called the station to request your mom?"

"'Um, *hiiiii*,'" I cooed in my best bored, hot receptionist voice. "'I'm calling on behalf of Levi Stoooone? He's doing, like, a benefit concert for this dyyyyyying girl? And he's requesting an interview with—'"

"Okay, okay. Got it." Stevie scanned The Square for the umpteenth time. "Seriously, if he doesn't—oh! I forgot to show you this!" She knelt down and pulled a small silver disc from inside her heel.

I cocked my head. "Super Jane Bond of you, but I don't get it."

"The battery to my dad's cell, so when your mom calls to cancel—"

"—he won't get the message," I finished. I could have thrown my arms around her, but we weren't there yet, and hopefully after tonight, we would never have to be. "Nice touch."

"Uh, guys?" Zander summoned us via mic. "We kinda have a show to do." He looked back and forth between Stevie and me with a hopeful, yet slightly panicked glaze in his eye. It was the same expression Mom got when she realized she hadn't heard a peep out of Ella and the house was too quiet for comfort.

"We're good." I reached out and let Zander pull me onto the stage, his hand warm in mine. My legs felt wobbly, and I kicked off my heels and nudged them out of the way. "So let's try that song once through, and then maybe Stevie can rehearse one of the Hard Rock Life numbers?" Reluctantly, I released Zander's hand.

"You're assuming I need the practice." Stevie leaned against the stage. "Which I don't."

"Good," Molly called. "'Cause it's *time*! We're opening the doors." She and Nessa pulled open the doors to Silverstein, and The Square filled almost instantly, sending the temperature in the courtyard to packed-El-car-in-July level.

I surveyed the crowd. Quinn and his buddies hung in the back by the refreshments, and my old Channel M director, Carlos, sauntered in wearing a pair of stiff skinnies. Molly hung by the doors while Liv and Nessa snapped shots of The Square with Nessa's cell. Dr. Phil and Sean stood awkwardly off to the side. I wondered how long it would take them to pink-slip me for bringing in an unauthorized musical guest.

"What's up, Marquette?" Zander yelled into the mic. "I'm Zander Jarvis—"

"And I'm Kacey Simon!" I slipped my hands around my mic. At the very back of The Square, I spotted Paige slipping through the doors. Her head was down and her shoulders were slumped.

"And this is Gravity!" Zander cheered. "We'll be holding it down all night, and we're here to rock!"

"Musical guest! Musical guest!" chanted a group of sixth graders in the back. "Woooooo-hoooooo!"

"Uh, thanks, guys." Zander stole a bewildered glance at me. I shrugged. "Here we go. One, two, three, four."

We tore into our first number, a cover of one of The Beat's favorite Springsteen tunes. Soon, the courtyard was so full that kids were packed around the stage, dancing and singing along. A few fans lifted iPhones high in the air, recording our debut.

I sang with everything I had. The mic carried my voice to the corners of The Square, making me feel powerful. I closed my eyes and imagined a screaming crowd in a huge venue. Pritzker Pavilion, maybe. After tonight, anything would be possible.

"Zander Jarvis on guitar, guys! Give it up!" I shouted into the mic as Zander shredded an insane guitar solo. When he finished, The Square erupted in cheers, whistles, and applause. I lifted my hand, and Zander high-fived it. His chest rose and fell to the beat of the song we'd just played.

"Thank you. Thanks, guys. Awesome turnout tonight. Let's get a hand for Kacey Simon on vocals, Kevin Cho on bass, Nelson Lund on keyboard, and last but not least . . . The Beat! On! Drums!"

"Yeahhhhhhhhhhhhhh!"

Energy from the crowd pulsed around us. I smiled and waved as some girl from sixth snapped our photo with her cell.

"And now, we're gonna try a new song. A duet. We hope you guys like—"

At the foot of the stage, Stevie waved frantically. I recognized her flailing as the international signal for *The major pop star you ordered to sing to your non-dying friend for the purpose of breaking up our parents is here.*

"Uh, actually, guys," I interrupted. "We have a special treat for you tonight. The surprise musical guest you've been waiting for is here!" Goose bumps prickled over my entire body. This was happening. Actually happening. I'd pulled it off.

"Huh?" Zander's confusion was swallowed whole in the cheers of the audience. He looked to me, and I tried to send *You're gonna love this* vibes. But the swinging lights above us flickered over his face, making it hard to read.

"I'm gonna let your Party Planning Committee chair do the honors, and then we'll bring him in!" I motioned to Molly, and she hurried to the stage. Nelson, Kevin, Zander, and The Beat stood dumbfounded, but there wasn't time to explain. I jumped barefoot into the audience and followed Stevie as she elbowed her way through the wall of middle schoolers.

"You rock, Kacey!" somebody cheered.

"WHERE IS HE?" I yelled at the back of Stevie's head.

"HEMINGWAY," she yelled back, without turning around. We reached the edge of The Square, and she yanked the door open. I slipped inside, and she locked it behind us.

The guy standing in front of me looked nothing like

the Levi Stone I'd pieced together in my mind from the MTV cameos and iTunes album covers. He was only a head or so taller than me, and thin like Zander, with shoulder-length brown hair and dark brown eyes. The beginnings of a beard shadowed his cheeks and jaw line, and he was dressed in wrinkled jeans, a brown T-shirt, and sneakers. With the exception of the whole successful facial hair thing, he didn't look much older than us. High school, maybe.

"L-Levi Stone?" My whole body felt like it was asleep. "Seriously?"

"Seriously." Levi's grin was adorably crooked, with one of his front teeth overlapping the other. He adjusted the guitar strap that crossed his chest. The strap was frayed at the edges, like Zander's.

"Levi, this is Kacey Simon. She's Sterling Simon's daughter!" Stevie's tone was cheerful enough to freak me out a little. "And she's good friends with Paige. The"—she leaned in—"*goner*?"

"Yeah, hi." I stuck out my hand. "Thanks for coming."

"No worries. And, uh, sorry about your friend."

"Yeah, well." I lowered my head.

"And this is my manager, Mick. He's the one who got your mom's e-mail."

"Hey there." An older guy with a gray ponytail stepped

out from behind Zander. He was skinny, with puckered lips and warm blue eyes.

Stevie and I nodded. "Hey."

Outside, the kids started chanting. "Mystery guest! Mystery guest!"

"No problem," Levi said. "So where is your mom? Does she wanna do the interview now, or . . ."

"We just talked to her," Stevie assured him, while shooting me a *Where is she?* look over my head. "She had to get her crew together, but she's on her way."

Levi bobbed his head. "Cool. So maybe I could meet Paige? I was thinking if she wanted, I could bring her onstage for a song or two. As long as she's not . . . contagious?"

"NO!" Stevie's voice started to quiver. "I mean, no. Paige is über-self-conscious about her green . . . ness. She'll probably be hiding in the back so you can't see her face."

My toes curled. "Verticopolus." I exhaled a shuddery breath. "The silent killer."

"Tragic." Stevie ground her heel into my big toe.

Mick the Manager eyed us.

"Mystery guest! Mystery guest!"

Levi cracked his knuckles. "Let's do this. Lead the way?"

"Yup. Follow us." I unlocked the door to The Square and shoved through the doorway. The chants slowly morphed into ear-piercing whistles.

"Out of the way, people," I shouted, clearing a path to the stage. "Levi Stone, coming through." I wished I could freeze time, just for a second, and take it all in.

Molly exhaled into the mic as we got closer. "Marquette! Make some noise for the one and only Leeeviii Stooooone!"

I pressed my fingers into my ears to salvage what was left of my hearing, then stepped back while Levi took the stage. Molly shooed Gravity off the other side of the platform.

"What's up, Chicago?" Levi dragged a stool in front of the mic and started tuning his guitar. "I'm stoked to be here, and I just want to give a shout-out to a super-special girl. She's the reason I'm here, and she knows who she is."

I scanned the crowd, looking for Paige, but didn't see her anywhere. *Phew.*

"Here we go. And one, two." Levi strummed the opening notes of his latest single. The ground beneath me shook.

"Don't look," Stevie yelled. "But your mom's in the back, there. Six o'clock. By the refreshment table."

I whipped around to see Mom powwowing with Jankowitz, her executive producer, and their entire crew. The camera guys dispersed into the crowd, filming shots of the stage and the students.

Stevie and I high-fived as she mouthed the word: *Done*.

LEVI WAS HERE
Friday, 8:30 P.M.

"Mom? What are you doing here?" I was going for utter surprise, with a twist of panic. I even threw in a hand to the chest, for effect. "Is everything okay?"

Mom looked relieved when she spotted us. "Girls!" I could barely hear her over the music. She'd changed into a rumpled black suit dress, and her hair was pulled back in a lopsided ponytail. "Everything's fine. I'm here for work. To interview that kid, I suppose." She squinted at the stage. "Apparently, he requested us at the last minute."

"Cool." Stevie nodded, her lips pinched into a thin line. "He's totally a big deal."

"And he's doing this show for free? Charity, or something?" Mom shot me a quizzical glance. "I thought Gravity was supposed to play."

I leaned in and gave Mom a kiss on the cheek, pretending not to hear. "So what about Gabe?"

"I don't know. I've been trying to call, but his cell's going straight to voice mail." Up close, Mom looked exhausted, all her sparkle from earlier gone. The tiny lines at the corners of her mouth were deeper than usual. Even her auburn bob had lost its sheen. "If we can do the interview in the next ten minutes or so, I can still make it."

"Oh," I said. "Good." I eyed Stevie warily. With Levi only playing one song, there was the distinct possibility that Mom could finish the interview and get to Gabe in time for his high-altitude love proclamation. I crossed my fingers for an encore. "So let's wait inside. It's quieter in there."

I nudged everyone into Silverstein and closed the door, muffling the screaming crowd.

"Oh. Jankowitz. This is Stevie, by the way." I leaned against the closest locker. The chill of the metal sent icy shivers down my spine.

"What's up?" Stevie nodded.

Jankowitz grunted a hello. He never really said much, but I'd always liked him. He'd produced news segments all over the world, and had met, like, thirteen world leaders. Once he told me that at a White House Correspondents'

Dinner, he'd caught Clinton picking an atomic wedgie after the salad course.

"I wonder what's going on with your dad's phone?" Mom looked to Stevie before she tapped her touch screen and pressed it to her ear. "Nothing." She shook her head.

"Dunno." Stevie shrugged. "He's pretty irresponsible. Maybe he just turned it off and forgot about y—"

I elbowed her sharply in the ribs.

Mom turned to Jankowitz. "You're sure he requested us specifically, Bob? Can't we get one of the entertainment reporters out here?"

"Sorry, Sterling. Kid wants you, apparently."

"I don't have the slightest idea why." Mom closed her eyes for a few beats. Her mouth turned down at the corners.

Jankowitz shrugged. His potbelly heaved upward, then settled over his belt again. "This is gonna be pretty good for ratings, though. I hear the kid's pretty popular."

"That's *great*, Mom!" I said brightly, squeezing her arm. "You can always use good ratings, right?"

"I guess there's always a bright side." Mom tried a smile. "I just . . ." She looked down at her cell again, then shook her head and dropped it in her purse.

The noise level swelled again, and I looked up to see Zander shoving through the door. Traces of sweat darkened his T-shirt, and his face was flushed. "Levi Stone," he said. "Here? On my stage?"

"Can you believe it?" I grinned. "It's so—" My voice caught in my throat as I watched Zander's face. Instead of lighting up, it darkened.

"Well, hey there, Zander," Mom said warmly.

"Hey, Ms. Simon. What are you doing here?" Zander's steel eyes acknowledged Mom, then settled on me again. He shook his head. My body went hot. What was going on? Why wasn't he excited?

"We're here for Levi," Mom said. "But off the top of my head, I can think of a few other musicians I'd rather be watching up there."

"Yeah, me, too," Zander said coldly, without taking his eyes off me. "Can I talk to you for a sec? In there?" He jerked his head toward the nearest classroom. "It's about band stuff."

I looked to Mom, then Stevie. Stevie took a step back.

"Go ahead," Mom said. "I'll be right here, I'm sure." She glanced down at her watch, a worried look in her eye.

"'Kay." My voice sounded shaky. I followed Zander silently down the hall, staring at the purple polish on my toes. He threw open the classroom door, not bothering to flick the light switch on the wall before he turned on me.

"Tell me you didn't do this. Tell me this wasn't your idea, Kacey."

"What are you talking about? It's Levi Stone!" I kicked the door closed. Inside the classroom, the air was stale and smelled like chalk dust. "I thought you'd be happy!"

"Happy that some famous guy stole my set?"

"Okay. First of all? It's not *your* set. It's *ours*. And second, he's not taking the whole set. He's just here to play *one* song!"

Zander stuffed his hands in his pockets and turned his back to me. "Wrong," he spat. "Everybody loves the dude. They don't wanna see Gravity up there! We'll get booed off the stage!"

My stomach twisted into a knot. I hadn't even considered that. "I thought it would be good publicity," I whispered. "Can't we just go out there when he breaks and tell him we want to play?"

Suddenly, he spun around and slammed his palm against the desk. I jumped back. I'd never seen him this angry before. Not even when I'd ditched the band to star in the middle school musical.

"Tell him *we* want to *play*?" His laugh was bitter. "What is this, elementary school? I can't believe you did this, Kacey. I can't believe you screwed us over on purpose."

"But I—" The room swam in my field of vision. "I didn't mean—"

"You *did* mean to. Nobody asked you to bring this guy in here! You wrecked our big shot." Zander pushed past me, knocking me into the desk.

"Zander! Wait!"

"Okay." Stevie opened the door just as Zander reached for the knob. "What's going on with you guys?"

"Oh, please. Don't play dumb." Zander was almost shouting. "I knew the two of you were up to something. You've been acting weird all day. I can't even—I gotta get out of here. And don't expect me onstage for the rest of the night." He stormed out without even looking at me.

I opened my mouth to say something, but nothing came out. "I don't get it," I finally managed. "Doesn't he know I didn't mean to . . . I didn't think . . ."

"He'll be fine." Stevie hung by the door, looking unconvinced. "But I think your mom's about to leave. She says she thinks she can make it if she goes now."

"What? How could you let that happen?" I slid off the desk.

"So now it's my fault your mom's desperate?"

"Uh, yeah. My mom's desperate for *your* dad. Please." *Focus, Simon.* Stevie was right. I could fix things with Zander later. But for now, the most important thing was keeping Mom away from Gabe. I led Stevie back into the hall, my heart thumping in my chest.

"Everything all right?" Mom asked when we reappeared. "Zander looked upset."

"Fine," I said, as breezily as I could manage. "We just couldn't agree on which songs we wanted to play later. That's all."

"Okay, then." Her auburn brows arched. "Well, I think I'm going to try to catch Gabe."

"Wait." I reached out and grabbed her arm. "What about the interview?"

"Jankowitz offered to do it."

"Oh. Great." I glared at Jankowitz, who was too busy picking at a patch of dried mustard from his tie to pay attention. "Only don't you think you should do the interview, since Levi asked for you specifically?"

Mom glanced at the door, then back at her producer. "What do you think, Bob?"

"Go on, Sterling. Before I change my mind." Jankowitz whacked her awkwardly on the shoulder. "Have a good time."

I narrowed my eyes at Stevie.

"But—" I started.

"Okay! I'm going!" Mom was suddenly beaming beneath the fluorescent lights.

"O-okay." I didn't know what to say. It wasn't like I could stop her, thanks to a certain meddling middle-aged matchmaker.

"So go, then." Jankowitz doubled over and hacked up a lung. "Get outta here."

"I'm going!" Mom planted a rushed kiss on my cheek. "Don't wait up!"

"DON'T EVER SAY THAT TO ME AGAIN," I bellowed.

"Sorry! Here I go." She waved and disappeared through the doors.

"Whatever. I'm gonna check on Zander," Stevie said disgustedly. She followed in Mom's footsteps, leaving Jankowitz and me alone in the hall.

"AHHHHHHHHHHHH!" I banged my fist against the locker until it throbbed.

"He makes her happy, you know that?" Jankowitz hiked up his pants. "In all the years we've worked together, I've never seen her this happy. Remember that, kiddo, the next time you beat up a locker."

When he left, I pressed my forehead against the locker, the cool metal doing nothing to soothe my pounding head. How had everything gone so wrong, so quickly?

"Kacey?" I heard the click of the door behind me and turned.

"Hey, Paige." Even my voice sounded hollow.

"What's wrong with you?"

On any other night, I would have turned the question back on her. Paige's eyes were rimmed with pink, and her hair was matted to one side of her face like she'd just woken up and forgotten to brush it. Her clothes were wrinkled, and she kind of smelled like imitation cheese.

"I had a fight with Zander. I'm going home."

Her eyes searched mine. "Good," she said after a few seconds. "I don't really want to be here, either. Can I spend the night?"

I gave her a small smile. It was the best I could do to thank her for not asking questions. "Come on. Let's get out of here."

NORAH JONES AND TAPERED SWEATS
ARE THE FIRST SIGNS OF TROUBLE
Friday, 9:32 P.M.

We left without telling Stevie or Molly and the girls. After getting off the El, Paige and I trudged toward my house in silence, Clark Street's pavement glistening with the thin sheen of an evening rain. Friday night was just getting started. Everything and everyone reminded me of Zander. The giggling college girls in skinny jeans and heels (Zander looks way better in skinnies), the couples walking hand in hand down the sidewalk (If I weren't such a scheming, lying loser, that could be us right now).

When we made it to my front door, Paige jiggled the handle. Oddly, the door was open.

"Ella?" I kicked my heels and my purse into a pile on the floor under the walnut console table in the hall. All the lights inside were on. "Are you here?" Norah Jones crooned from somewhere at the back of the house. *Uh-oh.* Norah Jones was never a good sign.

"In here." Ella's tiny, pained voice leaked from the kitchen.

"El? Are you here by yourself?" I rushed after her voice, and Paige trailed behind me. When we got to the kitchen, I stopped in my tracks.

At the table, Mom was cradling Ella in her lap while Ella stroked Mom's ponytail. There was a half-full glass of red wine on the table, and Mom was wearing her sad-divorcée sweats, the tapered ones with the elastic at the ankles. I'd only seen her in those sweats in the months after Dad left. Hadn't she pinky-sworn to burn them? Hadn't we decided *no one* deserved the tapered leg?

"What're you doing here? What about your date?" A good daughter would have taken her place at the table, next to her sweet sister and her clearly devastated mother. But I couldn't stand to get any closer to Mom than I already was. I didn't want to see the mascara streaks that would confirm she'd been crying.

"My date. *Oof.*" Mom groaned, shifting Ella on her lap. "My date is nonexistent. Hi, Paige." She twirled one of Ella's ringlets around her index finger and gave us a tired smile.

"Hey, Sterling." Paige slumped over the island in the kitchen. "So, you were out with Stevie's dad?"

"What about the hot-air balloon?" I asked. "And dinner? Did he stand you up?"

"No, no. Nothing like that. I missed the balloon ride. And Gabe thought—well, we decided to take a rain check on dinner."

"But—"

"Gabe said Mom needs to figure out her sororities." Ella's bottom lip stuck out three inches from her face, and her little fists clenched in her lap.

"Priorities, lovebug," Mom corrected her gently. "And he's right. I just don't have time for a relationship right now. Maybe in fifteen years or so, when you guys are in college and they drag me off the air."

"But you—he—he *dumped* you?" My whole body felt tight, like I couldn't fit inside my own skin anymore. "No way! He can't do that! What a jacka—"

"KACEY!" Mom said firmly. "Watch the language." She kept her eyes on me as she kissed the top of Ella's head. "Why don't you get your jammies on. Then you can come back down, and we'll have dessert."

"Only the new jammies," Ella said angrily. Her face was pinched like she was about to cry but had no idea why. "With the bunnies."

"Bunnies it is. Now scoot." Mom nudged Ella off her lap.

"Fine." Ella stalked past me, then whirled around in the doorway. "But Gabe *is* a jacka, Mom. So there." She stuck out her tongue and ran upstairs.

"Thanks for that, Kacey," Mom said dryly. Sitting at the kitchen table in sad sweats and full TV makeup, she looked like one of those depressed people on the commercials. *Are you experiencing depressed moods more than a few times per week? Do you have a monster of a daughter who just sabotaged your only chance at happiness for her own personal gain?*

"Sorry, Mom." My eyes welled up, and I twisted the dimmer switch by the door.

"Ooh. Better. Thank you." Mom lifted her wineglass and patted the seat next to her. "Not to worry. My great guy-repelling powers aren't contagious, girls."

I hated it when Mom talked like that, like we were friends hanging out in my room or something. Moms were supposed to say Mom things, like *Clean your room* or *Because I said so, that's why.* Moms weren't supposed to spend Friday nights moping around the kitchen because they'd just been dumped.

I dimmed the lights a little more and loitered at the fridge to grab a soda and a few extra seconds. The faint sounds of my phone ringing in the hall drifted into the kitchen. After a few seconds, the ringing stopped. Then it started again.

"What are you girls doing home so early? I thought you'd want to stick around and watch Jankowitz do the interview." Mom took a long sip of her wine.

"Nah. I'm not really a big fan of Levi Stone's anyway." I sat down next to her and popped the tab on my soda, even though I wasn't thirsty.

"But wasn't bringing him in your idea?" Paige wriggled next to me, shoving me halfway off the seat.

"Whatever. He's not that great."

"So I'm guessing you weren't in a dancing mood, either?" Mom asked Paige.

"Didn't Kacey tell you about the election?"

"I thought the results won't be in until Monday."

"They won't. But Quinn Wilder's running now, which means I'll probably lose."

"Oh, sweetie. I'm so sorry." Mom reached over and squeezed Paige's wrist. "That's tough."

"Wait. Aren't you supposed to tell me I'm being ridiculous? That I've worked too hard to lose, and I'm *so* the better candidate? That's what my mom said!" Suddenly, Paige looked panicked and confused.

"You're absolutely the better candidate," Mom assured

her. "And we'll all be rooting for you. But if it doesn't work out, that doesn't mean that—"

"*Mom*." I glared across the table, in case drawing her name out to four syllables wasn't getting the point across. Wasn't *I* supposed to be the recovering honesty addict?

"No, Kacey. She's right." Paige slapped on her best brave-soldier face and straightened up in her chair. "Rejection is a part of politics."

"And life." Mom sighed.

"MOM. Stop, already!"

"I know, I know. I'm sorry, girls." Mom's chair creaked as she leaned back. "Paige, you've run a fantastic campaign. And I can't wait to call you Ms. President."

"Don't mind her," I told Paige. "She's having a bad night."

"Yeah. Me, too." Paige slumped in her seat.

I shrugged. "Me three. And four."

"E! Nuff!"

We all jumped at Ella's unexpected cry. She stood in her doorway in her bunny pajamas. "Stop it! Be! Happy!"

"Come here, sweet one." Mom opened her arms, but Ella stood firm.

"No! You *have* to feel better." Ella's face was pink with frustration. "We need chocolate sauce. And marshmallows and bananas and strawberries. Now, Mom!" She ran across the kitchen and threw open the refrigerator door.

"Actually, I *could* go for some fondue," I said slowly.

"Me, too." Paige's lips curled into a crooked smile. "I mean, if it's gonna make you guys feel better."

"I'm convinced." Mom pushed up her sleeves and joined Ella in front of the pantry. "Heads up, Kace," she said, whipping a bag of marshmallow chicks from at least six Easters ago in my direction. Paige turned on the tiny black-and-white TV on the counter and twisted the dial through several static-filled stations.

"Hey, Mom." I palmed the bag and popped it open. It wheezed a welcome breath of expired sugar. "Maybe fondue'll give you the energy to get rid of that sad sack you call an outfit."

Paige's hand shot into my bag. "I like those sweats."

"You would."

Twenty minutes later, the kitchen smelled like the holidays. The sweet, gooey essence of melting chocolate mingled with the tart scent of fresh fruit and the warmth of cinnamon buns baking in the oven. The garbled hum of the television dipped and fell in the background.

Paige bent over the steaming fondue pot in the center of the kitchen table and closed her eyes. A blissful smile spread over her face. She looked like she was giving herself a chocolate steam facial.

"Get your face out of there! I don't want the contents of your pores in my fondue, thankyouverymuch."

"Kacey," Mom warned, balancing plates of fruit, cinnamon buns, and marshmallows along the length of her slender arms. She whisked them to the table and spread the plates out evenly. Sometimes I forgot that Mom had a life before she was Mom. She'd worked as a waitress in Streeterville forever ago to put herself through journalism school at Medill.

"It's unsanitary!" I protested, taking my seat next to Paige. Ella climbed me and started bouncing in my lap.

"Whatever." Paige rolled her eyes. "Do you know how much dirt we eat in a year? It's like sixteen pounds or something."

Ella screamed.

"INSIDE VOICE. And Paige was just joking."

"Okay, so I think that's everything." Mom blew a few wisps of reddish-gold hair away from her face. They fluttered down again and rested against her high cheekbone. "Dig in, girls." She slid a bowl of toothpicks to the center of the table, and we descended on them. Soon, the muffled sound of chewing filled the kitchen. I started to relax.

"Coming up at the top of our newscast tonight, a rising rock star strikes a charitable chord at a local middle school," the TV on the counter blurted. "I'm Lisa Winchester, and you're watching Chicago's own Channel Five. We're back in thirty seconds, so don't go away."

"Ohmygosh!" Paige lurched for the TV and started adjusting the dial. "Marquette's gonna be on TV!"

"No! Wait!" Reflexively, I bumped Paige out of the way. "Turn it off!"

"Kacey! Come on! I wanna see!" Paige reached to turn up the volume. On the screen, an elderly couple was riding their bikes down a tree-lined path, apparently unhindered by their adult diapers.

"But. No!" I strained for the OFF button, but Paige blocked me, so I yanked the cord until it came out of the wall and the screen went black.

"Kacey!" Mom shoved her chair back. "What in the world has gotten into you?"

Would you believe a green flesh-eating fungus? Chest heaving, I tried to think of an acceptable reason for my psychotic break. But my mind was more staticky than the television. If I could just stall for the next minute or so, I'd be in the clear. At least temporarily. I was so desperate, I actually wished Stevie were here to create some kind of diversion.

"Have you lost your mind? What is up with you?" Paige jammed the metal prongs back into the wall and turned up the volume on the TV, blocking my access to the plug.

"As promised, we've got a fun story for you tonight!" chirped Mom's tiny colleague. "Singer-songwriter Levi Stone, in town for a concert at our own Goodman Theatre, stopped by Lincoln Park's Marquette Middle School to play a charity concert for one brave fan." Lisa's face scrunched up, like she couldn't decide whether the piece called for a cheery smile or a somber nod. Amateur. "Channel Five's Bob Jankowitz has the heartwarming story."

This was not happening. The picture on the screen wavered. Or maybe I was just about to pass out. Why had my stupid mother insisted on a TV in the kitchen? Didn't she know THE FAMILY WHO ATE TOGETHER WITH MINIMAL DISTRACTIONS STAYED TOGETHER?

"Look! They're in Hemingway!" Paige slapped the counter as Levi's face came on the screen. He was standing in front of a row of lockers. Jankowitz stood out of the frame, extending a mic to Levi's chin. "SHHH!"

"Thanks for taking the time to talk with us tonight, Levi." Jankowitz's gravelly voice was like sandpaper on my aching brain.

"I'm stoked to be here, Bob. I wouldn't be where I am today without my awesome fans, and it always feels good to give something back."

"Which brings us to the reason you're here tonight. You got a letter about your biggest fan here in Chicago, is that right?"

"That's right, Bob. A super-brave fan who's suffering from a rare disease called Verticopolus. She wanted to hear me play, and I was, like, totally honored to help her out and raise awareness about this silent killer."

I tasted chocolate. *Don'tsayhernamedon'tsayhername-don'tsayhername.*

"Wait. Verti-what?" Paige turned up the volume.

"Is there a sick girl in your grade?" Mom looked confused.

I blinked at the screen, telepathically begging the segment to end, or a natural disaster to strike, or for one of those annoying telethons that raised money for the station to cut the newscast short. I silently swore to buy fifty tote bags if a telethon would magically appear RIGHT. NOW.

"Now, I'm not familiar with Verti—"

"Verticopolus, Bob." Levi nodded somberly at the camera. I couldn't decide which was harder to believe: what a moron Levi Stone was, or that I was still standing here, watching. My brain was screaming, *Run! Do something!* but my body wouldn't listen. "It's a rare, green, flesh-eating fungus. And sadly, it's fatal."

"I believe your manager gave us a picture to show

the effects of Verticopolus? Can we put that up, guys?"

Noooooo! But it was too late. Paige's seaweed mask picture, the one I'd e-mailed to Levi to convince him to come to Marquette, was officially on television. All over Chicago. Our grainy TV made the cracks and crags in Paige's face look even more gross than they had in real life.

The kitchen went silent for a full five seconds.

"Wait." Paige's mouth flopped open and she squinted at the screen. "Is that—"

"It's tragic," Levi's voice said over Paige's picture. "But Paige Greene is an inspiration to, like, all her classmates. I just feel really grateful that she likes my tunes, you know?"

This time, it was Paige who jerked the cord out of the wall. The screen went dark, twenty seconds too late. She turned to face me.

"Paige." I backed away slowly. "I can explain. I swear."

She opened her mouth, then closed it. She did this three times before she finally forced actual words out of her mouth.

"KACEY! YOU DID THIS?" Paige was shaking so hard, her glasses were bouncing on her nose. "But why—I don't—I can't even—"

"Oh, Paige. Sit down, sweetie." Mom slipped her arm

around Paige's shoulder and tried to nudge her toward the table, but Paige wouldn't budge. So Mom refocused her attention. On me. "I truly hope this was some sort of horrible misunderstanding." Her voice was like concrete. Cold, enraged concrete. "I want to hear an explanation this very second, or so help me, Kacey—"

"I didn't mean to! It just—I don't knooooow!" I backed into the island, the sharp edge of the marble slab stabbing me in the back.

"'I don't know' is most definitely not an option. You have one more chance. And I'll know if you're not telling the truth."

I knew she was right. A woman didn't spend twenty years as a reporter in a major market without learning how to tell when someone was lying. "I just—I—it wasn't just me. It was Stevie, too." My breath was shallow in my chest. "We didn't want you dating Gabe, so we thought if you had to go to work—"

"You *what?*" my mom said.

The color had drained completely from Paige's face. "You humiliated me in front of the whole CITY just so your mom wouldn't go on a DATE?"

"He's not good for her!" I choked. "He's not good for you, Mom! I did it for your own good! Remember how sad you were when Dad left?" I didn't know where to look: at

Paige's shock-stricken face, or in Mom's horrified eyes. So I stared at the floor.

"Kacey. Elisabeth. Simon." Mom stared blankly past me, her eyes unfocused. "I cannot believe . . ." Her voice trailed off.

"You are, without a doubt, the most selfish person I have ever met," Paige said softly. I wished she had yelled, or even shoved me. It would have hurt less than the stabbing pain in what little remained of my conscience. "I'm so outta here." She turned to look at me one last time. "Don't ever speak to me again. We're through."

AFRAID OF THE DARK SIDE
Saturday, 2:51 A.M.

I didn't bother with a toothpick as I sat cross-legged on the kitchen counter in the dark, cradling a cold bowl of thickened chocolate in my lap. Other than the tick of the grandfather clock in the hallway, the house was silent with fury and judgment. As was the cell phone balanced on my thigh.

After Paige had stormed out, my own family left me in the kitchen, alone with a table full of virtually untouched grub. I'd secured the plates of fruit, marshmallows, and cinnamon buns with plastic wrap. Perfectly, too: Every corner was even, every bit of plastic stretched tight enough for me to see my reflection. If I'd wanted to.

I dragged a rock-hard marshmallow chick in figure eights over the fondue skin. I wondered if Paige was asleep. Maybe she was up, too, regretting how over-dramatic she'd been. But even as the thought crystallized in my mind, I knew I was wrong. Paige hadn't been over-dramatic. Everything I'd done—all of it—was so, so wrong. I'd gone from being the girl who always told the truth to the girl who could lie too easily. And now everything had come crashing down.

I'd gone way too far. Paige might never forgive me. And the same was true for Zander. When it came to relationships, maybe I just didn't have it in me to make them last. Maybe I was no better than my coward of a father.

"I hope you're not planning on leaving that there." Mom stood in the doorway in her light-pink terrycloth robe, striped pajama pants, and socks.

"Mom! You scared me!"

"Kacey." Mom gave a sharp nod to the bowl in my lap. I looked down. The marshmallow chick was drowning in the middle of the chocolate.

"Sorry." I scooped it up, saving it, like I wished some-one could save me from this night.

"Can't sleep?" Mom slid onto the counter next to me.

I shook my head. "Mom—"

"What were you *thinking*, Kacey?" Mom stared straight ahead, into the dark. "Do you understand what you've done here?"

"Yes! I just—"

She cut me off with the razor-sharp edge of her disapproval. "I don't think you do. I think right now, you're thinking about how Paige and I are angry with you."

"Well, yeah, but—"

"I don't think you've considered the fact that you used valuable Channel Five resources for what was essentially a prank. I don't think you've thought about the fact that when this gets straightened out, my job could be in jeopardy. Or about how that job is what puts food on our table, since your father contributes absolutely nothing to this family. So maybe you could think about those things for a while."

"I'm so sorry, Mom." My body folded into itself. In that moment, I felt like she'd knocked every molecule of air from my body. My stomach heaved like I was going to be sick.

It wasn't until Mom's fingers brushed my wet cheek that I realized I'd been crying.

"I know you're sorry." She didn't hug me, but she dabbed beneath my eyes with a rough dish towel. It was the pink-and-white towel I'd crocheted for her at summer camp the year I was six. I didn't have to see it to know that the pink had faded, the white had dulled to yellowed cream. "And I'm sorry, too."

"Why?" I rasped.

"Clearly, you weren't ready for me to date. We should have talked about this as a family. I wasn't thinking. I just really thought Gabe could . . ." Her eyes were glassy in the dark. "I'm sorry."

Wait. She was sorry? She might as well have stabbed me in the heart with a fondue toothpick. I made some sort of a noise in response. A combination of a wail, a sob, and a desperate plea for forgiveness. Paige was right. I was the most selfish person on Earth. I'd just wrecked my mother's chance at happiness, and she was apologizing? My sobs overtook me.

"Oh, my sweet, sweet girl." Mom pulled me in, cradling me against her chest. "You know no matter what you do, I'll always love you."

"I'm sorry, Mom." I heaved into her robe. "Really. I can talk to Gabe, or—"

"It's too late, Kacey. But if you're this upset, maybe it's for the best."

I curled up in a ball and buried my face in her lap, tears streaming while she stroked my hair and whispered over and over the words I didn't deserve to hear.

"No matter what you do, I'll always love you."

HONESTY IS A DISH BEST SERVED WARM.
WITH FROSTING.
Saturday, 7:47 P.M.

"Paige. I know you're mad, and you have every right to be. But you have to call me back." I shivered, leaning against Sugar Daddy's glass storefront. "I mean, you don't have to. But I want you to. Please?"

On the other side of the window, Molly, Liv, and Nessa waved me inside from their perch on our usual couches in the back.

I stashed the phone in the inside pocket of my jacket, wondering if I'd ever get the chance to apologize to Paige in person. I'd lost count of how many times I'd called, how many messages I'd left.

Sugar Daddy was in chaos—screaming kids with colored frosting goatees darted around the antique student desks and played hide-and-seek behind the cupcake bar. North

Shore moms barked orders into iPhones and BlackBerrys while rocking strollers back and forth.

My North Shore mom should have grounded me, but she was too depressed to forbid me to leave the house.

I plopped next to Molly at the end of the couch, and she squeezed my arm. "Glad you're feeling better." Her voice was pinched, high.

"Huh? Oh, yeah." I'd explained my early exit last night as sudden illness. "Much better."

"I don't know. You don't look so good," Liv said cautiously. She tucked her feet beneath her and spread the hem of her colorful maxi skirt over her boots. It looked familiar, but I couldn't remember when she'd last worn it.

Nessa looked up from the *Trib* review of a French film playing at the indie theater down the road. "*C'est vrai,*" she agreed.

"I'll be fine." I sighed. I wanted to tell them everything. To come clean about Levi. About Paige. And about Zander. To start fresh.

"What's going on?" Liv prompted.

I gripped the plate of the cupcake the girls had gotten me so tightly, it should have cracked. "It's Paige."

"Ah." Liv nodded solemnly. "Are you worried about how devastated you'll be when she *passes on*?"

"No, that's not—"

"Did the news guy say whether she was contagious?" Molly asked worriedly.

"Ohmygod. She's not—"

"How have I never heard of Verticopolus?" Nessa sniffed.

"Because it isn't *real*!" I burst out. "Don't you think I would have told you guys if Paige was really dying? I made it up!"

Their heads snapped toward me.

My face felt hot. "It's kind of a long story."

"Does *Paige* know she isn't dying?" Liv asked.

"Ooh!" Molly's eyes glinted. "Don't tell her! She'd be all, 'And I bequeath to Kacey my ugly black shoe collection,' and you'd be all, 'Um, over my dead body. Oops!'" She burst into giggles, obviously proud of herself.

"*Bequeath*?" Nessa raised an eyebrow.

"What? I know words." Molly sniffed.

I smacked her arm. "Of course she knows she isn't dying." My head was spinning, and the smell of sugar was starting to give me a headache. I shoved my plate as far away as possible.

"We're going to need you to start from the beginning." Nessa folded the sleeves on her three-quarter tuxedo blazer and took a long sip from her mug.

Slowly, carefully, I explained everything about the Paige situation.

"My mom's miserable, and Paige won't talk to me, and Zander and I—"

I froze. *Zander and I.* Had I really just said that?

"Zander and you . . . what?" Molly swiveled toward me. I couldn't read her. Her eyes were clouded, but her mouth twitched like she was on the verge of a smile.

"We've kind of been hanging out," I croaked. "And I didn't tell you because I thought you'd be mad, and I'm really sorry, but it won't happen again because he hates me now."

The girls were silent.

I should have felt lighter. Now everyone knew everything. I had nothing left to hide from the people closest to me. I should have felt like my old self again. Instead, I felt a cold rush of dread welling up inside me as I waited for my friends' judgment to rain down on me.

"It's okay," Molly said quietly.

"No, Mols. It's not. I'm sorry." Why did people keep forgiving me when I didn't deserve it? "I've been a terrible friend, and it's not okay, and I'm gonna make it up to you. I promise. Just tell me what I can do to—"

"YoucanforgivemeforkindofholdinghandswithQuinn-lastnight," Molly said under her breath.

I glanced at Liv and Nessa, who nodded.

"QUINN?" I shrieked.

Molly scrambled backward on the couch. "I'm SORRY! But you've been hanging out with Zander!"

"I know! But Quinn? When did this—how long have you guys—" I swallowed, feeling some combination of relief and nausea.

"Just last night. And we only held hands, I swear. It was just . . . after the rally . . . all that *power*."

"What happened to the Girl Code?"

"I haaaate the Girl Code," Molly exhaled. "I mean, it's not really fair, right? You can't help who you like, and friends shouldn't get in the way of each other's crushes! Especially when they didn't work out. Right? Who's with me?" She jumped up and dropped down again. Her eyes were crazed.

Dumbfounded, I tried to take it all in. Molly and Quinn. Quinn and Molly. Actually, it made perfect sense. But was it weird, swapping boyfriends like this? Boys weren't like shoes or a favorite pair of jeans.

But we aren't swapping boyfriends, I reminded myself. Swapping would mean that Zander and I were still together.

"Okay." I bit my lip. "You're right. We shouldn't get in the way of each other's crushes. If you like Quinn, you should go for it."

"Ohhhmygod." Molly practically jumped in my lap

and threw her arms around my neck. "Thankyouthank-youthankyou."

Nessa and Liv sighed in unison, looking relieved.

"Just like I never should have gotten in the way of my mom and Gabe," I said sadly.

"So get them back together!" Molly chirped.

"Yeah," Nessa agreed. "One missed date shouldn't be enough to break them up for good. They really like each other, right?"

I nodded. "Yeah. They did. They do." I thought back to the sparkle in Mom's eyes at the Millennium Park skating rink. To the lightness in her voice whenever she'd talked about Gabe. To the way they flirted right in front of Stevie and me. That last part I could do without, but the rest . . . Well, who was I to take happiness away from my own mother?

"Okay," I decided, nodding at the girls. "We'll come up with a plan. But first I have to talk to Stevie. And maybe Zander." My eyes cut to Molly. She squeezed my knee.

"Good girl," Liv said warmly. She stood up and fluffed her skirt. The colorful fabric caught my eye.

"Hey. Did you make that?"

"Yeah. You want one?"

"Do you have any of the fabric left over?"

"I think so." Liv looked at me quizzically.

"Do you think I could borrow it?" The beginnings of a plan were starting to crystallize in my mind. The kind of plan that maybe, just maybe, could fix everything.

"Sure, of course."

Molly's lip protruded about six inches from her face. "Hey! No fair! How come she gets to know what's going on?"

"She doesn't," I said secretively. "Not yet, at least." I grabbed my messenger bag and hopped up. "I have to go. Call you guys later."

"Good luck!" the girls called after me.

"Thanks," I said, gratefully. I was going to need it.

HALLMARK SHOULD REALLY MAKE
A CARD FOR THESE THINGS
Saturday, 9:08 P.M.

I made it to Zander's blue door way too soon. I hadn't even finished prepping my apology speech. Not that it mattered. The second Zander appeared in the entryway, every word, every syllable I knew deserted me.

We stood there for a long moment, staring at each other like strangers.

"Goose. Let her in, man. It's cold out there." Stevie nudged Zander out of the way, ushering me inside. Her eyes were red and smudged with mascara. I wondered if she'd been crying.

"So, um, where's your dad?" I kicked off my booties and left them by the door.

"He went out." Stevie ran a hand through her hair. "He was really upset last night. I think we might've screwed up."

"I know."

Zander cleared his throat. "What are you doing here? It's not really the best time." The space between us was palpable.

"I came by to apologize."

He didn't say anything, just stood hunched in the same outfit he'd worn to the dance the night before. His shirt wasn't wrinkled, though, and I wondered if he'd even slept.

"Here. Sit down, at least." Stevie shoved Zander onto the couch, and he scooted to the far end. I dropped where I was.

"I'm not expecting you to understand why we—" I looked to Stevie. She slid onto the coffee table and gave me a slight nod. "—why *I* wrecked Gravity's shot to play the dance. And I'm definitely not expecting you to forgive me. I did a really stupid thing, and I didn't even take the time to think about what it would mean."

"No. You didn't," Zander said to the floor.

"I know. And I know this is the second time I've let you down in a major way, and I can't expect you to keep forgiving me." My toes curled into the scratchy rug. I expected the patterned fibers to blur at any second, but somehow my eyes remained dry. Maybe I didn't have it in me to cry any more.

"Nope. You can't."

"I *know*, Zander. That's what I just said."

"And I don't get to say it, too? That what you did was totally unfair? That it's not okay that you went behind my back?" The tendons in Zander's neck throbbed every time he opened his mouth. "You know what burns me up the most? We've already been through this once! Why can't you trust me?"

"I *do* trust you!"

"Bull," Zander spat. "If you really trusted me, you'd have told me what was going on! I could've helped you figure out a way to deal with it that didn't involve lying or screwing over my band."

"*Our* band." An electric pulse of fear shot through me.

"Whatever. I would have understood."

"*That's* bull." Now it was my turn to get mad. "Okay, fine. I should have been honest with you sooner. And yeah, pulling the stunt with Levi was wrong on, like, fifty levels. But don't *ever* tell me you would've understood, Zander. *Your* parents are still happy."

"She's right, Goose," Stevie said quietly. I'd completely forgotten she was there. "You can't wrap your head around how crazy divorce makes you. Not unless you've been through it."

Thanks, I blinked. She blinked back.

"So just because my parents are happy, I'm not allowed to be pissed about this?" Zander's eyebrows shot up.

"That's not what we're saying, Goose, and you know it."

"*We?* Since when are you guys on the same team?"

Zander's blatant irritation fueled me. Where there had only been fear and remorse, now there were tiny sparks of anger. "Wait. You *wanted* us to like each other! And now that we do, you're mad about that, too?"

"Hold up, hold up. Who said anything about liking each other?" Stevie jumped in. "Don't put words in my mouth, Simon."

Even Zander should have smiled at that.

He didn't.

"Whatever. I'm out." Zander started to get up. In a flash, Stevie's palms shot out and collided with his chest. He fell back, surprised. "What was that for?"

"For being a closed-minded jerk." Stevie stood up. "You at least have to hear her out. I'm going upstairs, and you're gonna sit here and listen if it kills you."

"I just need a minute. And then I'll go," I promised.

Stevie flicked her hair over her shoulder and made a point of knocking one of Zander's sheet music binders off the table before stalking up the green ladder that led to one of the loft's sleeping areas.

Zander bent over and retrieved his binder. "Okay. I'm listening."

"I don't know what else to say," I blurted out. Instantly, I regretted it. Now was my chance. Zander had actually agreed to hear me plead my case, and all I could think of was *I don't know what else to say*? "I just wanted to tell you I was sorry and to explain."

"Stevie explained." His voice was raspy.

"Oh."

"And she told me some other stuff, about what it was like when her folks split and stuff. She'd never told me any of that stuff before." For the first time, he looked up at me. His eyes were conflicted. "You never tell me any of that. You never talk about your dad."

I closed my eyes. "I don't talk about him to anybody."

"Yeah, well. I'm not just anybody."

"Well, I didn't know you wanted to know about any of that stuff. It's not exactly a fun topic."

"Of course I want to know!" He leaned forward. "It's part of your life, part of what, like, makes you tick and stuff. And I wanted to know those things because I *liked* you, Kacey. Like, really liked you."

Liked. Past tense. Goose bumps rushed from my wrists to my shoulders.

"I liked you, too," I said quietly.

"She still does!" Stevie yelled from upstairs.

"No one's asking you!" I yelled back, even though she was right.

Zander didn't say anything. Every passing second filled me with more humiliation.

"Well, I guess that's that," I said.

A slow Barry White song blared through the loft.

"Ow ow!" Stevie catcalled from upstairs. "Don't you kids do anything I wouldn't do!" She stood at the top of the green ladder, gyrating her hips like the belly dancers at that Middle Eastern restaurant Ella liked, where you couldn't eat your hummus without some lady in a coin bra shaking her ta-tas in your face.

Zander and I hurled leather throw pillows at the ladder. They made it as far as the dining room table.

"Fine, fine." Stevie disappeared, and the music stopped. "You lame-o's are no fun." She shimmied down the ladder with ease and plopped down on the couch where I'd been sitting. "So, is your mom as depressed as my dad?"

I nodded. "She's a wreck. We messed up."

Stevie chewed her bottom lip and nodded. "We really did."

"But I think I might know how to fix this." I told her about Liv's skirt, about how the colorful fabric had ignited the beginnings of a plan.

"A skirt. You're basing a plan on some skirt."

"No, I'm basing the beginnings of a plan on some skirt. The rest, I need your help figuring out. But I'll do it without you, if I have to."

She shrugged. "Fine. I'm in. Although if they decide to get married or something, I'm going to reevaluate my position. And can we get something to eat first? I'm starved." She jumped up and headed for the kitchen.

"I should help her—" I tried to get up, but Zander grabbed my arm.

"I, uh, I'm happy to help your mom out and stuff, if there's a chance they'll get back together. But other than that, I don't know. I'm not trying to be mean or anything, I just want to be honest. Okay?"

A lump rose in my throat. "Okay."

And then he let me go.

AND THE ELECTION GOES TO . . .
Monday, 12:01 P.M.

Zander, Stevie, and I spent the rest of the weekend plotting, and by Monday, everything was set. I floated toward lunch period feeling lighter than I had in a long time. Maybe Zander would never forgive me. Maybe Paige would never speak to me again. But at least I was doing the right thing for Mom and Gabe. I owed them that much.

Briiiiiiing! The lunch bell echoed through The Square. I snapped to attention and pressed myself against the wall next to the Hemingway entrance. Paige had already slithered out of my reach at least seven times so far today. But she had to come through this door to hear the results of the election. And when she did, I'd be ready.

Next to me, the door flew open, spewing kids and noise into the courtyard.

When the initial stampede subsided, I spotted her.

"Paige!" I leapt in front of her and grabbed her wrist.

"Ow! Kacey! Are you crazy? Get off!" She wrenched her arm away.

"Ohmygod." A kid from Sean's American Government class was the first to step into Paige's wake. She gaped at me in horror. "Can't you see that she's getting weaker by the second? Leave her alone!"

"Ew, don't *touch* her!" someone else exclaimed.

A dull ache pulsed in my jaw. All morning, kids had been avoiding Paige like the plague. Which everyone thought she had. One girl had even worn a surgical mask to school, and a few kids had left a wilting trio of sympathy balloons at Paige's locker. She hadn't even tried to argue. It was like she'd completely given up.

"Paige, you have to hear me out." I tried to keep my voice down, but kids were starting to stare. "Look, I know you're mad, but I need you to hear me out. And I'm not giving up until you do. Even if I have to interrupt the election announcement." I checked a nonexistent watch on my wrist, for effect. "Looks like Sean should be here aaaaany—"

"Fine," she caved, sounding exhausted. "You have one minute. Or until Sean makes the announcement, whichever comes first."

I dragged her along the wall until we were out of earshot. "First, it was so awful that you had to see that newscast Friday night." My fedora slipped, and I knocked it back into place. "And I'm really, really sorry."

"Sorry I saw it? Or sorry you lied about me having some made-up disease in the first place?"

"Both," I said, truthfully. "I thought I was protecting my mom, but I was wrong. And I went about it in a really stupid way. I never should have dragged you into this."

"No, you shouldn't have." Paige looked past me.

"I don't want to sound dramatic, but have you ever woken up in a cold sweat in the middle of the night, wondering if your mom would be okay when you left for college?" I said. "Or worrying about who will help your little sister with her spelling words or make sure she eats something other than sugar cereal for dinner?"

"College? But Kacey, that's like—"

"When you go out to dinner with your family, do you have to be on the lookout for every jerk guy who hits on your mom when he notices she's not wearing a ring?"

She shook her head, looking abashed. "No. Never."

"What I did was wrong and stupid, and I wish I could take it back, but that's why I did it."

"You couldn't just fake sick and tell your mom you had to go to the doctor or something? That's what I—I, uh, this girl I knew did once to keep her mom out of parent-teacher conferences the one semester she got a B-plus."

"Test. Test." At the center of The Square, Sean stood with a cordless mic. "Can I have your attention, please?"

It took about half the time it usually did for a room full of seventh graders to listen to Sean. He adjusted his square frames on his nose, looking pleased with himself as the chatter died down.

"Thank you. As you guys know, I'm here to announce next year's eighth-grade student body president." He paused, apparently expecting a parade, but all he got was a polite golf-clap from a band geek.

I searched the crowd for Zander but couldn't find him. Now that our scheming was over, that was probably how it would be now. He would slowly fade out of my life like a flickering boy hologram.

I reached out and grabbed Paige's hand, but she pulled away before I had a chance to let her know that even though she was about to lose, I wouldn't desert her like I had after she'd lost in fifth.

"This year, we had two very strong candidates," Sean lied. "Incumbent Paige Greene—"

"Awwwwwww." The crowd sighed like a pity soundtrack.

I rolled my eyes.

"And basketball team captain Quinn Wilder. With your votes, you've used your political voice. As a country, we're privileged enough to have this voice heard every—"

"USE YOUR VOICE TO TELL US WHO WON!"

I recognized Aaron Peterman's yell and located Quinn and his friends at the very back of The Square. Quinn hair-tossed three times in a row in a transparent effort to appear calm. It would be a miracle if he didn't give himself whiplash by the end of the day.

Sean coughed into the mic. "With an impressive margin of victory, next year's student body president will be . . . PAIGE GREENE!"

When Paige's name left Sean's mouth, time froze. For a split second, I could hear nothing but the rustling of balloons and the heavy beat of my heart. Then . . .

"AHHHHHHH!" I didn't know if that was Paige's scream, or my scream, or both. We threw our arms around each other. Waves of shock and elation pumped through me like a steady backbeat.

Everybody clapped as Paige pulled away, tears hovering just beyond her lashes.

"Okay, okay. Let's take it down a notch, folks." Sean waited for the applause to die down before he tried again. "Would our candidates care to come up and say a few words? Quinn?"

Quinn made his way through the crowd with his chest puffed out but his head down. His sandy bangs fell at a humbled angle across his forehead. The crowd parted, with every kid tossing Quinn a clap on the back or a pity five. The tiniest part of me felt sorry for him. He'd probably thought he was invincible, that he'd always be on top. I knew what that felt like. And I knew what it felt like to fall.

Sean gave Quinn an *Atta boy* shoulder punch and handed him the mic.

"What's up, Marquette?" Quinn's words were more deflated than Paige's *Sorry you're about to croak* balloons.

"You rock, Wilder!" Jake Fields yelled through cupped hands.

"Goooo, Quinn!" Molly's disappointed chirp followed. Across The Square, Nessa linked arms with Mols and Liv.

Quinn managed a meager fist-pump in Molly's direction.

"Uh, thanks. I just wanted to say that even though it blows to lose, it blows even more to have a killer fungus. So I'm glad you guys voted for her."

Instantly, The Square was consumed with the kind of awkward, palpable silence usually reserved for the period lecture in health class. Paige stiffened. Sean rubbed his face in his hands. And that was when I knew: Paige had gotten the pity vote. She'd won because of my lie.

"I know Paige is gonna make a great president," Quinn said earnestly. "Plus, this is prob'ly the last cool thing that's gonna happen to her before, you know—"

"Thank you, Quinn." Sean batted the mic out of Quinn's grip. "Let's hear it for your eighth-grade class president, Paige Greene!"

Everybody went wild, from an appropriate distance, and doused themselves with hand sanitizer. Paige shot me one last half-confused, half-ecstatic smile and headed for the center of The Square.

"Hey, uh, Marquette." Paige took the mic from Quinn, who practically dove back into the crowd.

"Fight, Paige!" somebody yelled. "Don't let go!"

"Okay." Paige lifted the mic to her lips. "Let's get two things straight, Marquette. First thing is this: You guys rock for voting for me, even if you did it 'cause you think I'm dying. And second? I'm. Not. Dying."

"You're so brave!" A girl from Finnster's class cheered. "That's totally why I voted for you!"

"No. Really!" Paige protested. "I'm not dying. I don't have a killer fungus. I don't even think killer funguses are a real thing!"

"Fungi!" Jilly Lindstrom corrected her.

Somebody booed before I could.

"This whole thing happened because—" Paige looked directly at me. Dancing light from the balloon-covered ceiling reflected off her lenses, making it impossible for me to read her expression.

Please. Don't. I held my breath, hoping. If anybody else found out what I'd done . . . I didn't even want to think about what the rest of my middle school days would be like.

"Well, I don't know why this whole thing happened," Paige said finally. "But if I had to guess, I'd say it was a desperate last-minute ploy on the part of my opponent's supporters to keep me out of office."

I felt like a huge slab of concrete had been lifted from my chest. Heat and cleansing antibacterial fog rushed into my lungs. I didn't deserve it, but she'd saved me. Just like in some bizarre, twisted way, I'd saved her campaign.

"But it doesn't matter anymore," Paige said excitedly. "I can't wait to get to work for you guys. You won't regret this. Thanks, Marquette!"

A few confused, staccato claps punctured the air. Then I clapped. Loud. After a few beats, some of the kids around me started to clap, too, and soon there was enough applause for Paige to hand over the mic and blend into the crowd again.

"Well, I guess that's it for now." Sean's voice boomed over the loudspeakers. "Enjoy the rest of your lunch period."

I found Paige giving an on-air interview to a stiff Abra Laing, who stood at a safe distance and extended her mic as far as possible in Paige's direction. I smiled at the look of pure bliss on my friend's face. It was the same look Molly got when she was party planning, the same look I saw in Liv's eyes when she was sketching a new design, and the same look Nessa had when she was steamrolling through an easy test. It was probably the same look I used to have when I was on air—or on stage with Gravity.

"SO, PAIGE! WHAT DO YOU SAY TO THOSE WHO SAY YOU WON AS A RESULT OF, AND THIS IS A DIRECT QUOTE FROM A CONFIDENTIAL SOURCE, THE 'PITY VOTE'?"

Paige looked Abra directly in the eye. "I say it doesn't matter how I got here, only that I'm here. And I'm going to prove to my constituents that they made the right decision."

"DO YOU HAVE ANYONE YOU'D LIKE TO THANK FOR YOUR VICTORY?"

"I'd like to thank everyone who voted for me, of

course." Paige flicked her bangs out of her eyes and straightened her glasses. "And there's someone else who's responsible for this win. She knows who she is. And I just want to say . . . you're forgiven."

SOME ENCHANTED EVENING
Monday, 5:11 P.M.

When the doorbell rang eleven minutes late that afternoon, my stomach got all fluttery. It wasn't like I was
the Simon about to experience the world's most rocking
date in the history of love. But my nerves were inevitable.
Stevie and I only had one shot at reuniting Mom and
Gabe in a perfect, romantic setting. If this didn't fly, we
were sunk.

"Coooming!" I peeled off the yellow rubber gloves I'd
worn to scrub the kitchen floor and whipped off Mom's
KISS THE WOMAN WHO CALLED FOR TAKEOUT apron. The apron
hadn't gotten much use over the years, but at least it had
protected my new leather sheath dress from the bleach,
candle wax, and silver polish I'd been battling with since
I got home from school.

The doorbell rang again. Twice.

"Holdonholdonholdon." I slipped into the closest shoes I could find, a pair of magenta flats under the kitchen table, and sprinted to the door.

"Just for the record?" I gasped. A stabbing cramp sliced through my side. "You're way late, and—ohmygod."

Standing on my doorstep was Zander, toting his guitar, two mics, and a couple of music stands. Behind him was Liv, lugging her flute case full of accessories and a bolt of colorful fabric as tall as she was. Behind her were Molly and Nessa.

At least I thought it was Molly and Nessa. I could only see the top of a blond head and a few wayward sprouts of dark pixie cut over the top of the overflowing grocery bags.

"Guys, this isn't exactly a party. It's just a date. For two people. You know that, right?" I looked quizzically at Zander.

He shrugged, but the pained look in his eyes told me he'd been subjected to a Molly jab or two before I made it to the door. "They were waiting outside when I got here. Can I come in? I can't feel my face."

I stepped aside. When Zander passed, his leather jacket brushed against my shoulder. Feeling the familiar softness, even for a nanosecond, was comforting.

The date crashers shuffled by and headed for the kitchen.

"Before you say anything, let us explain." Molly leapt into my path as soon as I entered the kitchen. Static electricity sent her locks wisping toward the ceiling.

I spat out a few strands of her hair. "Okay. Go."

"I know Ness and I weren't invited, and it's not like a *party* party, but we did just put on a pretty amayyyzing party Friday night."

"True," I admitted.

"And everything has to be, like, perf, for this to work. Right?"

"That's the plan."

"And this is my *thing*, Kacey. I'm *good* at it."

I couldn't help but smile at Molly's pink cheeks and the hopeful lift of her brows. I'd never seen her this invested in anything. To be honest, I'd expected her to have moved on to a new extracurricular by now.

Nessa stepped up and threw her arm around Molly's waist. "So this one basically bullied Liv into giving us the details this afternoon."

"Whatevs. She wanted to tell." Molly sniffed.

"Hey!" Liv wobbled a few steps forward with her fabric bolt, then a few steps back. Finally, she gave up, and it went crashing to the floor.

"Watch it! I just waxed that!" I barked. "I mean, be careful. Please."

"Anyway, we're here to help. As far as moms go, yours is pretty cool." Molly batted her lashes at me innocently. "We pinky-swear to leave when they get here. And we brought sparkling cider and strawberries . . ."

I glanced at the clock. Five fifteen. "We *are* running late."

Ding-dong!

"That's the French bistro delivery guy!" Why was I shouting? "Cash! Does anybody have cash?"

"Ooh! Me!" Mols smacked her denim behind, then whipped a few bills out of her pocket. "I got this." She made a beeline for the front door.

"Okay." Nessa took off her coat, folded it in half, and draped it neatly over the freshly scrubbed countertop. "So what do you need? Actually, it looks pretty great in here already."

"Thanks." I surveyed my work proudly. Every inch of the kitchen gleamed, from the slick stainless steel appliances to the buffed wooden table. I'd scattered every surface with various sized pillar candles on sterling silver bases. Louis Armstrong crooned over the speakers, and there was an explosion of birds-of-paradise in a silver vase at the center of the table. I'd voted for roses, but Stevie said these weird-looking things were Gabe's favorite.

"Okay, um." My head was spinning. "Ella convinced Mom to take her to the movies after picking her up from school. They won't be back for another twenty minutes or so. Stevie's bringing her dad over at the same time. We've got the food and the candles, so all that's left is dinner music and the last of the decorations."

"I've got the music covered." Next to the sink, Zander twisted his mic stand and raised it without looking at me.

"I'll take care of the food." Molly lugged two armfuls of plastic delivery bags into the kitchen and heaved them next to the sink.

"I'll light the candles!" Nessa volunteered.

"And we can finish up the decorations." I kicked off my shoes again and dropped to the floor next to Liv. "Scissors?"

Liv popped open her flute case. "Fabric shears, regular scissors, hair-cutting scissors—"

"Fabric shears."

"Where do you want the Brie?" Molly yelled from the sink.

"There should be a silver platter somewhere—"

"Got it! And where do you keep champagne flutes?"

"The hutch in the dining room. And if you break one, we're both moving to Mexico."

"'Kay! Gracias!"

I shifted my focus back to Liv. "Okay. So we want to cut long strips of fabric, and then we're gonna hang them from the center of the ceiling to the walls."

"I don't get it."

"You don't have to," I teased. "You'll get it when it's done. Now hurry. They're gonna be here any second."

Liv was a total rock star, just like I knew she would be. In under ten minutes, she'd cut the fabric and hung it so that it dipped from the ceiling over the kitchen table to the walls, then tumbled to the floor. The bright fabric canopy billowed over the blazing arrangement of candles in the center of the kitchen table, looking exactly like—

"A hot-air balloon? Was that what we were going for?" Liv asked once we'd finished. "'Cause I can fix it if not."

I gave her a hug. "It's perfect. I love it. And you."

"Somebody's cell!" Zander called as my phone started to buzz on the counter.

"Ooh! Me!" I grabbed it with trembling hands.

STEVIE: 2 MINS AWAY.

"PLACES!" I bellowed. "Stevie and Gabe are almost here!" I hurried to the wall and adjusted the dimmer switch to the *loooove* setting. "Somebody turn off the music!"

"Kacey Simon." Zander settled onto one of the stools by the sink and strummed a few chords. His easy laugh blended perfectly. "Chill out. It's gonna be fine. You did good."

"Really?" My breath caught in my throat. "You think so?"

"Kacey! Where are our places?" Molly's face was panic-stricken. "We didn't rehearse for this!"

"Your places are out of sight, remember? Back at your house! Sugar Daddy! I don't care! Just so you're gone when—"

"Yoo-hooo!" Mom called from the entrance hall. "Anybody home?"

"Too late," I hissed. "Just be quiet." I dimmed the lights a little lower and met Mom and Ella in the hall.

"Hey," I said breathlessly.

"HEY!" Ella screamed in her best outside voice. "WHAT'S UP?"

"Hey. Hey. You look nice, Mom! Really pretty!"

"Thank you?" Mom looked at me strangely as she unbuttoned her coat and dropped her keys on the console table. "What's going on with you two?"

Ding-dong!

"WE'LL GET IT!" Ella and I yelled at the exact same

time. We steamrolled past Mom and threw open the door.

Not to be creepy or anything, but Gabe actually did look really handsome. He was still wearing jeans, since apparently anthropologists don't bother with nice pants, but he wore a blue V-neck sweater that made his eyes stand out. Stevie had coordinated her outfit with mine: black leggings and a silky black tunic that tied at the hip. We wanted to blend into the background so Mom and Gabe could focus on (ew) each other.

"Hey, guys! Come on in," I said too cheerfully. "Hey, Mom, look who's—"

"Gabe?" Startled, Mom took a couple of steps back. "What—what are you doing here?"

"Stevie said you needed help moving a piece of furniture, which I'm just now realizing does not exist." He eyed his daughter warily.

"Won't you please like to come in, anyway?" Ella offered politely.

Gabe stuffed his hands in his pockets. "I don't think we should. Listen, Sterling, I'm really sorry about this."

"Please come in, you guys. Just for a second. Stevie and I have something to tell you. It'll only take a sec."

"Yeah. It's not like you have anything better to do, Dad." Stevie steered Gabe into the hall, and I shut the door. Then I gave Ella a quick nod. She took her cue like a champ and snuck upstairs.

A giggle escaped from the kitchen.

"What was that?" Mom asked.

"Nothing. Listen. Okay." I took a deep, slow breath. "We just wanted to say this is all our fault."

"Yeah." Stevie nodded somberly. "Kacey's really sorry."

"Um, so is Stevie," I said through clenched teeth. "Who happens to be equally responsible."

"Debatable." Stevie beamed at her dad. "But we wanted to make it up to you. Since you missed the hot-air balloon Friday night—"

"Ow!" Molly shrieked. "Quit it!"

"Okay, that's it." Mom hurried toward the kitchen. "What in the world is going on he—" She gasped.

I did, too. Even though I knew what to expect, stumbling onto the scene for the first time was magical. The candles cast the kitchen in a flickering, romantic glow. Perched on his stool, Zander smiled and started strumming his guitar. And the table was brimming with elegant trays of Brie and crackers, fruit, olives, and chocolates. Two glasses of sparkling cider fizzed at Mom's and Gabe's places.

"SURPRIIIIIISE!" Molly, Nessa, and Liv leapt up from the window seat.

"Oh! Well, um, thank you, girls!" Mom smiled. "Are there any more of you back there?"

"Nope! We're on our way out," Molly said cheerfully. "Enjoy your date." She slapped my palm as she passed. Liv flashed me a peace sign, and Nessa squeezed my hand.

"Thanks, girls."

"Kacey," Mom whispered. "What did you do? A hot-air balloon?"

"I'm really sorry, Mom. I didn't mean to . . . we just . . . can you have your date now?" My voice cracked, and a lump rose in my throat. "Please?"

"Oh, baby." Mom bent down and scooped me into a hug.

"So?" I turned to Mom and Gabe. "What do you think?"

Mom's eyes shone in the candlelight. "I think this is the sweetest thing you've ever done, my precious girl." A tear glistened on her cheek.

"This is really beautiful," Gabe agreed, kissing Stevie on the top of the head. "And even though time is fleeting, and life itself is transitory, this is a moment I'll never forget."

"Ohhhhmygod." Stevie's head dropped. "Dad. Sit down already."

Mom glanced up at Gabe. If it hadn't been so dark, I

would've sworn she was blushing. But the very idea was too gross to consider. So I didn't.

"They *did* work really hard on this. Do you think we should sit down?"

"Ladies first," Gabe said kindly. "Which certainly isn't meant to imply that I view women as any less equal than—"

"DAD."

"Sorry. Sorry." Gabe and Mom walked side by side to the table and took their seats, just as Ella barreled into the kitchen in black tights, a black dress, and a glittery bow tie I'd found in her costume trunk.

"And is this our server for the evening?" Mom smiled.

"Mom!" Ella whispered excitedly. "It's me! Ella!"

"And for your entertainment." I nodded to Stevie and we took our places next to Zander. "One, two, three, four . . ."

Zander's fingers picked at the fret board, and the opening notes of the song he'd written filled the kitchen. The notes overwhelmed me with a rush of feeling, and I blinked away tears. Stevie and I leaned into the mic.

"*Outside the world is gray, and I listen. As the minutes tick away, I'm just wishing.*" Stevie looked up and rolled her eyes. By now, I'd known her long enough to know that an eye roll was Stevie-code for a hug, or at least a wink. *"For the one who makes me feel like it's all gonna be okay."*

At the table, Mom and Gabe clinked glasses, then leaned toward each other. I looked away. I was glad they'd agreed to the date and everything, but please. There were limits.

~~THE END OF THE BEGINNING~~
~~THE BEGINNING OF THE END~~
THE FINAL INSTALLMENT
Monday, 6:25 P.M.

After we finished our song, Gabe leaned back in his chair and clasped his hands together. For a second, I could almost see what Mom saw in him. There was a kindness that played around his eyes, even when he wasn't smiling. "Your timing is perfect, girls. Well, not perfect, of course, given that everything in this life is flawed."

"Of course." My temporary brain-haze cleared. Gabe was nothing more than an old guy with a penchant for reciting from *The Big Book of Buddha Quotes*. But he was nice. And he made my mother glow. Which was worth something.

Mom laughed and rested her hand on Gabe's arm. I looked at Zander, who was watching them with a small smile, and I realized how much I'd missed him over the last two days. Not just Crush Zander, or the feeling of excitement that overwhelmed me when I thought about our stairwell kiss. But Real Zander. The one who knew me and made me feel better when I was down.

"What I mean is, your timing is appropriate," Gabe decided thoughtfully. "There's something we—Stevie and I—wanted to share with you."

"Like a surprise?" Ella gasped.

Gabe nodded. "Kacey? Do you want to sit down?"

We *wanted to share?* My skin went clammy. "I'm good," I said carefully. "Go ahead."

"I got a call from the department head at U of C this afternoon." Gabe kept his eyes on Mom. "They offered me a permanent faculty position."

"Gabe. Stop it." Mom's lower lip dropped in shock. I would have laughed at Mom's adolescent reaction, had I not been consumed with the news that—

"You're *moving?* Here?" My head snapped toward Stevie. She crossed her arms over her chest and looked at the floor.

Gabe nodded. "As soon as we can get everything packed up in Seattle. I'll start teaching a full course load this summer."

Mom let out some kind of humiliating hyena shriek, and Gabe gathered her in an airtight hug.

Stevie, Zander, and I just stood there awkwardly. Not group-hugging. Not saying anything. Which was fine by me. I wouldn't have known what to say if I'd wanted to.

"Chicago? That's . . . awesome," Zander said tentatively, checking for my reaction.

"Yeah. Totally," I managed.

Stevie shrugged. "I guess. If we have to move, at least I'll start out someplace where I already know people."

"Yeah. Totally," I said again. "Is it hot in here?" I clawed at my neckline, wishing Mom and Gabe would break it up already.

"Outside?" Stevie was at the door before I could blink.

"Yes, please."

The three of us made our escape and settled onto the front stoop, Zander between us. Poetic.

Stevie was the first to speak. "So is this gonna be weird?"

"Dunno," I admitted.

Zander didn't say anything. Straight ahead, the sky was starting to dim. I wished I could see his face better. I wished I knew what he wanted. Who he wanted.

Stevie cocked her head toward me and brushed her hair out of her face. "Just so you know, I get that you've got your own thing going here. I'm not trying to wreck it."

"I set you up," I blurted to my feet. "At the aquarium."

"Yeah. I know."

"It was a sucky thing to do. I'll tell your dad. And for what it's worth—"

"Yeah. I know."

I couldn't even look at Zander. I didn't want to see even a trace of the disappointment, the anger I knew was waiting for me.

"I, uh, I'm gonna go check on my dad," Stevie said suddenly. "See you guys back in there?"

"Yeah," Zander and I said together.

With the careful click of the front door came a sudden rush of nerves. I didn't know what to say or do, or where to look. So I just stared at my feet, waiting for the reality of the news to come crashing down.

"You set her up?" Zander's tone was even.

"Yup." It was almost freeing not to lie about it anymore. "And you can't say anything about it that I haven't already said to myself."

"Stevie and I had this long talk last night."

"Great." I didn't mean for my voice to sound so bitter.

"About you. Or at least, we talked more about divorce and stuff. And she just kept telling me how I wasn't getting it. How I had no idea what you—anybody, I mean—would do to protect your family, and your life, and everything."

I blinked. "It's not just some excuse."

"No, but it's a reason. And it's not the worst one in the world."

A chill breeze swept down Clark Street, making the hem of my dress flutter. Everything in me wanted to scoot closer to Zander, to bury my face in his shoulder and have him tell me everything was going to be fine. But I settled for resting my palm on the cold, rough brick between us. And, luckily, he took it.

"No more pranks, or schemes, or anything. Seriously, Kace. I can't take it."

"I swear." Warm calm settled over me. With my hand in Zander's, I felt anchored. Safe.

Zander squeezed my hand in a gentle rhythm. I didn't know if he was assuring me that we'd be okay and that Stevie wouldn't come between us, or if he was just being there for me, being a friend in spite of everything I'd done. I didn't care.

Just as long as he didn't let go.

ACKNOWLEDGMENTS

It takes a team of creative geniuses (present company excluded, of course) to make a book happen, and I'm so blessed to have been surrounded by just that kind of team as I wrote these pages. At the helm: Lanie Davis, Sara Shandler, Les Morgenstein, and Josh Bank at Alloy, and Cindy Eagan, Elizabeth Bewley, and Pam Gruber at Little, Brown. Each of you has made this process everything it should be: unbelievably fun, challenging in the best possible ways, and so very exciting. Thank you for giving me the space to grow these characters as I needed to, and for stepping in to offer your wisdom when I needed that, too.

Thank you to Rebecca Friedman at Hill Nadell. You're a talented agent, a sounding board, a therapist, a brilliant mind, and a friend. To Kristin Marang for your website genius, your kindness and enthusiasm, and for answering my e-mails so cheerily, even when I clearly should have directed my questions elsewhere. Thanks to Mara Lander and Jessica Bromberg at Little, Brown for spreading the word in such cool, creative ways. To Carolyn Sewell, who executed the most perfect cover for this book. I'm continually amazed by your work. To Beth Clark, Liz Dresner, and Aiah Wieder for working your collective magic and producing such a beautiful book. And a huge thank-you to Katie Schwartz for getting this party started.

As always, my love and gratitude to my family: to my mother, Mimi, who is the single most encouraging presence in my life. To my father, Hugh, who's always there to lend an inspired sentence or two ("It was a dark and stormy night . . ."). To my beautiful sister, Molly, and to her husband and my new brother, John—who bought every copy of *Braces and Glasses* off the shelf before anyone knew it was out. That's awesome. Also, next time maybe you could leave a book or two for someone else.

Finally, my deepest thanks to the teachers and administrators of Episcopal School of Jacksonville, who shaped me as a writer and a human being, and who gave me a home away from home. You know who you are and what you've done. Not just for me, but for every student who has come through your doors. This book is for you.

mh

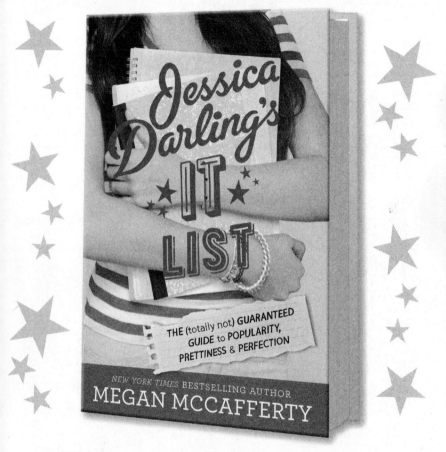